# *What Happens in* IDAHO

## BONNIE JO PIERSON

Text copyright © 2024 by Bonnie Jo Pierson

Cover Illustration © Nat Mack
Distributed by Simon & Schuster

ISBN: 978-1-998076-12-3
Ebook: 978-1-998076-13-0

FIC027270    FICTION / Romance / Clean & Wholesome
FIC027020    FICTION / Romance / Contemporary
FIC027410    FICTION / Romance / Medical

#WhatHappensInIdaho

Follow Rising Action on our socials!
Twitter: @RAPubCollective
Instagram: @risingactionpublishingco
Tiktok: @risingactionpublishingco

*For Richard, my one true love*

# What Happens in IDAHO

# Chapter 1

## Liliana

Twenty miles per hour ... fifteen ... ten miles per hour. *Ten?* I'd survived the past twenty hours driving through traffic in cities across the country, and now I was stuck behind a tractor going slower than a first-year med student suturing a wound.

My fingers twitched, and I tapped the dash in a staccato beat. Each time I blinked it took longer to lift my eyelids, as if miniature weights had been latched onto my lashes. My tire thumped over a pothole, and my eyes jolted open.

Only seven more minutes and I'd be out of my car—if I could get around this John Deere. I'd moved away from one-lane gravel roads and this farming community for a reason.

For a lot of reasons.

My front bumper approached the massive planter attached to the tractor which spanned beyond either side of the road. The gleaming blades spaced evenly along its metal bars made it resemble a medieval torture device. Maybe it wasn't a planter. My parents had moved me here when I was ten, and I'd never gotten involved in the agricultural community.

Channeling my inner NASCAR driver, I weaved from one side to the other. My mother, the illustrious Renee Hutchinson, expected me at nine o'clock for a late dinner, and on time was my middle name. I'd used "punctual" as one of the words to describe myself in my interview at the hospital. Never mind that I wasn't looking forward to being back in Renee's house, or the fact she'd coerced me into coming here.

The farmer finally turned left onto a crossroad, and I sighed.

"About time you got out of my way," I muttered and pressed my gas pedal to the floor, angling around the tractor. Only then did the large black and white animal rooted in the lane become visible. It lifted its head to meet my stunned stare.

*Shit.* Cow. Brakes.

My muscles tensed. I screamed and swerved hard to the right. The scenic countryside whirled around me, blurring into a haze of green, gray, and the red-orange glare of the sun. I lost track of the cow as my car launched off the road.

A telephone pole whizzed past my window, taking off my side mirror. I slammed into a metal fencepost, barbed wire tangling around my car. Dark sludge spattered onto my windows seconds before my airbag blasted into me, solid as a brick wall. My car lurched to a stop, the white bag already hanging like a windsock on a calm day.

Acrid fumes engulfed me and stung my eyes. I gagged and flung my door open, waving smoke out of my car.

The stillness of the landscape amplified my pulse thrumming in my ears. Steam hissed from under my dented hood. I focused on the bags of spilled Corn Nuts and gummy worms littering the passenger seat and took in a few gulping breaths.

I'd swerved. I saved lives for a living, and a cow's life counted too. What did I get for my effort? I got stuck in a flooded corner of a field. Pushing the pedal down, I shoved my shifter into reverse and willed The Force to pull me to the gravel lane not thirty feet from my position. My Audi's engine revved, rocking the car side to side, but though it moved, it didn't progress forward. It sank.

*Crap dammit!* I slammed my hands against the steering wheel and stared at the rows of potato plants stretching for miles in front of me, disappearing into the blood-red sun fat on the horizon.

I rubbed at a twinge in my neck and scanned the gravel road, endless fence lines, and pastures for any sign of civilization. Nada. Nothing. Zilch. With the tractor gone from view, and no houses springing up from this land barren of people, I was on my own. It wasn't like I could call an Uber in this forsaken place.

This used to be home.

The black-splotched cow sauntered into the field in front of my car, swinging her hips like a diva. I turned off my engine. With the sole of my sneaker, I shoved the barbed wire out of my way and plunked my feet into silky, wet slop. Four inches of standing water drowned the few remaining potato plants still fighting for life.

Potatoes, the one crop—aside from corn—that I could identify on sight.

I stood and my legs wobbled under me. This was my own fault. If I hadn't been so intent on getting around the tractor, then I wouldn't be in this situation. I should know better than anyone the damage that one thoughtless act behind the wheel can cause.

What if the cow had been a jogger? What if I hadn't swerved in time? What if I'd been the one to rob someone of their happiness?

The cow plodded around to the back of my car and casually munched on potato vines as if it hadn't just brushed with death. I glared at her. Life often poured spoiled milk on my plans, but this time, it'd thrown a whole fetching cow in my way.

She mooed at me, a vine hanging out of her mouth.

Potato vines were toxic to animals. Even I'd gleaned that much information from living here. I fluttered my arms at the black and white cow, but she didn't move.

"Fine. Die a slow death," I muttered.

I searched my dash, where my phone had been before the accident, but it wasn't there. Hunching over, I shoved my hand under my seat. The tip of my index finger grazed the smooth corner of my phone, bumping it further out of my reach. I groaned, straightened, and yanked the back door open.

My phone's screen lit up where it lay on the floor mat, but my eyes traveled to the purple stain it rested on. I brushed my fingertips reverently over the frayed carpet fibers, then closed my eyes, shoving the memory to the back of my mind.

I gripped my phone and shut the door, cutting the stain from my view.

Its screen faded to black, but I'd already seen the time. It was 9:02. I was officially late. I shoved my phone into my back pocket.

The cow's large, glassy eyes followed my movements. I bent, dipped my hand under the standing water, and grabbed the most substantial clump I could.

"You stupid cow!" I yelled and launched the mud at the animal. Once it left my hand, it came apart, spreading in different directions, splashing into the water before it reached my target.

I didn't ask for much. Simple things like a shower and a meal made me happy. Maybe a cup of Starbucks coffee in the morning. Paved roads shouldn't be too much to ask for.

No cows. No muddy fields.

The brisk wind shifted, carrying a hint of the smell of cow manure, and the sun's rays weakened further. I'd forgotten how cool summer nights could be in this part of the country. Goosebumps zipped along my legs to the tips of my fingers, as my T-shirt and jean shorts were no longer sufficient.

Nothing had changed in Clear Springs, Idaho in my absence. What had I hoped to gain by coming back? My mother, the sole person anchoring me to this place, would never change.

I eyed the cause of my predicament and broke into a cold sweat. Cows weighed up to three thousand pounds. What if it tipped on top of me, or charged at me? I'd be like a baby aspirin to a major heart attack. A slight annoyance. Ineffective. A mere suggestion.

Surely Hippocrates wouldn't view refusing treatment to a cow as a violation of his oath, even if said cow had a death wish. I glared at the asinine animal as it stooped to ingest more vines.

I took a deep breath, hating that I couldn't let it be. Widening my stance, I stepped toward the cow. Naturally, it lifted a hoof and stomped it.

"You're going the wrong way, you dumb thing. Can't you see that I'm trying to save you?" My voice grew louder with every word, but still she backed away from me.

Snot hung out of the animal's nose. She tossed her head at me, and I squealed, ready to bolt. Cow boogers flung onto my shirt and smacked against my face.

"Ew. Ew. *Ew.*" In rapid succession, one hand after the other, I wiped at my cheek. The goo smeared and stuck to my hands, forming strands between each finger.

*She slimed me.*

The cow watched me the whole time. She stuck out her pale tongue and inserted it into her nostril, looking at me as if she'd intentionally boogered me.

Fear forgotten, a red haze clouded my mind, and I charged the cow, screaming all sorts of obscenities. Not caring which way the cursed animal ran, I lunged forward, slipped, and landed face-first in the muck. The cow skittered further into the field as I sank into the deepest mud pit of my life.

I lifted my face, now covered with an au-natural mask, and reached for my phone. My back pocket was empty. I groaned. What had I done to upset karma this badly? If only my fellow physicians could see me now: Dr. Liliana Chase—literally shit-faced.

Oncoming headlights interrupted my thoughts. A navy-blue truck slowed as it passed me. Its brake lights turned on, followed by bright-white reverse beams. Hallelujah. Help had arrived. I scrambled to my knees, but my hands slipped in the wet silt, and I fell onto my chest. Gritty bits of soil—and heaven only knew what else—crunched between my teeth.

A pair of polished cowboy boots with jeans overhanging them landed in the gravel, a cloud of dirt puffing into the air. They progressed around the truck until *he* came into full view and stopped at the edge of the field.

He wore a pearl-snap, plaid blue shirt, and a baseball cap, but he might as well have been wearing a tuxedo for the way I stared at him. Though the daylight had faded, the expanse of his shoulders, his suntanned arms, and his lean waist permeated my bottom-up world.

I blinked.

I was beyond caring about how dirty I'd get. I rolled onto my back and sat up, resting my arms on my bent knees. My ab muscles burned with exertion. I tugged my T-shirt into place and scrubbed at the snot-mud on my face, but it was useless.

"Hey there." He waved with one hand, the other shoved into his pocket.

My greeting vanished down the back of my throat at the sound of his rich voice. I waved in response.

He crouched, tucked his jeans into his boots, and waded into the field, carefully maneuvering over the busted fence. "You look like you could use some help."

I bobbled my head. Not quite a yes, not a definite no. He held out his hand to me, and I grabbed it. Mud squished between our fingers; his other hand slipped to the small of my back as he lifted me out of the pit.

My left foot sank deeper, but at least I was on my feet. "Thank you, um—"

"Blake."

His nearness, the smell of his cologne—a woody musk with a hint of spice—the field, the cow, and the absurdity of my situation left me speechless. Warmth from his hand on my back seeped into my cold muscles.

The last time I'd been this close to a man was with Michael.

I jerked away from Blake, swinging my right leg toward my car, but my left remained anchored in the sinkhole. I fell backward, my arms pinwheeling like a cartoon character as I tipped dangerously low. He caught me around the waist and pulled me against him. The rhythm of his heart echoed in my ears.

"Whoa, hold on." His voice reverberated in his chest. He teetered on one leg, and for a couple of horrifying seconds, we wobbled back and forth until he steadied himself. "We're in a bit of a pickle."

Understatement. A long line at the coffee shop when you're already late for work was a pickle. This was an entirely new level of complicated. In post-op appointments, I'd seen men naked and touched their bare skin, but outside of the hospital where male bodies weren't broken things needing to be fixed, they made me uncomfortable. Here I was with my face pressed against a very male, very solid chest.

Dark splotches stained his pale-blue shirt.

"I'm so sorry. I've ruined your shirt."

"No worries. It had a mustard stain on it. I was going to get rid of it anyway." His voice had the effect of a fuzzy blanket on a chilly afternoon.

"You're just trying to make me feel better."

"No, really, it was a stain the size of Texas."

My laugh was rusty from lack of use. I tried tugging my left leg free, but it didn't budge, and my right leg slid further between his, entangling us even more.

"Sorry, uh ..." He paused. "You never told me your name."

"Liliana." With my cheek tight against his chest, I glanced up at him.

Color drained from his face, and he straightened his elbows until he held me an arm's length away, tweaking my left leg at an awkward angle. I twisted out of his grip and righted myself. After double checking that I was stable, he interlaced his fingers in front of him, looking everywhere but at me.

WHAT HAPPENS IN IDAHO

Did he know me, or, a more important question, did I know him? I'd remember someone who had such a commanding presence.

He rubbed under his nose and left behind a streak of mud like a mustache. I stared at it and folded my lips together, containing my laughter.

"Liliana, that's a pretty name." He shifted his eyes to the road and back to the cow. "I—"

The cow interrupted him with a moo. She clomped toward us, flicking her tail back and forth.

"He's not talking to you," I called to the animal as she lifted her tail and dropped a fresh cow pie. It landed with a loud *splat, plop-plop*.

"Oh, please." I gagged on the smell and waved my hand in front of my nose.

Blake smiled and tugged his cap lower over his eyes, even though the sun's rays glowed behind the distant mountains, and a few stars appeared in the twilight. I held my breath for a split second before I released it. With his country-boy charm, he could be a greater threat than the cow, but I would survive another five minutes, and then I wouldn't have to see him again. I looked at his truck—at the small cab.

Either I would be trapped in a confined space with him, or I had to walk to my mother's house. An easy choice. "Thanks again for helping me, but I can walk."

He wrinkled his eyebrows while I yanked at my left leg. With a loud slurp, my foot emerged, minus a sneaker. Blake burst out laughing.

This wasn't happening. I'd lost my car, my phone, my *shoe*, my hair hung in muddy ropes around my face—and some small-town Hottie McHotterson stood there laughing at me. What else could go wrong?

My feet shifted under me, and I bumped into Blake's shoulder. His laughter ended with a shout as he fell. I swung my arms for balance and managed to stay on my feet while Blake created a tidal wave on impact. Startled by his fall, the cow jumped and bolted over the section of fence I'd torn through. Then she slowed her pace and moseyed across the road, back through a hole in another barbed-wire fence.

I covered my mouth with my dirty hands. "I'm so sorry. I didn't mean to—"

Once again, the rumble of his laugh filled the air and halted my apology. I offered him a hand, and he took it. The glint in his eye caught me off guard. For a moment, I thought he might pull me down, but he didn't, and the look disappeared. I anchored myself and helped him up.

"At least we solved the problem with the cow." His shirt was more brown than blue now, and his fitted jeans were soaked.

Mission accomplished ... but at what cost?

"Thank you for your help. I've got it from here." Not bothering to find my shoe, I left him standing in the field and maneuvered through the downed wire to the road. Mud dripped around my feet and slipped off my backside in sync with my uneven gait.

I only had liability coverage on my car. Since I was the one to cause the accident, my insurance wouldn't pay me a dime. If I reported this crash, I could say good-bye to my good-driver discount.

I took a breath. First, I needed to get to my mom's house and find my way to a good night's sleep. I'd make better decisions in the morning.

"Wait." His voice carried through the wind behind me. "What kind of a man would I be if I let you walk away without a shoe?"

A man who grinned all the time. A man who should have kept driving. A man too good looking to live in this middle-of-nowhere town. I didn't stop walking until a sharp pain stabbed into my heel. Hopping around on my one sneakered foot until I faced him again, I sat in chair pose and examined the source of my injury. A thorn pierced deep into my skin, and I pulled it out.

Damn devil weeds. I straightened and placed my foot back on the ground. Damn Idaho. Damn cow. I proceeded to curse everything within my sight until my eyes settled on Blake. Damn him. Damn him for being too good.

I rubbed my temples in a circular motion. The mud on my knuckles tightened and cracked as it dried.

"I'm going to check your engine." Blake gestured to my Audi and wiped his hands on the last clean fabric of his jeans. "If there's nothing too damaged, I can pull your car out tomorrow morning."

I nodded and let my hands fall to my sides.

White, puffy clouds billowed into the air as he lifted the hood.

Blake let out a low whistle. "Looks like your radiator's cracked."

"Meaning? Can I still drive it?"

He shook his head. "You could, but I wouldn't recommend it. For one thing, your airbags deployed. Another issue is that your engine could overheat, and then you'd warp the heads and blow the pistons, turning it into a square block of metal only good for recycling."

Warped heads? Blown pistons? What was he talking about? "In other words, I'm back to walking."

"Unless—you wouldn't mind if I give you a ride? I'm driving past your mom's house anyway."

"Wait." I took a step back. "You know my mom?"

# Chapter 2

## Blake

"This is a small town," I responded. Of course, I knew her mother.

Renee was constantly stopping by the garage to check the progress on her most recent project car—and my daughter adored her. That was why I'd trusted Renee when she'd told me to attend the singles 'Connection Mixer' event tonight.

I'd driven forty-five minutes one-way to attend a function ripe with single women, and it'd been not only a total bust but my personal nightmare. I'd seen only one semi-familiar face, Angie. She'd moved back to town to take care of her parents, but this was the first time we'd socialized. Angie had come right out and asked my age—thirty-six. Angie told me she was thirty-four, same age as Liliana, according to Renee.

I closed my eyes and took hold of my wandering mind. Long story short, it was Renee's fault I had waded into thick ditch water, dealing with her daughter.

The pictures hanging on Renee's walls were far outdated, and the grainy image in the newspaper clipping covering the car accident wasn't exactly detailed—which was why I hadn't recognized Liliana.

The universe was a royal jerk. It'd thrown a completely off-limits woman at me, as if it was telling me, '*Good luck, pal, there's no one for you.*' Even if she overcame the differences in our economic status, she'd never forgive me for what I'd done. I leaned away from the engine and closed the hood.

"Do you have stuff you need me to grab?" I continued to mask the irritation caged inside me.

Her sigh floated over to me. What the hell was she sighing about? Her terrible driving had landed her in this field, not me.

"I suppose, if you don't mind grabbing my purse and suitcases ..." She took a couple of steps toward her car.

I held up my hands to stop her. "I can handle this."

She shot me a sideways glance, looked away, and then her gaze returned to me, her chin tipped slightly down. I'd been on the receiving end of these pointedly interested looks before, including dozens of times tonight, but for the first time in a long time, I didn't hate it. My ears grew hot in the cool air. I flipped my baseball cap around to do something to disguise the warmth climbing the back of my neck.

"Besides, we wouldn't want you to lose your other shoe." A smile teased its way across my mouth.

Her laughter caught me off guard. The sound of it mirrored the rush of finding a 1968 Pontiac GTO with a functioning engine. My irritation receded, and I didn't care that my nicest pair of boots were dirty.

She moved toward my 1977 Ford F150 and stared at the logo on its side. *Blake's Place: Let me get your engine going.* At one time, I'd thought my slogan was hilarious, yet as I watched her read it, I wasn't so sure. She looked over her shoulder at me. I re-focused on the bags in her trunk as my neck burned hotter.

The door to my truck closed, and I glanced up to see her sitting in the passenger seat.

Three years ago, Renee had set me up on a blind date with Lili, days after my divorce had finalized. No way in hell would I have gone on our date, and apparently Lili had felt the same way. She'd bee-lined it back to St. Louis the next morning, and now I'd found her planted like a potato in a field.

I grabbed the first two bags and took them to my F150, wrangling my way through the destroyed fence. I'd come back to fix it in the morning. The barbed wire would be way simpler to deal with than the woman who'd damaged it.

Murky water splattered onto my jeans with each step. My boot sank into a bottomless hole and the water crested over the top, soaking my socks. I took a steadying breath. Nothing was worse than wet socks. Of course, this had to happen on my final load. I looked down at my submerged foot as I pulled it from the sludge, the tip of my boot catching the barely discernible square form of a phone. It had to be Lili's. I fished it out of the puddle and wiped it on my jeans. Not that it did a lot of good.

After gathering her last bag, I closed the trunk of her Audi A8. My entire bedroom could fit in the luggage she'd brought. With the phone in one hand and her suitcase in the other, I splashed to the truck.

I climbed into the cab and gripped the steering wheel. I glanced at her to find her staring at my hand—was she looking at my empty ring finger? She turned away and leaned against the passenger door.

"Sorry about all the luggage," she said.

"No problem." I tossed the muddy phone to her. "I found this. I thought it might be yours."

Unfortunately, she didn't catch her cell, and it landed in her lap.

"Yes! Thank you." Placing a hand to her chest, she sagged against her seat and fiddled with the blank screen. Within moments, she cussed under her breath. "It won't turn on."

"Sorry." I started the engine and maneuvered back onto the road. I'd been working my ass off the past two days, practically living in my truck, running from one call to another. With all the soda cans and fast-food trash on the floor, she probably thought I was a slob.

I reached for my phone, but before I touched it, Lili pointed to the police scanner on the dash.

"Are you going to alert the police about the damage I caused to the field?"

She was clearly trying to joke, but her voice wavered.

"Nope, don't worry about it. The fence can be easily fixed, and the plants in that part of the field were dying anyway. I volunteer as an EMT and a firefighter. The radio comes with the job. Well, jobs—I guess." I pulled my phone off the dash and waved it in the air. "I know the traffic is really thick, but do you mind if I make a call?"

"Not at all." She relaxed against the seat.

I dialed home.

"Hi, Daddy." Maddie's voice rang through loud and clear. My six-year-old daughter sounded even younger on the phone. I braced myself. I hated disappointing her.

"Hey honey. I'm not going to be able to make it home for bedtime."

"I can't do bedtime without you." Tears edged into her voice.

Nothing I said would stop the oncoming fit, but I tried anyway. "I'm sorry. I have to help someone. I'll be home as soon as I can."

"Who are you helping, Daddy? Is she a girl? She's more important than bedtime? I hate hurry-dating."

She must have overheard Irene and I talking. Had Irene told her where I was going tonight? Either way, I regretted not making the call outside the truck. Speed-dating. Renee had described it as efficient and easy. Which was a load of bull. Tonight was anything but easy.

I peeked at my passenger. Though she drew her eyebrows together, Lili showed no other outward sign that she paid attention to my conversation.

"Maddie—" I said in a gentle reproach.

I sensed Liliana stiffen next to me. I took a quick look at her and was surprised by the raw sadness in her eyes, but when I peeked at her next, she was composed, her hands tucked in her lap.

I heard the patter of Maddie's feet as she ran to find Irene. It took a while longer before my babysitter's voice sounded in the receiver.

"Hello?" Irene's elderly voice crackled, and she cleared her throat.

"Hi, Irene. Sorry, I'm running late. Would you mind putting Maddie to bed?"

"Huh?"

I raised my voice. "Will you put her to bed?"

"Oh, sure. Did you meet anyone special tonight?" Irene asked.

The ladies in her Bunco group would, no doubt, appreciate fresh gossip tomorrow night. I had a copy of her schedule on my fridge.

I looked at Liliana. "Nope. Bye, Irene."

"But you don't do bedtime right." Maddie's sob echoed in the background before I ended the call. Every night, bedtime was the same. Nights like these were avoided at all costs, and Liliana was costing me.

"Sorry, my babysitter is hard of hearing." I cleared my throat. Liliana knew I had a daughter. Better to rip the Band-Aid off quickly. "Renee told me you were coming to visit. She didn't know exactly when, though."

"I didn't tell her I was coming until I got off the freeway. I was supposed to be there over an hour ago." She kept her gaze focused out the window as if mesmerized by the passing fields. "How long have you known Renee?" she asked without looking at me.

Renee, not Mom. Ouch. Things must be even worse between them than Renee had led me to believe.

"I've known her since I moved here." Small towns were great, but only after integrating yourself as one of the locals. I'd worked hard to build my reputation along with my business. Renee had befriended me, which had helped a lot. "I met her at church."

The similarities between mother and daughter were unmistakable. Renee had given Lili the same bright green eyes as she had, and they shared a similar shade of brown hair. Their profiles were nearly identical, and they had matching dimples, but Renee was quick to share hers. Lili was not. "It's been a while since you've been in Clear Springs, huh?"

"Yeah."

"Since you're all dressed up, you want to grab a burger at the Tractor's Grille?" I said with my practiced thick hick accent.

She laughed but then firmly said, "No."

Wow, she was as tightly wound as a rusty nut on an engine block.

Her one-word answers and cold tone made it clear that she didn't want to talk. Liliana was still mentioned at the gas station, the grocery store, and at church. In this small town they loved to relive their greatest hits no matter how heavy the memory.

*The high school valedictorian.*

*She ditched town right after the accident. She couldn't handle the constant reminders.*

*Medical school in the most dangerous city in the nation, can you imagine?*

I guided my F150 into Renee's circular driveway and cut the motor. The dirt on my hands didn't hide the grease and oil stains lining my cuticles.

"Thank you for your help." The muscles in her arms flexed as she pulled against the stubborn passenger door handle.

"No problem. Here, let me." I leaned across her lap to open the door out of habit—but this wasn't my daughter sitting next to me. My arm brushed against Lili's chest, and I quickly shoved the door open.

"There you go ... Um ..." I lost my train of thought. Damn. "Tell Renee hi for me."

"Looks like I won't have to. She's coming out of the house. Thanks, again." Liliana hopped out faster than a jackrabbit and closed the door.

I rolled my window down so I could hear them.

"Blake? Lili?" Renee gestured with her hands back and forth between us. "What in the world's going on?"

"I found her in a field on my way here." I purposefully didn't mention the 'Connection Mixer' in front of Lili.

"What were you doing in a field, Lili?" Renee asked. She'd already gotten dressed in her pajamas; a matching light pink set covered in llamas.

"Hi—Renee." Leaving the question unanswered, Liliana gestured to the mud all over her body and avoided Renee's outstretched arms.

"Wel... welcome home." Renee's voice faltered, a sheen in her eyes.

"You've lost weight," Lili said in an even, unaffected tone.

"Yeah." Renee tucked her chin to her chest. "Over seventy pounds."

I watched, knowing I could and should leave, but the awkwardness was palpable. Apparently, I was becoming one of the locals, seeing how entertained I was by their stilted reunion. Simple life, simple pleasures.

Renee straightened. "I'm looking pretty good now, huh?"

"You've always been beautiful, Mom." Liliana let the words slip out along with a breathy sigh.

Mom? Not Renee? Beautiful? The prickly shell had a heart.

With slumped shoulders, Liliana continued with uneven steps to the tailgate and pulled on the handle.

"Wait. I should get"—the tailgate crashed down and slammed against the chain— "that." I climbed out of my F150 as Liliana tugged on the strap of her largest bag. "Here, let me."

"Yes, let him," Renee said.

"I was going to." She clenched her jaw and glanced at the sky for a fraction of a second. "Thank you, Blake." She hesitated, as if she wanted to say more, then she shut her mouth, and walked up the front porch steps, into the house.

"Are you going to tell me what's going on?" Renee asked as soon as the door closed. She scooped up the smallest bag and shuffled up the steps.

"She slid off the road," I said.

"Oh dear."

Light from inside the house broke into the early night as I walked through the front door Renee held open for me. Her face changed from concerned mother to conspirator in a blink of an eye. "How did the *other* thing go?"

I set the bags on the floor. Clumps of drying mud fell off my boots. "It was miserable. I'm good with being single."

"You can't give up." Renee dropped the small bag and stepped back outside.

"Actually, I think I can."

Renee walked me to my truck, laughing. I opened the driver's side door and grabbed her casserole dish from behind my seat.

"Sorry." I blew on it and rubbed specks of dirt off the Pyrex dish. "It's a bit dusty."

"I forgot you had that." Renee took it from me. "Don't give up on dating after one night, okay? You're dipping your toe in the pond, testing out the temperature."

"The water is too cold for me. Might as well stay on dry ground," I shot back.

She laughed again and held the dish close to her chest. "Thanks for your help tonight."

"No problem. With Lili here, are we still on for dinner Monday night?" I asked, half hoping Renee would say no.

"I'm not missing Monday night dinner for anything. Plus, Maddie is planning on it."

That was true. It was best to stick to the schedule when it came to Maddie. "Tell Lili not to worry about her car."

"Okay. Put it on my tab at the shop."

"Sounds good." I climbed in my F150, and with a final wave, Renee went inside.

Although her farmhouse was a money pit, I couldn't help but admire it. For the last three years, I'd spent my spare time putting down fresh gravel in the circle drive, removing torn window screens—Renee was supposed to be looking into replacing the windows—and patching the

WHAT HAPPENS IN IDAHO

cracks in the concrete. These to-dos would have been done long ago if Renee's husband were alive. He died when Lili was little.

Renee didn't pay attention to home maintenance or have the skillset to do it herself. Sure, she could hire someone to do it, but it would cost her a fortune. I was more than happy to help out. Monday night dinners had started, as a thank you for my help, and Renee had become the grandma that Maddie desperately needed.

The chipping paint drew my attention. I'd been planning on painting it for months and had finally set aside time to get it done next week. It was a job that I wasn't looking forward to.

The rocking chair on the front porch moved back and forth in the wind. I started my truck, flipped on my headlights, and drove away. Ten minutes later, I parked in my driveway and got out of my truck.

Maddie's screams carried through the front door and onto the porch as I jogged up the steps.

"I want Daddy," she wailed.

I didn't catch Irene's muffled response, but her tone remained steady. She'd dealt with Maddie's fits several times before. Careful not to hurt my daughter, I pushed open the door.

Somehow Irene had managed to get Maddie dressed in her Tinkerbell pajamas and wrangle her long black hair into two braids. Maddie paused long enough to meet my eyes with her large blue ones before collapsing on the floor.

Irene shot me a sympathetic look. "Good luck," she said next to my ear while she collected her purse from the coat stand. She backed outside and closed the door behind her, leaving Maddie and me alone.

I scanned the floor around Maddie for anything harmful while she flailed on the carpet next to the entryway. As usual, Irene had already tidied the house, and nothing was in Maddie's immediate vicinity.

"It's all right," I said in soothing tones, trying to calm my daughter. "I'm home."

My words only made her scream louder, so I slid my muddy boots off in the tiled entryway and sat on the shoe bench. Dirt crumbled from my jeans onto the recently mopped floor and I grimaced. Leaning my head back against the wall, I closed my eyes, occasionally peeking at Maddie.

Several minutes passed before her sobs eased into hiccups, and she stilled. I moved to her and lifted her into my arms, ignoring the dust transferring from my shirt to her pajama top. She didn't care about the dirt and wrapped her arms and legs around me in a panda hug.

"You played in the mud—without me?" she managed to say between her erratic breaths as I paced toward my room.

"I fell in the mud, helping a woma—lady—girl." Sheesh. Obviously, I was an expert in talking to my kid about my dating life. I closed my mouth and stopped talking. After walking through my open door, I set Maddie on my chair next to my dresser.

Fresh tears trickled down her cheeks. "I could have helped you help the lady-girl."

I placed my hands on the armrests and crouched in front of her. "I'm sorry Maddie, but I had to be alone tonight."

Her bottom lip jutted out, and her chin quivered. She angled her head down and looked up at me through her eyelashes. "Can I sleep with you tonight?"

I needed to say no—good sleeping habits and all—but I couldn't resist that look. "Sure, honey. Why don't you change into new pjs while I get cleaned up?"

I hoped that she would fall asleep while I showered but she didn't. She'd tucked her ratty, blue teddy bear and an orange kitty stuffy in bed next to her. I closed my closet door, got into my pajamas, and climbed into bed.

She snuggled up next to me. No matter how bad I'd screwed up in life, I'd done one thing right—loved my sweet Madeline.

I'd wished for a loving home as a child. At one time, I hadn't even had a mattress to sleep on, just a dirty blanket. I remembered curling up on the cold tile floor in my corner with that blanket, listening to the echo of the TV well into the night. Abandoned. Alone. Unwanted.

"Sing the song, Daddy." Her request was buried under her yawn.

"Twinkle, twinkle little star. How I wonder what you are ..."

I continued to sing until Maddie's breathing became deep and rhythmic. I brushed a stray piece of hair behind her ear. I would do anything for my daughter.

Since the divorce, things had worsened with Maddie's meltdowns. Her diagnosis had left us with more questions than answers, and like the coward she was, my ex-wife had abandoned us. Every case of autism was unique, and I viewed it more as Maddie's superpower. Most people who interacted with my daughter didn't know, although some aspects about it made being a single dad even harder.

The next woman who I invited into my life would have to get Maddie's approval first.

Liliana.

Her name flew into my mind followed by an image of her standing above me, covered in mud. It was clear that Renee wouldn't mind me being her actual son, and I wouldn't put it past her to spend all weekend plotting. Liliana would never forgive me if she discovered the reason I'd struggled to accept Renee's friendship, or why I kept a newspaper clipping of the accident in my wallet.

Not even Renee knew my connection to the green Bronco—the one that had changed their lives forever.

# Chapter 3

## Liliana

I walked into the sunlit kitchen, to the Ziploc filled with rice and my dead iPhone I'd left on the counter the night before. My muscles throbbed. My head ached. My car was still sitting in a field. Renee crouched in front of a cupboard.

I tugged at the bottom of my shirt, futilely attempting to smooth the suitcase wrinkles.

Renee stood. A pile of pots fell out of the open cupboard and clanked to the floor at her feet. The air, thick with bacon grease, smelled like a breakfast diner, but Renee had never cooked breakfast in the eighteen years that I'd lived under this roof. She'd always been gone before the sun rose to work at the bakery, or the restaurant, or harvest potatoes, but she'd never held a job for long.

"Ah, shit." She looked down at the pots. "Morning, Liliana. You've finally come down from your room." The clattering of pots and pans resumed as she bent down and stacked them back into the cupboard. "I made you French toast. It's over by the microwave. You may have to nuke it for a few seconds; it's been there a while. I made some bacon, but then I remembered you like to eat healthy. I could go buy some grapefruit if you want."

It was Monday morning. Renee shouldn't be at home. "Don't you have to work?"

"Who spit in your coffee this morning?" Her shoulders slumped. She shut the cupboard and stood once again.

I took a breath. While there wasn't any need to cause more damage to our non-existent relationship, I wasn't here to pretend everything was hunky dory either. "I don't know, but I won't leave them a tip."

Hopefully, the joke was enough to smooth over my crankiness. My roommate, Tiff, and I usually only had time for a cup of coffee before we ran out the door.

"I took time off work when I got your message." She brushed at her knees and pointed to the French toast. "Now go over there and fix a plate for yourself before everything is wasted."

I opened the bag and dug for my phone. Grains of rice rattled onto the countertop as I tapped the screen. Still dead. I frowned. I should have upgraded to the new model, the one that was completely waterproof.

"If you want something else, I'm more than willing to run to Nora's Market and get it for you. It's a little pricier than the WinCo, but the selection is better. I guess if you don't mind waiting, the forty-minute drive might be—"

"It's okay." I didn't want to share a meal with my mother, but she had put forth the effort to welcome me with a home-cooked breakfast. The least that I could do was eat it.

That didn't mean I forgave her for my childhood. It was just breakfast.

Strawberry jam sat on the table next to the pile of French toast and a plate full of black bacon. I looked at the burnt edges of the French toast and again at Renee. She expected me to eat this? I took the least burnt one, covered it in jam, and set it on my plate along with a charred piece of bacon.

I sat at the table, different than the one that we'd had when I was a kid. The kitchen had the same basic layout that I remembered, but the laminate floors were tile, the counters were a light, speckled granite, and the cupboards were new.

As a kid, I'd cooked the meals. Most nights, Renee had been passed out on the couch with an empty bottle of Smirnoff Ice next to her. I squeezed my eyes shut and shoved bacon into my mouth.

"The kitchen looks nice." I choked down a bite. "Did you double up on shifts to pay for it?"

"Oh, Blake helped me with most of the work, so all I had to pay for were the supplies." Renee joined me at the table with her customary hot chocolate and shuffled through the newspaper on the table.

Blake. The sexy mustard-stain guy.

"You mind if I borrow your cell phone?" I asked.

"Sure; lock code is 0315."

Renee slid a phone older than mine across the table. I plugged in the numbers. "You know, you're not supposed to use birthdays for passwords."

"It's easy to remember."

I clicked on the message icon, typed in Tiff's number, and sent her a message. *I made it home. This is Renee's phone. (Which means, don't text this number.) My phone is dead.*

The response came back immediately: *Glad you made it safely. Next time, fly.*

27

*And pay that much money to be crammed next to strangers. No, thank you.* Flying equated to the most uncomfortable way to die. I refused to do it.

*Whatever. Good luck with your mom. Why is your phone dead?*

*A cow crapped on it.*

*What???* A wide-eyed emoji was tagged on to the end of her message.

I didn't respond. She was going to kill me. I deleted the text strand and handed the phone to Renee.

"Thanks."

"No problem." Renee left her cell on the table.

I nibbled on my French toast and tried to think up a way to start a decent conversation, but 'How have the last three years treated you?' or 'I'm a licensed doctor now, need any medications?' or 'Will you just give me the stuff Dad left for me so I can be free to go?' sounded lame even in my own head.

"Would you mind if I borrowed your car? I had a run-in with a cow."

"And you survived?" Renee asked with mock sincerity.

"Fear of farm animals is a real thing." Zoophobia.

Renee flicked her eyes away from her newspaper to look at me. "So, what did you think of Blake?"

Of course, Renee chose to fix her interest on him. "He's nice—"

"Did you think he was handsome?"

I dropped my head in my hands. "I didn't pay attention to the way he looked," I lied.

What was all this talk about Blake? The breakfast she cooked, and the undercurrent of happiness were both out of place in this house. If Renee mentioned his name one more time, I would scream. In my experience, people didn't change, especially absentee mothers.

"Anyway, I didn't come here to tell you all about my life and have some mother-daughter moments," I said. The corner of Renee's lips took a sharp turn downward, and a twinge of guilt ate at me. "In your voicemail, you said Dad left something for me."

"Yes, I did." Renee's voice flattened. "I didn't expect you to come back right away. It's not ready yet."

"What do you mean, it's not ready yet?"

Renee flipped her newspaper between our faces.

I pushed the paper down. "When *will* it be ready?"

"In a couple of weeks."

"I won't be here for a couple of weeks. I have to get back to work." I'd only requested a week off. How could I possibly extend it when I was the newest addition to the trauma team? They'd have to scramble to cover my shifts. I was finally done with my education, so close to financial freedom. Fellowship had almost killed me. I couldn't risk upsetting Pete, the trauma attending.

I let go of the paper and fell back into my chair. "Okay. I'm going to call a tow truck." First step car, next step freedom. I'd leave with or without my father's gift—if it even existed.

"Oh, that's already been taken care of."

"What?"

"Blake took the car to his garage. He said it wouldn't be a problem. I'll bet he's working on it right now. Since you're so fixated on your car this morning, how about we run over there and check it out? I'm sure he wouldn't mind, and then you could meet dear little Madeline. You know, the other day she said the darnedest thing—"

She chattered endlessly about Blake's offspring while she gathered her keys, purse, and sunglasses. I blocked out my mother and pushed back the resurfacing memories of my own baby girl, who never made it past two-years-old. According to the therapist Tiff had forced me to go to one time, this was my coping mechanism. My daughter would be thirteen now. What would she have been like at six?

We walked out the door. Instead of Renee's rusted Chevy Malibu, a restored, sky-blue Ford Mustang sat in the driveway. Its chrome rims and whitewall tires gleamed in the sunshine. The rest of the car sparkled.

I stood in the gravel drive while my brain made sense of what my eyes saw. "What happened to the Malibu?"

"It's still here. I park it in the back." Renee nudged my ribs. "The Mustang's pretty, isn't she? Blake did it. Wait 'til you see under her hood."

Renee walked to the driver's side and climbed into the car.

Of course, this car came from Blake. He'd replaced me as Renee's biological child. He'd even provided her with a living grandchild to fawn over.

"I thought you wanted to go to your car!" Renee yelled out her open door.

With a nod, I unlatched the door and sat in the passenger seat. My Audi was the last connection I had with Michael, so yes, I wanted to see my car—just not the mechanic working on it.

# Chapter 4

## Blake

"So—uh—boss, tell me again. How'd ya get a butt print on the passenger seat of your truck?" Chuck scratched his head and leaned his arm on the open passenger door.

I glanced at Maddie. She sat in the same place she had all morning with her wireless headphones over her ears, tinkering with her lawnmower. It had no blades, springs, or anything on it that would harm her, but it kept her occupied.

My other employee, Pedro, stood with his hands tucked in his overalls next to Chuck. Pedro yawned and rubbed a hand over his full mustache. "Sorry. I forgot how hard having a newborn was."

"I'd think you were an expert since this is your fifth one," I said, hoping to keep them distracted.

He shook his head and returned his focus to my seat. "I told you not to do the suede." He yawned again.

I set my rag down. I'd already told them my story. Twice. Our conversations too often involved my personal life instead of the job at hand. Most of the time, it didn't bother me, but today I shook my head at them. "Get back to work."

Earlier, I'd panicked, lied, and told them that I'd helped one of Peterson's stranded employees. If Chuck found out it had been Lili in my truck, he'd start asking the kind of questions I didn't want to answer.

Chuck had been able to keep my involvement in the accident quiet all these years, and I had no reason to think he would say anything to Lili. Why was I suddenly worried? Just because women gravitated towards him like he was a country music star who happened to spend his spare time at the gym didn't mean that Lili would. And what if she did? Like I cared.

The fact was, if word got out about the Bronco, I'd be sunk, left without a way to provide for my daughter. If I didn't have a job, neither did Chuck or Pedro. Pedro had a family to provide for, and Chuck, no matter how much of a womanizer, was dedicated to caring for his ill mother.

"Which one of Peterson's workers did you say you picked up last night?" Chuck asked as he pulled a tube of cherry lip gloss out from under the seat.

Chuck tossed the gloss to Pedro who caught it single-handedly. "This color would be great on a Stingray, but I'll bet it looked better on her. Did it taste good too?" Pedro asked.

Both of my employees busted up laughing.

Chuck's toothy grin widened. "Pedro, smell it."

"Why?"

"Knock it off, you two," I said.

"How else will we know what your woman smells like?" Chuck asked.

Pedro opened it and took a whiff. "Mmm. Strawberry cheesecake?"

"That's enough. Toss it here." I held up my hand. It had to be Lili's. I knew Maddie didn't own anything like that. "It's Maddie's."

Pedro tossed the tube to Chuck, and I gave up.

Chuck read the label and murmured under his breath, "I don't know what Smashbox is, but I know Nora doesn't carry that brand." He handed the gloss back to Pedro.

I ignored them and turned my attention to Lili's Audi. Once I had the parts, replacing the radiator would take an afternoon to fix, but they'd take a week to arrive, maybe longer. I could work on the body damage while I waited for them to come or press the easy button and order in all new panels.

I couldn't just fix this and send her on her way.

Why did she drive around a dented, over twenty-year-old car, anyway? Her V8 engine put out 350 horsepower and, at one time, this had been one amazing machine, but it wasn't anymore. Why keep it around?

The bell on the door in the office jingled. I left Chuck and Pedro to their work.

It was Lili, and Renee filed in right behind her. Oh, great.

Lili wore a white shirt, pants that extended just beneath her knees, and heels that did all kinds of things for her calves—and not an ounce of mud hid her sexiness. Why would she wear heels like that in a town like this? We only had a few feet of sidewalk in front of the grocery store.

Receipts were scattered on the front counter. I'd been working on a quote right before the stupid 'Connection Mixer.' A couple of cashews hid under the slips of paper, leftovers from my trail-mix dinner.

"Hey, Chuck, Pedro, come meet Lili!" Renee yelled in the direction of the garage.

In an instant, both of my employees came through the door. I checked to make sure Maddie was still by the lawnmower before the door swung closed.

"Ma'am." Pedro stepped forward and tipped his head, but then he let out a jaw-cracking yawn. "Is this yours?" he asked through his yawn, holding out the bright lip gloss. "It looks expensive. I know my wife can't go without hers for more than twenty minutes. Did you buy this on Amazon?"

"Oh. Thanks." Lili took the tube from him. "No, I order this from my salon. I could have sworn I had it in my pocket yesterday. I'm so glad you found it."

Chuck's penetrating gaze was on me through this whole exchange. His eyebrows lifted, and his mouth sagged open. The pieces of my faulty story fully assembled before him, in black heels and patterned, skin-tight pants.

# Chapter 5

## Liliana

We walked into the reception area of *Blake's Place* to see if he *'got my engine going.'*

The smell of oil and tires dominated the air, but also something pleasant: cedar, perhaps? Pictures of cars and their parts were perfectly aligned on the gray walls. Three chairs and a table sat in the corner of the room next to a fake deciduous tree. Renee strolled over to two men. They were likely Blake's employees. Renee talked with them while I approached Blake's cluttered countertop to discuss the repairs for my Audi with him.

His gaze glided over me, but he kept looking from me to his employees as if he was nervous about something. His dark blue coveralls and his hands were already dirty, as if he'd been working since the break of day. Before he told me how long the repairs would take, the part I was most interested in, Renee interrupted.

"Lili, this is Chuck and Pedro," Renee gestured first to the taller man, and then to a shorter, stockier one by his side. "Boys, this is my daughter, Lili."

The two men wore the same coveralls as Blake, their hands equally dirty. Pedro rubbed at his heavy-lidded eyes. The accompanying bags underneath made me think he hadn't gotten a good night's sleep in a long time.

"Sorry," Pedro spoke through a yawn. "I have a newborn baby."

I acknowledged his comment with a polite nod, ignoring the stab searing my heart. In another lifetime, I'd cradled my own precious newborn. Slamming the door on memories of tiny feet, soft coos, and the smell of baby lotion, I refocused on the present. Pretending to be fine was easier than facing the pain. I'd perfected this over the past decade of medical training.

Renee brought my attention to the other man standing in the small office.

"You remember Chuck," Renee said as if I knew every person ever born in Clear Springs.

"Hey, Lili." Chuck waved at me. "Haven't seen you in a while."

His thick, chestnut hair hung over his eyes, and he was well over six feet tall. He did look vaguely familiar.

"Is your brother John?" I asked.

"Yeah."

"You were in middle school when I graduated." I laughed.

"I'm not anymore." He leaned closer to me, smelling fabulous, and when he flashed a genuine smile, his teeth and lips were stunning. So were his eyes. He'd grown into a more handsome man than John, and John had been voted best looking my senior year. Out of the corner of my eye, Blake's expression hardened.

"Clearly, you've grown up." I took a couple steps back.

"Some would argue not," Blake said in a flat voice.

Chuck began moving toward the garage. He didn't appear intimidated by his boss. "I'm sorry about your car," he called over his shoulder.

Pedro nodded at me and followed Chuck.

"Let me apologize for those two." Blake shoved his thumb toward his employees. "They were born in a barn."

"A barn converted into a birthing clinic," Pedro hollered as the door swung closed.

"Before we were interrupted," Blake began, "I was about to say, it's going to take a couple of weeks to have your repairs completed."

"Two weeks? Seriously?" If my OR was run like this, I'd be losing patients left and right. What else could I do?

Couldn't he sense my urgency? My restraint would bleed out well before two weeks in Renee's house. It'd be dead within days. Would this take weeks if I were in a decent-sized city, one large enough to have a stop light and a car wash? Probably not.

"It's the best I can do. The parts will arrive in ten days, at the earliest."

I sucked in a lungful of air through my nose. This wasn't his fault—it was mine. My impatience had landed me here. He held the door open for me, and my Audi, still muddy, sat in the farthest garage bay.

We weaved through car lifts and tool chests. My black heels clacked against the concrete. Even though the garage was the cleanest one I'd ever been in, I worried my clothes would get dirty. I kept my hands close to my sides as I walked between the three bays, impressed at all the tools hanging orderly on the walls.

*Hammer. Screwdriver. Drill. Weird pair of pliers resembling alligator clamps. Twisty thingy.* Clearly, my calling was fixing people, not cars. The only tools and parts out of place belonged to the dissected lawnmower in the center of the room.

We reached the Audi. The last of my hope faded. It looked like it'd been in a fight with a giant dirt clod and lost.

How was I going to get around for the rest of my stay? I'd be stuck catching rides from my mother like a thirteen-year-old. Maybe she'd let me borrow the Malibu if it was still in running condition. More importantly, how was I supposed to get back to work? Fly? I shuddered at the thought. Rent a car? How would I get my car home?

Would the hospital let me, their newest trauma surgeon, extend my vacation?

The mud and low light had hidden the damage from me last night. I pressed my fingertips to the back passenger window and, as usual, the stain on the floormat drew my attention.

My defenses were down, and all I could think about were Michael and Bug. Dressed in his pink button-up shirt, Michael had driven us to the park for a picnic of grape juice boxes and peanut butter sandwiches. On the way home, our little Bug didn't want to give up her juice. I was too tired to fight her, and Michael didn't care if she kept it. I'd known it was a bad plan. Moments later, she'd turned that box upside down and squeezed. Purple grape juice had saturated the floor mat.

Out of frustration, I'd yelled at her, ruining the moment, spoiling the day … all because of some juice. Here I stood, over ten years later, with only a purple blotch as proof that they were once my whole world. How I longed to return to that day, to run my hands through Michael's hair, to feel the weight of my daughter in my arms again.

I remembered removing the car seat for the last time. Tidbits of food had fallen out, Cheerios and hardened fruit snacks, all dropped by my daughter. The fingerprints were wiped off now, the car vacuumed, and only the purple stain on the carpet remained.

"Lili, are you okay?" Blake's voice came to me through a tunnel.

"Yes," I lied as I walked toward the exit. "I'm fine." I had to leave. I had to get out of here. Fast.

I passed the lawnmower, which straddled a custom hole giving access to its underbelly. A little girl popped out of the small pit. I skidded to a stop. My heart pounded against my ribcage.

I pressed my hand to my chest. "Oh my—you scared me."

"I'm sorry." She climbed out of the pit and strode directly toward me.

Her head reached my midsection, and her striking blue eyes, framed by dark eyelashes, locked onto me. Two untidy, black pigtails bordered her face. One of them dripped oil as dark as her hair.

"Are you my daddy's lady-girl?"

She couldn't be more than six or seven years old. I followed an oil droplet with my eyes, down to the bright blue embroidered nametag sewn onto the coveralls. Maddie.

"No. I'm not your daddy's lady-girl." I looked behind my shoulder at Blake. He'd followed me when I'd practically run away from my car. "You told your daughter you were with a woman last night?"

"No, that's ... not like that," Blake stuttered.

"Were you at the hurry-dating place?" Maddie remained focused on me.

"No." I half-laughed. "I wasn't."

"So, you can't tell me what hurry-dating is," Maddie stated under her breath and frowned.

*Hurry dating?* What in the world was she talking about?

"Madeline ..." Blake walked to Maddie's side.

Renee, having followed us into the garage to continue her conversation with Chuck and Pedro, left them and joined us.

"But, Daddy," Maddie whined. "You won't tell me, and I want to know. What is hurry-dating, *dammit*."

Blake's expression darkened. "Madeline Cynthia Richardson. We have already discussed the use of that word. Go sit in time out." He thrust his finger toward a room situated off the back of the garage. The visible vending machines led me to believe it was the break room.

"Fine, but I only say it when I'm frust-er-rated, like you."

"We will talk about this later." Blake leveled his stare on her until she started moving.

"I don't know what the big deal is," Maddie mumbled.

"I'll go talk to her," Renee said, like some devoted grandma.

Wait a second. Hurry-dating. Hadn't I overheard something in his truck about— "You went speed-dating?"

I couldn't quite stifle my chuckle. With his good looks, women must flock to him like white blood cells to a virus. Why would he need to go to a speed-dating night? They were reserved for people like me who had no idea how to date, let alone find someone to do it with.

"Yeah. I did."

No embarrassment colored his words. His confidence spiked my jealousy. I didn't lack self-assurance as a surgeon, but in the dating game I was a lost cause.

"Yet you were headed to Renee's before the sun went down," I countered. My desire to knock him off his game was petty.

"To return her dish. Lucky for you I was, or you'd still be stuck in a field."

Okay, maybe he had me there. I bit my lip, not sure what else to say.

"By the way, you look nice now you've cleaned up." He didn't wait for my response and walked back to my car.

"Thank you," I said, almost as a question. The beginnings of a blush burned in my cheeks.

I opened the door leading to the lobby and my freedom.

"Hey, Lili? Don't forget your shoe," Blake called out.

I turned. My white sneaker soared through the air toward me. Dirt crumbs cascaded into my bra as I caught it against my chest. Blake, rather triumphant, curled his lips into a mischievous grin, and his eyes sparkled.

I straightened my shoulders and tamped down my annoyance; he had, after all, taken the time to find my shoe. I met his smirk with a tight smile and left the garage.

# Chapter 6

## Blake

A meadowlark sang from his perch on a fence post across the street from Renee's house. The bed of my truck, weighed down by four five-gallon buckets of Behr paint and primer, sagged on its rear suspension springs. After spending weeks looking at samples of different white tones for the color of her house, Renee had settled on a shade called Polar Bear.

I never understood why there were so many options for white. It was the absence of pigment, and they all looked the same to me anyway.

Chuck and Pedro were running the mechanic's shop, and Irene had agreed to babysit Maddie this week so I could paint Renee's house. It wouldn't weather another winter the way the paint was chipping.

Renee's Mustang wasn't in the driveway. Maybe she and Lili had gone to breakfast or something. Hopefully, they had. I'd get a lot more work done without Lili here to distract me.

All weekend, I'd wrestled with driving to Renee's and confessing my role in the accident, but fear of being on the receiving end of Lili's hatred stopped me.

Sleep was fleeting, mind-numbing, and physical labor was a godsend. I'd made the long drive to Home Depot and back, leaving my house at five a.m. and arriving at Renee's by eight thirty. I grabbed the tallest ladder I owned and pulled it off the rack on my truck. Shoving the paint scraper into my toolbelt, I fully extended the ladder, and leaned it against the south side of the house.

The morning sun brightened the clouds in the sky, and cool air brushed against my arms. I adjusted my baseball cap and slid my sunglasses into place. Whistling along with the meadowlark, I leveled the ladder feet, and climbed to the top. I shoved the scraper back and forth over the peeling paint.

With each pass I scraped my way back to the night in the field, the minutes before Lili had told me her name, when I was just a random guy helping a woman. I might have asked for her number, taken her on a few dates, and shown her around town. Flecks of paint fluttered downward and scattered in the wind.

Movement in the open, full-length window caught my eye. Lili walked into the far side of the bedroom in jean shorts and a bra, holding a bag of—rice? Although I knew I should look away, I couldn't help but admire her long legs, smooth midsection, and how alluring her messy bun was. She met my gaze, screamed, and dropped the bag. Rice exploded on the floor.

I jumped, dropping my scraper. I bent over the ladder to watch it hit the ground.

*That sucks.*

An instant later, Lili clutched my hands in a death grip.

My attention snapped upward, my sunglasses slipping to the tip of my nose, to find my face was mere inches from her breasts. What the heck was happening? Why was Lili hanging out the window, half-dressed?

I turned my head and closed my eyes out of respect as my heart rate skyrocketed along with my desire.

"What are you doing here?" Lili asked.

"Why don't you put a shirt on before we begin this interrogation?" I kept my voice light. I didn't mind her being half naked, but if she was going to stand there like that, I would never get a good night's rest again. Her lavender bra gave her great cleavage, and try as I might, it wasn't something I could ignore. I closed my eyes to preserve my future sanity.

Lili let go of me. A minute later she announced, "It's safe now."

She'd thrown on a green T-shirt that matched her eyes. Lili tucked her bottom lip under her top teeth in an alluring way.

I shoved my sunglasses back in place. "What was that? Did you think I'd fall?"

She nodded. Too bad I didn't; I wouldn't mind being her patient.

"Why are you here, on a ladder, looking into my bedroom?" she asked.

"I'm here to paint the house. Didn't Renee tell you?"

"Does she tell me anything?" Lili left me at the window and pulled her phone from the bag of rice on the floor. I figured the question was rhetorical, so I didn't say anything until she continued. "She's not here. She had to go into work. Her coworker's kid is sick." She held her phone in front of her until it jingled. "Yes! It works."

"Oh good." I couldn't think of anything else to say, so I climbed down to get my scraper.

"You know it's not safe to be on a ladder without someone holding the bottom." She leaned out the window to look at me.

I paused mid-way. "Is that concern I hear in your voice?"

"Only concern for myself when I have to save your sorry ass."

I laughed. "I guess it's only dangerous if there are women standing around in their bras."

Her mouth sagged open. "I was getting dressed. You're the Peeping Tom."

"Peeping Painter," I corrected with a smile.

Her hard-earned laughter floated down to me.

"Aren't you supposed to be working on my car?"

"I've ordered the parts. They'll be here next week."

"Next week? You weren't joking." She covered her face with one hand. "Pete's going to kill me."

"Pete? Your boyfriend?"

"No. Chief of Surgery."

"Do you have a boyfriend?" The question was out of my mouth before I could stop it. "I mean. He might care if you're away a week longer than planned."

She gave a short laugh. "Thanks for your concern," she said flatly. "I don't have time for relationships."

No boyfriend. Good news—sort of. Even if the forbidden fruit was available didn't mean I'd be welcome to partake. The 'no time' comment made it clear she wasn't interested.

"I'll have to get my shifts covered." With a soft groan, she closed the window.

I retrieved the paint scraper, climbed back up the ladder, and found myself alone. Ignoring my disappointment, I refocused my energy and moved the scraper back and forth over the peeling paint, the methodical movements clearing my mind.

"Didn't you hear me?"

Lili's yell destroyed my focus. I looked down to where she stood with her hand resting on one of the lower rungs.

"You shouldn't be up there without someone holding your ladder."

"Painters and construction workers stand on ladders all by themselves all the time," I called.

"And they end up in my OR from nasty falls."

"Look." I shoved the scraper along the wood siding. "Unless you're going to hold the ladder all day, there isn't anyone else available to waste their time doing it." I paused long enough to check on her reaction.

She gripped the side rails and didn't move, determination written in her glare.

"Seriously?" I asked.

"The last thing I need is for my mechanic to break."

I shook my head, making my disbelief evident. When she steadied her stance, I made a little bet with myself. If she stuck it out for more than an hour, I'd show her one of my favorite places. If she didn't, I'd drown my sorrows and share a Coke with Maddie tonight.

Half an hour later, I'd scraped everything within reach. I climbed down; Lili didn't let go until my foot touched the ground. The breeze carried a coconut scent from her to me, making me want to bury my nose into her neck and breathe it in. She licked her lips and kept her eyes trained on the grass while she stepped back.

Only then did she look at me.

I shifted the ladder to a new position. "Do you have a problem with heights? You seem a little paranoid."

"This coming from a guy who almost died from falling off a ladder a few minutes ago."

I laughed. "No, I didn't. You just thought I was falling."

She shrugged and walked into the house, leaving me to level the feet alone. Just like that, I lost the wager with myself. No date. One Coke, straight up, headed my way ... then she returned minutes later, sunglasses and a book in hand.

She hadn't quit. I kept my expression cool, but on the inside, I cheered.

"Your commitment to my safety surprises me."

"I need you," she said, and then scrambled to fix her comment. "I need my car. And it seems, in this small town, I can't get one without the other."

"Uh-huh."

She let out an exaggerated sigh and shoved her sunglasses onto her face.

We continued this way, me whistling and scraping and her reading with one hand always on the ladder. She could be inside with air conditioning, but instead she was out here keeping me safe. I didn't have it in my heart to tell her that her foot resting on the bottom rung did little to no good. No matter how many times I tried to believe her reason—she needed me to fix her car—I sensed, no, *hoped*, that she kind of liked me.

"Hey," Lili called to me after a while. "You're getting paint chips on my book." I looked down at her and choked on a laugh. White flecks speckled her brown hair.

"You should see your hair."

She patted her head and groaned as the debris fell to the ground. "How long is it going to take you to paint the house, anyway?"

"At least five days." I scraped off a large chunk of paint. It fluttered back and forth in the wind until it touched the ground. I was covered in sweat, dirt, spiderwebs, and flakes of white. Five days of this. *Good times.*

"Do you have a sprayer thing?"

"I do. And if I had another person helping, it'd probably cut the time down to three or four days."

"I'm helping."

"You're reading."

She snapped the book shut and dropped it on the ground. "If I do more than hold the ladder, you'll be done sooner, right?" she asked.

"Yup. But I might die in the process if you don't."

"Ha. Ha."

"You want to get rid of me so much that you'd be willing to do this?" I gestured at the mess covering me.

"I can do dirty."

I closed my mouth on the shout of laughter I'd almost let free as her eyes widened.

"I mean that I can work hard."

I laughed and made my way to the ground, hungry and thirsty. Lunch couldn't wait any longer. "I'm starving." I stepped onto the grass.

"Are you finished for the day?" She didn't even try to bury the hope in her voice.

I shook my head. "Not even close. This is a sunup to sundown kind of job."

A crease formed between her eyebrows, and her lips dipped downward. I wasn't sure she'd be capable of sixteen hours of hard labor. Doctors worked long hours, but manual labor exhausted you in an entirely different way.

A welcome blast of air conditioning rushed across my hot skin when I opened the front door. I waited for Lili before I entered. She looked at me funny when she passed, as if men didn't hold doors open for her often. On my way to the kitchen, I took off my sunglasses and shoved them onto the brim of my hat.

"Be right back." I walked to the bathroom and washed my face and arms. I grabbed one of Renee's old towels from below the sink, knowing not to use the matching sets on the rack. She kept old towels in here for the days I came over to work on the house. Everywhere, she'd set aside small conveniences for Maddie and me.

It was hard—knowing and feeling like I belonged here when I was sure Lili felt the opposite.

I returned to the kitchen to find Lili digging through the fridge. She rummaged in the deli drawer for some lunch meat and cheese, checking the expiration dates before handing them to me. I set them out on the counter.

"Would you like ham or turkey, or both?" she asked.

"Both."

"Sounds about right."

The central air unit hummed while I put together our sandwiches. I placed a club sandwich in front of her and filled two tall glasses with ice water.

Lili took a bite of her sandwich. "Mmm." She ate another bite. "I'm so hungry. Renee's cooking is the best diet I've ever been on."

"I'll sneak you some food if you get desperate." I laughed, sat on the barstool next to her, and took a large gulp of water.

"Do you always make yourself at home here?"

I paused with my sandwich halfway to my mouth. "Yeah."

Renee was the grandmother I'd always wanted for my daughter, and for that, I would do anything for her. Gifts like painting a house and keeping up on repairs were nothing compared to what she'd given me.

"I didn't realize you also owned a painting business. How much do you charge per house? If you don't mind me asking." She continued eating her sandwich while she waited for my answer.

"I'm not a painter, but I have plenty of experience, and I'm not charging Renee."

She coughed and swallowed the bite in her mouth. "You expect me to believe that you, a businessman, aren't charging for five days of labor?"

"I don't see why it's hard to believe. Her house needs painting, and I'm painting it. It's what we do in small towns. Or have you forgotten?"

Her lopsided grin was the only answer I got.

# Chapter 7

## Liliana

I stared at Maddie, and she stared back at me. A bowl of cookie dough sat on the kitchen counter between us. Heat from the oven warmed my back.

The tips of my hair dripped water onto the floor, still wet from my shower. Blake had left when Renee had come home from work, only to return an hour later. Apparently, Blake and Maddie had a standing invitation to dinner on Monday nights, and I couldn't tell Renee who she could and couldn't invite over. I didn't have a place in Renee's life, and I was okay with that.

Luckily, Blake was in the backyard grilling steaks with Renee, and I'd been left alone to bake the cookies—until Maddie had entered the kitchen. I didn't have the patience for this. My body ached. Soreness from the cow incident compounded with the pain from the lactic acid build up after a day of scraping old paint off an *entire* house.

"I'm here to help with the cookies." Maddie broke the silence first, stating her purpose like an agent on a mission.

Her red summer dress, covered in little strawberries, kissed the floor. Grease-stained tennis shoes poked out from under the hem. Noise-canceling headphones sat on her head, and a skewed red clip embellished her long, black hair.

"Okay." I handed her a spoon. While I would rather not endure this evening, it was clear to me that Maddie was excited to be here. "Would you like to scoop up the cookie dough?"

"I'm not touching mushy dough. Renee has a scoop." Maddie went to a kitchen drawer and grabbed two cookie scoops.

She handed one of them to me, ran to the pantry, and came back, dragging a stool behind her. She pulled it to the counter and climbed on up. *Good gravy.* She had her own stool *and* knew where everything was in the kitchen.

Renee had made space for this little girl. She'd never made cookies with me—or my little Bug. Try as I might to keep the fury tucked away, it started to scorch through my invisible, protective walls.

"Are you listening to some good music?" I pointed to the headphones, desperate to survive this.

She looked at me like I'd asked her the stupidest question. "I don't play music on these. It hurts my brain."

"Sometimes, music hurts my brain too." I forced a smile.

"Really? What kind?"

The timer beeped for another batch I'd already prepped and baked. I opened the oven and retrieved the pan of cookies. It was warm through my thin oven mitt.

"Oh, I don't know. Heavy metal? Rap?" As I thought on it, an image flashed through my mind of my little girl wearing her favorite pink dress and princess shoes, her voice ringing out the lyrics of "Girls Just Want to Have Fun." That song hurt my brain and my heart.

My chest tightened as if it were bound in compression bandages. If only memories were like tumors, and they could be surgically cut out. An empty hole was better than remembering what had filled it.

The pan grew hot through the mitt, and I set it on the counter.

"Lili?" Maddie tilted her head to the side. "Are you okay? You look afraid, like there's monsters under the bed."

"I'm fine," I choked out.

"If you say so. I asked you if these looked good, but then you didn't answer." Maddie displayed her work.

The clumps of dough lined the pan in straight rows, each one evenly spaced from the other. Had she hidden a ruler in her dress? "Yes, they look great."

I put Maddie's pan in the oven and offered her one of the cookies from the batch I'd placed on the cooling rack ten minutes ago.

She shook her head. "Dad says I can't before dinner."

What kid turned down a cookie? What kid followed the rules? "Do you always listen to your dad?"

"I obey rules that make sense."

I stifled a laugh. If only adulting was this simple. I could think of so many hospital policies I would love to throw out the window because they didn't compute with good patient care.

A problem I couldn't find a solution for entered the kitchen, wearing a blue plaid shirt and khaki slacks. Mr. Mustard Stain, I-Paint-Houses-For-Free, himself. Not wearing a baseball cap for once, he'd gelled his hair in place. No grease, sweat, dried paint, or coveralls got in the way of his McHotterson vibes.

"Oh." My response to Maddie came out delayed.

"Oh ... what?" Blake asked.

Rather than explain the whole conversation, I said, "Nothing."

"It's never nothing when it comes to Maddie."

In one statement he had revealed that he focused his entire life around his daughter. I tamped down my growing admiration for him.

Renee walked in behind Blake carrying a plate of very well-done steaks. At this point, well-done was their distant cousin. Maddie climbed off her stool and ran to Renee's side.

"Dammit, Dad. What took you so long?"

This kid was growing on me.

"Maddie." Blake kept his voice soft as if he talked to dynamite. "We talked about this."

"What?" she countered.

"Stop saying swear words."

"Why? You say them all the time."

Renee placed a hand on Maddie's head, avoiding the headphones still securely in place. "Because they're not nice words, honey. You can say them when you're older."

Saint Renee, to the rescue, and full of bullshit as always. During my teenage years, she could cuss a sailor into submission. The ones not in the Bible were her favorites. Instead of arguing with Renee, Maddie became her shadow, arranging the food on the table, mimicking her every move.

I leaned against the granite counter. Maddie might have replaced my daughter in Renee's life, but she would never replace her in mine.

"How are you doing this evening?" Blake asked in his annoyingly deep voice.

I scooted further away from him. Distance was my friend, but dammit, Blake was well-armed. He smelled as good as a funnel cake at the county fair. I tucked my hair behind my ear. "I'm—uh—doing fine."

*Come on, Lili. Get control of yourself.* I was made of stronger stuff than this. I shoved bowels back into place, stabbed tubes into chest cavities, and stitched my way through shredded muscle fibers on a regular basis. I could handle one guy.

"You two want to join us?" Renee called from the table.

"There's still three minutes on the timer for this batch of cookies." I wished I could stall dinner indefinitely. I bit my lip to keep from saying anything out loud. Thanks to Maddie, however, I was feeling rather unsure about my ability to stay strong.

Blake took a couple of steps toward the table, but Renee waved him off. "You stay and help Lili."

As if taking a pan out of the oven required two people. Maybe this was why Renee had wanted me here. It had nothing to do with my father and everything to do with her adopted son.

Renee was wasting her time.

"Sorry about Maddie. She needs to spend less time in the shop." Blake folded his arms across his broad chest, and I tried so hard not to check out his waistline in comparison. In truth, I couldn't stop my assessment. Like any good nurse doing an H and P—a history and physical—I was quickly gathering information, though, in this case, I really didn't need it.

Blake had blue eyes like an Idaho sky, a smile worth several thousand dollars, and a body built for hard work and summer sun. No doubt the muscles tucked away under those clothes were hard-earned. I could think of a few women at the hospital who'd fight to give him a sponge bath.

Hell, I might even volunteer for the job.

The pearl-snapped shirt did me in. His vibe tonight was all cowboy and American-made truck.

"No apology needed. We all learn those words somewhere," I said.

"To tell you the truth, I don't think she'll ever learn her lesson. I even washed her mouth out with soap."

I smirked in the face of his cruelty. Renee had soaped my mouth on several occasions. "How'd it go?"

"Well, she willingly sat on the bathroom counter and opened her mouth for me. When I squirted a bit of soap in it, she made a face, ran her tongue under the faucet for a few minutes, then turned to me and said, 'Damn, that tastes bad.'"

I laughed. Blake unleashed a smile of pure delight; one I hadn't seen before. It caught me off guard, as it transformed his entire face, and—*crap dammit*—he was beautiful when unguarded joy lit up his eyes.

The three minutes ran out. I silenced the timer, and we both bent to get the cookies. In an instant, Blake's face was a few inches from mine, his hand was on my knuckles as we both reached for the oven handle, and my security blanket of distance had been effectively removed. Baited by his cologne and hooked by his vibrant, blue eyes, I didn't pull away. He didn't move either, his hot gaze stopping my breath.

I came to my senses. I didn't want this romance—or him. "Sorry—um—I didn't mean to—" I pulled back, only to smack my elbow on the raw edge of Renee's granite countertop. A sting ran up my arm. "Ouch."

Blake let go of the oven and turned to me. I grabbed my arm and, sure enough, blood coated my fingers—not a lot, but enough to capture his attention.

"Let me look." He lifted my arm in his palm, careful not to brush my wound. "Hey, doc, I think you'll be okay. It's just a scratch ... but a good one. Let's grab you a Band-Aid."

Together, we walked to the bathroom. He pulled out a small first aid kit. I bit my lip to keep from saying anything. First off, he knew right where to find the Band-Aids. Granted, he had a six-year-old daughter, so I could roll with that, but he didn't bother to clean the wound or wash his hands. He'd showered and cleaned up, but his nails were still lined with black.

He applied the Disney princess Band-Aid, his thumb gently rubbing around the edges of Ariel and Flounder, sending goosebumps to my shoulder and into my back.

"You're not a terrible patient, Doctor." He nodded at his handy work and looked at me.

"Thanks." My voice squeezed past my tense throat. I swallowed.

Some unseen force connected us, and I stared into his eyes, trying to define it. Attraction? Intrigue? Basic lust? I forgave him for not following sterile procedure, and if he continued to rub my arm in such stimulating circles, I'd give him my medical license.

"Are you two coming?" Maddie called from the kitchen, severing the moment.

"Of course we are, Maddie." He let his hand fall from my arm but didn't look away. "Maybe later, I'll give you a sucker for being good." He shot me a half smile and turned to join Maddie and Renee.

I shook my head, and a corner of my mouth lifted almost without my consent as I trailed after him. With each breath, I cleansed my system of its desire to cling to Blake. I sat at the opposite end of the table from him, took a blackened steak, and started sawing it. The others weren't touching their food, so I paused.

"What?" I asked.

"Renee, you didn't tell Lili the rule?" Maddie leaned toward me. "If you eat anything before the prayer—you'll get a tummy ache."

Wow. We'd never prayed over our food except for the one time we went to my grandparents' house for Thanksgiving. I awkwardly interlaced my fingers.

"Will you say the blessing, Maddie?" Renee asked.

"Okay." Maddie bowed her head over her plate. "Dear God, thank you for Renee, Lili, and thank you for Daddy. Help me to not say the *d*-word anymore—"

I opened my eyes and peeked around the table. I caught Blake looking at me and squeezed my eyes shut.

"Please bless the food, in Jesus' name, Amen."

Everyone echoed in agreement except me. I ate, contributing occasionally with stilted conversation. I'd managed to swallow most of the edible bites of food on my plate when the air filled with the scent of smoke.

Blake sniffed. "Does it smell like something is burning?"

"Oh, I forgot to bless the cookies," Maddie said.

"*The cookies.*" I jumped up and sprinted to the oven. I yanked open the door, releasing smoke into the room.

Maddie came to my side, while Renee ran around the kitchen throwing open the windows. Blake was quick on our heels.

Maddie's eyes welled with tears. "I made those cookies."

I pulled the pan from the oven and set it on the stove. She went to grab one of them, but I stopped her, afraid she'd burn herself. "I'm sorry, Maddie. It was an accident."

She grabbed a spatula and pried one off the pan. Her chin quivered and then, without warning, she used the spatula to catapult the cookie at her father. It caught Blake right between the legs. He flinched and braced himself on the counter, taking a deep breath.

"Wow." He coughed. "That's a dense cookie."

I burst out laughing, imagining the complaint in the ER *Reason for the visit? Cookie to the crotch.* Even Renee barely contained her mirth.

"Did you teach you daughter how to aim?" I asked.

"Obviously not," he choked out.

Maddie looked at me and scrunched her face analytically as if weighing her options of continuing her fit or joining in the fun.

Blake's pain-filled laughter mixed in with mine and Renee's. "I just don't think she wants any siblings."

I laughed even harder.

"Maddie, dear, you can't throw things." Renee held her open palm out to Maddie.

"Siblings are brothers and sisters, right?" Maddie placed the spatula in Renee's hand.

"Yes," Blake grunted.

"I want a little brother. Can you get one for me right now?"

"No. You can't go out and buy a brother. It takes more than that." Blake stood upright, his face softening.

"Why?" Maddie asked.

She sure was inquisitive and demanding, and I could appreciate both of those traits.

"Babies aren't bought. Um ... they're made when two people..." Blake paused.

Curious, I gauged his level of unease about this subject. The human body and its functions should always be addressed in an age-appropriate way, but Maddie wasn't mine to educate. When he couldn't come up with anything, I interjected with a safe and vague answer.

"When two people who love each other, tango?" I supplied.

"Yes—*tango*." He straightened, glancing at me with gratitude in his eyes.

"What's tango?"

"It's a dance," he said. "A special dance."

"Have you and Lili ever done tango?" Maddie asked her father with a matter-of-fact tone.

"No," Blake answered quickly.

I shook my head to the point my neck twinged, still sore from my accident.

Renee laughed out loud while I met Blake's eyes for an uncomfortable moment. He coughed again. It appeared that some things could knock him off balance.

No tango for me. The only love I had waiting for me in St. Louis was my profession. It was all I had time for, and besides, my heart would always belong to Michael. The intense stare down in the bathroom, the one laced with primal desires, was a base need that I could control, and did.

My jovial disposition fled. If Blake was ever interested in me, in *that* way, could I resist him?

Thankfully, Renee's cell phone rang, taking the heat off us. She pulled it out of her pocket. "Hey, Nora."

Renee listened, and we all watched her take the call, not sure what to do on the tail end of the sex talk.

"I'll be right over." She hung up and looked at me. "Nora needs a sewing needle. Hers broke and the store is closed. Would y'all mind if I ran one over?"

Since when did my mom sew?

Maddie bounced on her tiptoes. "Can I go with you, Renee? Please. Her mama cat had kittens."

Renee looked to Blake and part of me hoped he'd say no and go home with Maddie. Another part would be disappointed if he left.

"I don't mind if Maddie goes," Blake said. "I'll clean up while you're gone."

"I'll help," I chimed in, not wanting to be considered useless.

"Sounds good." Renee took Maddie's hand, and they walked out of the room.

"I hope there is an orange stripey one. Those are my favorites." I heard Maddie say.

A minute later, the front door closed, and I was alone with Blake.

We cleaned the kitchen, speaking only about the dishes and where to find kitchen towels. When we finished, Blake grabbed a couple non-burnt cookies and sat down. I joined him, and he offered one to me.

I took it. "So ..." Having a normal conversation with a man was harder than removing an appendix. "You're a mechanic who can gnaw through Renee's steak."

He chuckled. "Guess so. You're a doctor who wears high heels."

"Guess so." I didn't mind the comfortable banter, but where was this headed? How many times had Michael and I sat right here talking?

Too many to count. I'd met Michael my first day of Chem. 101 at the community college, and we'd married six months later.

"What did you major in? In college?" Blake asked.

"Microbiology." I relaxed. School was something I could talk about. "I was a student researcher for a professor."

"What did you do for research?" He tore off a piece of his cookie and tossed it in his mouth.

"Counted bacteria colonies."

"Oh, boy, does that sound exciting or what?"

I glared at him while still smiling. He didn't understand. Microbes were the key to solving Earth's greatest mysteries. "Poke fun all you want. I also irradiated a bacterium known as *deinococcus radiodurans*. They are the most radiation-resistant bacterium on Earth."

Blake pretended to doze off, and I dissolved into giggles. I nudged his shoulder. "Stop. I loved that job."

His eyes crinkled at the corners. "I'm joking. It sounds like important work, and I'm glad there are people out there who do it—people like you."

Michael used to tease me relentlessly about my affinity for the microbes I worked with. "What's that supposed to mean, Michael?" I took in a sharp breath and covered my mouth. I couldn't believe I'd called Blake Michael. How could I be so flippant? Michael had been floating on the surface of my subconscious this whole conversation. His name had slid off my tongue, like a fetching Slip 'N Slide.

"I'm so sorry. I didn't mean to—"

"It's okay. Michael was a big part of your life." He placed his palm on the back of my hand.

"Yes. He was." Every inch of me still missed him. Gentle. Kind. Detail-oriented. Disorderly in all the right ways. Michael.

"We can talk about him if you want."

I shook my head. "I want to talk about him as much as you probably want to talk about your ex."

"I'll tell you whatever you want to know." He let go of my hand and leaned back in his chair. "Tell me about him."

"No." I took a breath. "I can't. And please—*please* don't say his name, ever again?" I softened my request, keeping the edge out of my voice.

He nodded as I stood and walked toward the hall.

"Lili, wait."

Blake's calloused hand grasped my upper arm. I turned and shifted from his touch.

"I didn't mean to upset you."

"Listen. You're a nice guy." My voice cracked. "But I'm tired, and I'm only here for a few days."

He nodded, sadness weighing on his features. I left him alone in the kitchen. Through the large window in the living room, I saw Renee's Mustang pull into the driveway.

I ran upstairs to my bedroom, slumped into my comforter, and buried my face. No one could understand my loss, could comprehend how much I'd loved Michael.

It wasn't long before I heard Blake's truck leave. Sure enough, with his departure, Renee's footsteps creaked on the stairs. I lay still on the bed. I couldn't handle a confrontation with her right now.

She paused outside my room, the shadow of her feet visible in the small space between the edge of the door and the floor. Renee stood there for a good five minutes before she went back down the stairs.

# Chapter 8

## Liliana

I'd barely slept. Something about being in this house with a man and his little girl brought everything I'd buried back to the surface. I gripped the edge of the kitchen sink as the remnants of my nightmare flickered through my mind. It was the first I'd had in years.

*Michael sat next to me at the table in our apartment, our breakfast illuminated by a ray of sunshine coming through the window. I rubbed Michael's arm. "Good luck at work today. You're going to nail the interview."*

*"I hope so. We could start being grown-ups if I get the promotion." He squinted behind his thick-rimmed glasses.*

*"Having a baby didn't make us grown-ups?" I squeezed my Bug's shoulders.*

*My baby girl squealed in delight. She dangled her legs in her booster between us.*

*"Mommy, please I have more bacon?" Bug held up her plate with her greasy hands.*

*"You are bacon." Michael tousled our daughter's curly brown hair.*

*"I not bacon, I just Bug."*

*Michael's robust laugh mixed with the heavy smell in the air.*

*I joined him. "Your name is Madison, not Bug."*

*"No. I Bug."*

*In her two and a half years of life, everyone used her nickname. It was no wonder she thought her name was Bug.*

*I touched the side of Michael's face and leaned in to kiss him. He stood, wrapped his arms around me, and spun me. He set me down on the stiff brown carpet and turned away. My smile sagged when I saw the roses on the counter in the plastic pitcher.*

*"No."*

*The petals on the roses drooped and dripped blood. It pooled at my feet.*

*"No, Michael, don't go." My throat constricted around my words.*

*He locked hands with Bug and walked away into a portal of light. I shielded my eyes and started to run toward them. Each time I grabbed for them they were out of reach.*

*"Stop. Don't go." My yell became desperate. "Take me with you."*

*Our apartment door slammed shut. Complete and utter darkness consumed me. The sounds began, quiet at first, but then grew louder. Over and over again the squeal of tires, and the soft thud of metal connecting with flesh reverberated in my ears.*

I hated that I recalled the details so vividly. This was my reality. I had diagnosed myself with PTSD, survivor's remorse, and Persistent Complex Bereavement Disorder, but knowing the labels didn't make the problem go away. I couldn't talk to my mom about it. Since I'd arrived here, Renee and I had danced around each other, sharing the same house but barely speaking.

I'd been grateful she'd been called into work until Blake had shown up with his paint scraper and the most annoying boy scout attitude. Why did he have to be so good? Painting Renee's house for free? People didn't do that, but Blake did.

In the heat the previous day, he'd kept his shirt on the whole time, much to my displeasure. What was it that made a hard-working, sweaty man so attractive?

Perhaps because of evolution we were drawn to a mate capable of hunting, gathering—killing invading hordes. It was this part of me, the basest core of my womanhood, that I smacked back into place whenever I looked at him. We'd evolved past an archaic patriarchal society. I didn't need a man to take care of me. Not now. Not ever.

I couldn't risk the pain. Raw wounds seared in my mind, reopened by my nightmare, ever-present in my thoughts. The sponge shook in my hand, and I plunged it back into the water.

Every time I moved, a new muscle cried out for attention. My upper and lower back ached, and I couldn't lift my arms above my head. On top of the muscle aches, I was a lobster. I hadn't thought to put on sunscreen or a hat when painting, and I was paying the price.

The soap bubbles crackled in the quiet. Renee had made sausage for breakfast. She'd cooked every meal since I'd been here, as if she was trying to make up for all the meals she'd missed when I was a child. Black remnants caked the pan next to the sink.

I grabbed its handle just as I heard the front door open. Maddie charged into the kitchen, paused for a second when she saw me, and then continued to the backyard.

*What the*—? I swung my head toward the front door even though it wasn't visible from the sink.

"Morning, Lili," Blake called into the house.

I forgot. People didn't knock in small towns or lock their doors. "I'm in here," I yelled.

Blake walked into the kitchen and set a package on the counter. "Renee asked me to order this for her on Amazon."

"Why doesn't she order her own Amazon packages?"

"She's unsure about putting her credit card information online, but I don't mind. We've got a system."

This was something I should know about my mother.

Did I still want nothing to do with her? I envied Tiff's relationship with her mom. They called each other every day, and her mother consistently sent home-baked goods to the apartment. Would it be possible to repair the damage with Renee and start over? I closed my eyes, blocking out the newly remodeled kitchen.

No. It was too late for us.

"I'll see you outside." Blake turned to leave.

I bit my lip and thought about the way I'd left him alone in the kitchen last night, and although he'd gone about it in the wrong way, he'd only offered help.

"Look." I still worked on the sausage pan. He stopped and turned around when I spoke. "I'm sorry for how things ended after dinner—"

"Don't worry about it."

He walked to my side as I scrubbed at the stubborn grease.

For no good reason, I leaned toward him and breathed in. The smell of him, like spiced pine shavings, tickled my olfactory nerve. I pushed harder on the sponge, ignoring my complaining forearm muscles.

"Whoa. You're going to scrub a hole in the pan. Here." He took the handle from my grip. "Let me."

"All right." I stepped away from the sink and dried my hands. He filled the pan with hot, soapy water.

He was offering to do the dishes. Could he get any more perfect?

# Chapter 9

## Blake

The frying pan surely thanked me as I set it to the side to soak. "I think you've scrubbed all the non-stick coating off this." She would have scrubbed her way to the center of the Earth if I hadn't intervened.

She shot me a sassy glare. "It doesn't help that Renee burns everything."

"Like your cookies," I retorted.

"It's your fault those cookies burned, not mine. If you hadn't distracted me—" She stopped and curled her lips together.

"Me?"

*I* distracted *her?* Was it possible the intense attraction I felt for her wasn't one-sided? Her cheeks were pink from her sun exposure yesterday, accentuating the freckles on her nose.

All night, I'd replayed our conversation, creating alternate realities where I didn't act like a total ass. Her grief weighed on me. I'd tried to tell her about the Bronco before she'd left the kitchen, but she'd stopped me from speaking.

Maybe my best move would be to keep quiet. Why cause her more unnecessary pain?

I took the other pile of dishes and dumped them into the soapy water.

"Oh, those dishes didn't fit in the dishwasher. I forgot to start it last night." Lili pointed to the bubbles where the dishes were no longer visible. "You really don't have to wash them."

"I think I can handle a few more." I could have told her that the others wouldn't survive a washing by her. Plus, I didn't want her pent-up frustration turned on me.

I followed Lili with my eyes as she walked to the table and grabbed two plates, but I focused on the sink as soon as she glanced my way. She set the plates on the counter next to me and went to clear the mugs. She came back and slid them in the soapy water.

I wished I'd spent more time on my appearance this morning, not that a pair of torn jeans and an old, paint-splattered T-shirt could be improved upon. Yesterday, I'd successfully kept my distance from her, except when I climbed up and down the ladder, but the more time I spent with her, the more I wanted to be close to her. She could be the woman of my dreams. Smart. Strong. Willing to work her butt off to help me finish one of my crazy projects. My ex-wife, Cindy, never would have done that.

The dishwasher whirred next to me. A *nice* woman. A possibly *pretty* woman, when she wasn't upset. *Not* the woman of my dreams. I couldn't afford to think of her like that.

With the table cleared, she leaned against the counter next to me. I faced forward, keeping her in my peripheral vision. She shifted her weight and put a hand to her mouth as if she was unsure of what to do or say next.

She retrieved a towel, and I handed her the over-cleaned frying pan. She rubbed the edges of the pan then moved to the center.

Her voice came out quiet and hesitant. She set the pan onto the counter. "I really am sorry." She breathed in deeply. "I usually don't lose control."

I didn't doubt that she kept her emotions tightly reined in. Her eyes remained fixated on the pan. She reminded me of Maddie after she'd gotten into trouble. Timid—and genuine.

"Don't worry about it." I flipped on the faucet and rinsed the forks and knives. I set them in the towel in her hands. Only then did she look at me. "I kind of deserved it. I shouldn't have been so nosy."

She laughed as she placed the dried silverware on the counter. "No. You shouldn't have."

I washed and rinsed a plate and set it down. "How about, if you forgive me, I'll accept your unnecessary apology."

She laughed again. "Deal."

She smelled like shampoo and flowers. Her hand paused over the sink and for the barest of seconds I imagined what it would be like to have a woman by my side every morning, helping me clean the kitchen or butter toast.

Maybe Maddie wasn't the only reason I'd created an online dating profile, or why I went to the speed-dating event. I'd become acutely aware of my loneliness.

The clasp on her bracelet came undone and it plummeted beneath the surface of the dish water.

She muttered something under her breath and reached in. "My best friend gave it to me."

Her shoulder brushed mine.

"Don't worry, we'll find it." I swept my hands on the bottom of the sink.

71

Our hands touched, hers smooth against my callused fingers. I didn't let my hand linger and continued searching for the bracelet. I brushed the metal strand with my fingers.

"Found it." I raised it out of the water. White bubbles clung to it.

"Oh." She shook off her hands. "Tiffany never would have forgiven me."

"Tiffany?"

"Yeah, we met in med school, and now we work in the same hospital."

"And she's your friend?" I asked.

"I didn't have a choice."

I laughed and looked at the bracelet, then to Lili.

She frowned and moved her hands toward the dangling jewelry. "You have no idea the torture I would have to sit through if I didn't come back with my bracelet. She made me promise."

Her fingertips gripped the chain, but I didn't release my hold on it as her knuckles brushed mine again.

"You have a habit of losing things she gives you?" I maintained my hold on the diamond bracelet. Her friend must be a doctor, too, if she could afford a piece of jewelry like this.

"One time I forgot a novel she had loaned me at a Cardinals game."

I pushed down my desire to run my thumb along her palm and interlace our fingers. "I'd be more concerned that you brought a book to a baseball game."

"I had it in my purse. I pulled it out the bottom of the eighth. It was a one-run game."

"Against the Braves?"

She nodded.

"That game was brutal." I shook my head. "If Martinez hadn't walked those two batters ..."

"I know."

I caught the way her eyes danced before she glanced down at our hands.

"Are you ever going to let me have my bracelet?" she asked.

I'd almost forgotten it. "I always make Maddie say the magic word." I lifted one side of my mouth.

She looked up to the ceiling and then back at me. "Please."

I shook my head. "Not the magic word."

"Well, what is it then?"

"Lug-nut."

She blew air out her mouth and brushed her hair out of her face. "So, if I say the *magic* word, you'll give me back my bracelet?"

"Promise."

"Lug-nut." Her lips broke and curved upward.

"See? It made you smile." I let go of the bracelet.

She rinsed and dried it but struggled with the clasp.

"Here. Let me." With slight hesitation, she held out her arm as I fastened it securely around her wrist. "Thank you, for allowing me to help you with the dishes, Dr. Chase." I let my fingers linger on her soft skin.

"Thank you for helping." She pulled away, dried her hands, and passed me the towel.

"Wait until you get my bill," I said.

She laughed, and that one sound made the rest of my day scraping paint and taping plastic over windows worth it.

73

# Chapter 10

## Liliana

The next few days, we found a rhythm: Blake would show up in the morning, he'd help me clean the breakfast dishes, and we'd go outside to paint. I told him about medical school and the hospital since they were my whole life. He told me about all the changes in Clear Springs, which weren't a whole lot.

Maddie joined him for two days after Irene came down with a stomach virus. I did my best to interact with her. I didn't think she cared one way or another about me. She chased cats, blew dandelion seeds in the air, and altogether acted oblivious to her father and me. Her headphones remained secured over her ears when I was around.

Then, Irene recovered enough to watch Maddie, and it was just us painting the house, all on our lonesome.

The more I spent time with Blake, the more I counted the years since I'd been with a man. Aside from a few stilted dating attempts in med school, I hadn't had a decent kiss since Michael. I found myself taking longer to put my hair in a ponytail, debating whether to place it high or at the base of my skull. I actually thought about putting on mascara in the morning.

A fat lot of good it did me. I looked terrible. Black and white blotches of paint marred my workout clothes, the only outfit I'd packed that was suitable for this kind of work.

An ache grew within me, a sadness almost like disappointment, something I hadn't felt in a while. This would be our last day of the house painting project.

But then what? My couple of days of peace looked quite barren now. Renee said her coworker wouldn't be back until early next week, which left me stranded alone in her house on Friday, not that being alone on a Friday night would be a new event for me. This was my vacation, the one time I was guaranteed not to get called into the hospital. I'd searched the house up and down for the keys to the Malibu and was convinced they were hopelessly lost.

Even as I plotted escape, a grudging admission pushed its way to my frontal lobe. I'd been shoving it back into the nether regions of my brain where thoughts went to die. I couldn't avoid it today. I didn't want to. I liked Blake, and I liked having him around.

Straddling the A-frame ladder, I dipped my brush in the black paint and smoothed it onto the exterior window trim. The house had transformed. I didn't remember it ever looking this good. Its wooden slats gleamed with a fresh white coat. Painting the trim proved to be more time-consuming than spraying the entire house. The sun hung low in the sky as we finished the last window.

The sunhat I'd stolen from Renee's closet scraped against the wet paint. I grunted and repaired the damage.

"I'm going to be done with the rest of this window by the time you get halfway across your board," Blake said from the ground. He'd already painted twice as much as I had, but I questioned the quality of his work.

The temperature had shot over one hundred degrees, yet Blake still wore his shirt. My fantasies of him wielding a paintbrush without one had gotten worse over the past couple of days. I angled my head to get a better look at him and stopped painting while I watched him work. Maybe he progressed faster than me for more than one reason.

He squinted in my direction, and as I jolted back to my task, my elbow bumped my full tub, and it tumbled off the ladder. I didn't get a chance to warn Blake. The entire bucket dumped over the top of his left shoulder, covering him in the thick, black liquid.

I hustled down the ladder. "I'm so sorry." I turned to inspect the house. "Did any of it get on the house?"

"No." He set down his own bucket of paint and flicked his left hand, spraying the grass with black. "I'm pretty sure I caught it all."

Not only was his arm covered, but the left side of his shirt and his jeans were goopy as well. I cringed. *Well done, Lili. More of his clothes ruined.*

He tugged his shirt over his head and used it as a rag to wipe the paint off his arm. Once he turned to face me, I broke out laughing. He had the worst farmer's tan I had ever seen.

"You look like you still have your shirt on," I teased to distract myself from his toned abs and nicely muscled back finally exposed for my examination.

He joined in with my laughter. "And this arm looks like Darth Vader."

I couldn't stop cackling. "Do you ever take your shirt off?"

"I don't want to get skin cancer, okay?"

He walked close to me, focusing his gaze on something on my forehead, but then his blue eyes locked on mine. All my teasing and joviality bolted, replaced by my fantasies of stolen kisses and paintbrushes.

"You have something black right here." He dragged his left pointer with a blob of wet paint on it from my temple down to my chin.

"Hey." I gripped his wrist and pulled his hand off my cheek, only to have the paint on his arm transfer to my palm. My phone buzzed in my pocket. Of course, it rang at that precise moment. "Hold on." I wiped my hand on Blake's shoulder, leaving black streaks on his pale skin. The rigid edges of puckered flesh brushed my hand. Possibly a scar? What type of injury had caused it? "There, I gave you some color."

I pulled out my phone and answered Tiffany's video call while he shook his head. I held the phone in front of me before he could retaliate.

"That's not fair." He frowned but then laughed.

"Who's that?" Tiffany asked as soon as the call connected. "I hear a male voice ..."

I turned the phone to keep Blake from view, but he stepped around me and waved at the camera. I had no choice other than to introduce him.

"Hey, Tiff." I moved the phone in Blake's direction. "This is Blake. Um. We're painting Renee's house together."

"Tiff, as in bracelet Tiff?" Blake asked in an overloud whisper.

She was silent for a second, but it didn't take her long to connect the threads of our conversation. "Tell me you didn't lose the bracelet I gave you for your birthday." Tiff shook her head.

"I didn't. See?" I held the bracelet in front of the camera and flinched. It was smeared with black paint, and I dropped my wrist to my side. If she'd noticed, Tiffany didn't comment.

"By the way, I agree with you. Reading a book at a baseball game is not okay," Blake called from over my shoulder.

Tiffany laughed. "Neither is leaving the book there and never returning it to her friend."

"Totally unacceptable." He waved his hand. "It's nice to meet you." Blake returned to the window trim, and I walked to the shade of the cottonwood tree.

"Tell me everything. Why didn't you answer my calls? How the hell did you end up with the hot painter? Have you done it yet?" Tiffany shot off her rapid-fire questions.

"*No*," I said. "And I don't plan on doing anything with him except painting the house. You know how I feel."

"Yes, but honey, we've talked about this before. Michael has been gone for over ten years. It's okay if you are attracted to another man."

I didn't say anything, but I looked in Blake's direction. He met my eyes for a millisecond before he dipped his brush in his bucket.

"So ..." Tiff dragged her voice out.

"So what?"

"Are you going to fill me in?"

With a sigh, I told her about the cow, the mud, and the man.

She popped a Wheat Thin in her mouth and crunched on it. Her brown hair pulled into a bun was almost the same shade as mine, but our similarities ended there. Where I had green eyes, hers were brown, and my twenty-thirteen vision didn't require Tiff's stylish glasses. "Oh, this is so much better than any of the gossip at the hospital—"

"Promise me you won't tell anyone," I cut her off.

"I promise, as long as you think long and hard about kissing the painter. If I could, I'd jump through the phone and do it for you."

"He's not a painter. He's a mechanic." Not that this detail made any difference.

"Mechanic, painter. Even if he was a sheep herder, I'd still want to have his babies."

I laughed. Blake had finished the last window and started to collect his tools.

"Whatever. I'll call you later, okay?"

"You better." Tiffany kissed the camera, her large lips taking up the whole screen. "Just in case you've forgotten how." She winked at me and hung up.

Tucking the phone in my pocket, I wandered to where Blake was spraying off the brushes and his arm. I fixated on the spot where my handprint stood against his pale skin. The scar I'd felt hid underneath the paint. He turned his shoulder away from me before I could get a good look at it.

"Here." He grabbed a clean cloth, put it in the stream of the hose and handed it to me. "For your face."

"Oh." I'd forgotten about the black streak across my cheek. "Thanks."

I scrubbed at the mark; the cloth rough against my tender skin.

"You missed some. It's right there." He pointed and I tried to get it, but he walked over to me, leaving the hose running in the grass. "Let me help."

He gripped the rag, and I let go of it. His touch was gentle. He focused intently on my eyes while he wiped at the paint. I stood there with my skin tingling anywhere the rag touched, frozen to the spot. Would he try to kiss me? Should I let him? Would I remember how if he did?

As I thought about kissing him, the normal fear clutched me. I couldn't betray Michael. In this life true love only came around once, and I had already found and lost mine.

"Thank you." I backed away. "I think I'll go shower. Do you need any of my help cleaning the rest of the stuff?"

"No. I can handle it."

I turned to go back into the house.

"Listen."

I faced him, but he didn't continue. "Yes?"

He looked at the ground and then back to me. "I thought this would take me longer than it did, but since you helped me, I have a day off tomorrow. Would you be interested in hanging out? In a friend kind of way, not in a I-want-to-date-you kind of way."

No matter how he put it, he was asking me on a date. No one asked me to go on dates with them. The male doctors, nurses, even medical students learned quickly to keep their distance. Caught off guard, I didn't have an excuse ready.

"We can hang out in the morning, so you'll be home when your mom gets off work. I don't want to take any time away from her."

I weighed my options. Stay at home alone, bored out of my wits, or have an adventure with Blake? It wouldn't be a date. Just two friends hanging out, as he put it.

"Fine."

His shoulders relaxed.

"But it's not a date," I added. I rounded the corner to the house and jogged up the stairs.

"I'll pick you up tomorrow morning at eight," he called as I opened the door and ran inside.

# Chapter 11

## Blake

I studied the rusted-through hose clamp I'd pulled from Lili's car. It could have failed at any second. The cow had nothing to do with it. Lili's car was in rougher shape than I'd expected. I wiggled the stubborn transmission hose off the base of the radiator. Oil, black as tar, leaked into my drip pan. She could have easily blown her gearbox before reaching the first state line on her trip.

Regular car maintenance. I'd write it up on a poster board and pin it to the back of her seat. Chuck and I had removed the front bumper of the Audi along with the headlights. Only one antifreeze hose connected the radiator to the car.

"Hey, will you grab me a hose clamp?" I asked Chuck. "This one on the antifreeze line is garbage."

Chuck handed me a new hose clamp, and I slipped it onto the black rubber hose.

"Looks like the water pump will also need to be replaced." He crouched down to look closer at the undercarriage of the car.

"Add it to the list of parts we still need." I pressed the button to lift the car higher and get better access to the bottom of the radiator.

"How about we order her a whole new car?" He laughed. "Even the body of this Audi has rust holes in the back quarter panels. It's probably totaled with the bent frame."

"She wants the car fixed, so we'll fix the car." I grabbed the flathead screwdriver and pried at the antifreeze hose. A stream of green fluid flowed out of the radiator once the hose came free. Some splattered on the ground, and I adjusted a bucket to catch all of it. "So, you knew Lili in high school?"

"Yeah." Chuck nodded. "My brother had a crush on her."

"What was she like?"

"Hot."

"That's it?" I set my screwdriver down and lifted the radiator free of the car.

"What do you expect from me? I was in middle school."

I leaned the old radiator against the wall, my back to Chuck. "I talked to her after the dinner at Renee's—about her family."

Chuck let out a low whistle. "Have you told her about the Bronco?"

"No." I moved back to examine the front end of the car. With all the time I'd spent in the last four days working on Renee's house, I'd had plenty of opportunities to tell Lili, but I couldn't. I didn't want to make her cry again. After all, I was familiar with emotional pain.

By age six, I'd been through two sets of foster parents. I kept bouncing from home to home until, in eighth grade, I was placed with Jorge, who'd taken it upon himself to teach me how to properly work on engines, rebuild transmissions, and fix steering linkages, while simultaneously teaching me Spanish.

Sadly, I didn't pick up the Spanish as well as the mechanics.

Jorge's brother, Marcos, originally bought the house and shop. It's because of him that I moved here. I hated to think about what my life would have looked like if Marcos hadn't offered me the garage and his place. Cindy and I had been dirt poor, which I could handle; Cindy could not.

Chuck stopped fiddling with the water pump and stood. He leaned against the Audi. "I don't know why you keep beating yourself up. Maybe if you tell her, you'll be able to move past it."

"I'm not sure that's the best idea."

"Secrets like this have a way of coming out one way or another." Chuck placed his socket wrench back into its holder.

I'd acted like an idiot the other night. Pressing Lili about her past, thinking I could—what? Fix her? Make myself feel better by figuring out that she wasn't still grieving? I'd been wrong.

"You should have seen her." I pulled two blue shop towels from the box on the floor and handed one to Chuck. "It was like it'd happened yesterday for her. Renee told me she was living a new life in the city as a successful surgeon. I thought maybe she'd recovered from the accident by now."

"Dude, she lost her family. It's not like she can rip off the Band-Aid and magically be better."

I knew this. Experienced it. Jorge's death left my life in shambles. I barely had any pieces to scrape together to figure out how to live without him. Every now and then, a memory of him would send a pang through my chest and, I'd be back at the funeral parlor burying the one man who'd ever believed in me.

Lili's grief impacted her every minute of every day like she'd never left the cemetery. I couldn't be the cause of more pain.

Chuck rubbed his hands clean. "Are you thinking that telling her would hurt her more than she is already hurting?" he asked, in tune with my thoughts as usual.

"Yes."

My confession would force her to relive everything. I didn't want to cause her to dive deeper into depression. No. The best option would be to keep quiet, finish her Audi, and send her on her way. Still broken—but with a functional car.

Bubbles clung to the edge of the bucket filled with green antifreeze. The bubbles rubbed together and disappeared to nothing. I bent over to pick up the bucket and empty it into the waste bin.

If I showed her how to enjoy life again, maybe then I could forgive myself. Michael would want Lili happy, and I could make that happen during her visit.

Chuck followed me to the waste bin with the old transmission fluid.

"Maybe I'll help her laugh more while she's here."

Chuck dropped the drip pan on the ground. "Terrible idea. You'll get attached to her, and then she'll leave and go back to her life in St. Louis."

"I won't get attached."

"She's not a charity you can donate money to and make it all better." Chuck shook his head as he wiped the oil off his hands with a towel. "Besides, you don't have anything to feel guilty about."

"Yes, I do." My quiet voice cut through the air. I rubbed at the grime on my hands. "I can't tell her. I'm afraid it'll push her over the edge."

"If Lili's anything like Renee, she's a strong woman." Chuck rested his hand on my shoulder. "And any other mechanic would have done the same thing you did."

The difference was that two had people died, and I would forever question if I'd missed a bad brake line, or if I should have replaced the master cylinder seals.

"I'll see you later. You going to Trout Fest?" Chuck asked.

"Yeah. Maddie has been excited about it all week. It's her favorite event of the year."

Chuck gathered the wrenches and sockets and put them in their drawer in the toolbox. "I'll see you Saturday." He headed toward the exit. "You sure about closing the shop tomorrow? Since you're done with painting the house?"

"Yeah." I straightened. "I'm hanging out with Lili. As *friends*," I clarified.

"Okay," Chuck said in a I-don't-think-you-can-handle-what-you're-getting-into kind of way. He shook his head and closed the door.

I cleaned up the rest of the tools and lowered the Audi to the ground. Chuck was somewhat right. I wasn't personally responsible for the accident, but I was still tied to it. If Lili found out, she would never forgive me. I mean, I'd been an immature twenty-five-year-old working in my uncle's shop, but if I could have one redo, I'd go back all those years ago to the day in Marcos's mechanic shop when that green Bronco came in for maintenance.

# Chapter 12

## Blake

With my arms full of ropes, harnesses, and carabiners, I turned toward Lili. Her bottom was planted on a rock a good distance away from the cliff, her eyes wide like saucers as she slathered sunscreen on her skin. She'd been quiet on the twenty-minute drive to the desert canyon.

Rays of sunlight beamed on the gray, lava-rock face, and reflected onto me. The air filled with the scent of baked stone, but the face of the cliff was still cool to the touch in the early morning light. I shuffled my rock-climbing shoes in the dirt, causing a cloud of dust to rise into the air, only to be blown away in the wind. I wished my anxiety could be eliminated as easily.

Why had I made a wager with myself? Taking her to one of my favorite places? What was I thinking?

If I discounted the events of this past weekend, I hadn't been on a formal date since well before Cindy and I split. This wasn't a date, as Lili had reminded me before she'd left yesterday.

Date or no, it wasn't the wisest thing for me to be here with Lili. I felt as though I'd eaten a handful of ball bearings for breakfast. Although I didn't know much about the dating scene, I knew that puking wouldn't be a good move. What other bodily functions were acceptable? Could one fart be the downfall of a relationship?

"Get it together, Blake," I muttered to myself before I continued to get the rest of the gear out of my truck, keeping all thoughts of the accident far from my mind.

I took a step in Lili's direction. "Have you done this before?" I followed up my question with what I hoped to be my most charming smile.

Without a sound, she shook her head. If possible, her eyes grew bigger. She looked more petrified than a piece of petrified wood.

"Ever climbed at a gym before?"

"I ... I think I played on the climbing toy at the playground when I was little." Her eyes fixed on the top of the ravine. "I don't like heights."

My arms dropped to my sides, and the ropes and carabiners landed in the dust. I should have been more considerate. Just because Maddie and I loved to do this together didn't mean that Lili would too. I'd suspected she might be timid about heights, but Liliana was such a strong woman, I never imagined seeing her face bathed in fear at the thought of scaling a cliff.

Dust devils twirled in the wind in the distance as I made my way to her side. I reached for her hand. With a slight hesitation, she placed hers in mine, and I pulled her to a standing position.

"I'm not going to force you to do anything you don't want to do." She relaxed beside me. "How about we walk closer to the wall, and I'll show you all the gear and safety harnesses? Then you can decide if it's something you'd like to try."

A strand of dark hair escaped her ponytail, blew into her face, and stuck to her glossy, full, very kissable lips. She tugged it free. "Sounds good. I wish I could say I'm always up for an adventure, but I'm not exactly an adrenaline junkie."

We made our way to the cliff. "Wait, I thought you were a trauma surgeon."

"Yeah, so?"

"Your life is an adrenaline junkie's dream. Don't you ever feel your heart pounding when you're operating?"

She laughed and traced her hand around a sharp edge on the rock. Instead of fear, her face now held mild curiosity.

"Maybe in the beginning, but now it's just what I do."

I shook my head. "I still say you're a closet adrenaline junkie. You act like you're a librarian or something. Librarians don't get soaked in blood daily or save lives."

"You've been watching too much TV drama."

I laughed and slipped my legs into my rock-climbing harness. "So, your ex-lover isn't sleeping with the new intern who looks amazing and sexy in scrubs at 3 a.m.?"

She rolled her eyes and chuckled. "No."

"Well, way to ruin it for me."

She laughed harder, and I loved it. Goal one: make her laugh every day I was with her.

I held up the harness I'd brought for her. "Okay, rock-climbing is quite safe when you're with someone as experienced as me." I sounded conceited, but maybe she heard the kidding tone in my voice. "This harness is clipped to a carabiner securely tied to this rope which is looped through a steel piece of metal drilled deep into the rock at the top of the ravine."

I tugged on the rope I'd prepped when we'd first arrived. "One person will be on this end of the rope and another person will be on the other end. They will be responsible for keeping the slack out and stop the other person from falling—"

She held up her hand. "You mean, I'm supposed to be able to hold your weight and keep you from falling?"

"Yes. *If* I fall. It won't happen." I reassured her. "But if I do fall, sit down in your harness, and you'll hold my weight just fine."

"And I won't be catapulted into the air?" Her face draped in doubt.

"Nope." I chuckled. "But wouldn't it be an adventure?"

"Not one I would like to go on." She rubbed her palms on her leggings.

"You won't have to, if I climb, I'll solo climb. So, no worries."

"Makes perfect sense to me." Sarcasm dripped from her words.

Instead of delving into the difference between solo climbing and top rope climbing, I explained all the other equipment I'd brought and demonstrated how to tie a proper figure-eight knot. Although still skeptical, her eyes reflected some of the fascination I had felt as a fourteen-year-old boy when Jorge had taken me on our first of many trips to the rock.

Rock-climbing had given me a sense of freedom like nothing else could. If I could climb up a cliff without fear, then I could do anything. Although, it'd still taken me years to free myself forever from the decisions of my former life. Involuntarily, I traced the scars on my left shoulder.

"Tell you what." Lili's voice brought me back to the present. "If I do this, while I climb, you have to answer some questions."

"Like, an extreme dating game?" Much better than any speed-date or app.

"Yes. *But* this isn't a date."

I flicked the rope behind me and fiddled with the carabiner. "How about when you fall, I get to ask you a question, and if I fall you get to ask me a question?"

"Nice try." She tilted her head to the side. "You told me you never fall."

"Exactly." I rubbed my chin. "I don't see the problem."

I was rewarded with her short laugh.

"I have another proposal," she said as I clipped her harness to the carabiner and double-checked the knots. "If I make it to the top without falling once, I can ask you any five questions I want. *And* you can't pass." She raised her eyebrows at me.

"Wow, you do drive a tough bargain." I looked at her, then at the top of the ravine. She'd more likely be able to swap out a transmission by herself than climb this run without falling. "I'll only give you three."

"Deal." She went up to the rock and said, "Belay," as I had instructed.

"Belay on," I replied.

With one big breath she lifted her foot off the ground and pulled herself onto the rock. She made it a quarter the way up before her legs began to shake like a sewing machine needle, and her body hugged the wall. Her foot slipped, and she nearly fell.

"Crap dammit," she muttered.

"What did you say?" I tilted my head to the side. "Crap ... dammit?"

"Can we talk about this later?" she called down to me.

"Sure." I pressed my lips together, but then couldn't keep them shut. "It's just I've never heard those two words combined before, and I've heard some creative swearing."

She lifted her foot again and tested out another foothold. *Atta girl.*

"A few years ago, a kid came into the ER needing stitches or something, and he said it any time something made him nervous or scared." She spoke through her panting breaths. "He was like four, I think, so he said it more like 'cwap dammit,' but you know."

I burst out laughing. "You got it from a four-year-old."

"It started as a joke, and now it's my go-to cuss word. I mean phrase—I guess." Her words came out strained with her exertion, but her shoulders relaxed, and she took in a deep breath.

Right now, I couldn't dream of a more perfect point of view, unless I was the cliff. My mind superimposed my body in the place of the rock, and it was a perfect fit. Her chest would be snug against my pecs and her legs would be wrapped around—

Her foot slipped again, and her tension returned in full force. My mind climbed back to a safer path. She closed her eyes and hugged the cliff. I'd never been more jealous of a rock before.

"I can't do this."

"You're doing fine. Remember, if you get stuck, put your foot in a secure place and stand up."

"Nothing is secure up here," she grumbled.

"You could let go and fall." I called up to her. "Then I'm off the hook."

She squinted one eye open and straightened her shoulders.

*Uh-oh.* I was in trouble.

Her legs slipped again in the same spot, and I thought I was in the clear, but she didn't give up. She clung to the rock, put her foot back on the small ledge, and stood up. In half the time it took for her to climb the first part of the run, she'd doubled her distance from the ground. She tore up the rock until she reached the top.

She looked down at me and yelled, "I did it. I did it. I can't believe I did it!"

She stood at the top of the canyon, breathing heavily, and I felt drawn to her even more. Her sweat glistened in the sunlight, and her face shined bright in the aftermath of her accomplishment. She looked like a goddess.

"Okay, now how do I get down?" She stretched her arms and arched her back, then bent to look at me. "Or do I get to ask my questions from up here?"

The rope shook when I laughed. "Just sit back in your harness. Keep your feet on the cliff face so you maintain control, and I'll lower you to the ground."

"You want me to *sit back* into nothingness?"

"You can count to three if you like. It helps Maddie."

"You bring Maddie rock climbing?" Her voice cracked. "She's so little. She could get a subdural hematoma, or contusions, lacerations, or she could break all her bones in her body. You have no idea how many—"

"Whoa, slow down. Of course, I bring Maddie. She loves it." I paused and made sure my gloved hand held fast to the rope. "Lili, if you live your life in fear of all the bad things that can happen, you aren't living. You become stagnant like still pond water."

"There are millions of bacteria in rotten pond water."

No way on God's green Earth could I have predicted that would have been her response. I grunted in mock frustration.

"Whatever." I laughed. "You and your bacteria can live a wonderful life together, but you still have to come down."

Her head jerked up and down. "Okay, I'm coming down. I just have to lean back," she repeated and turned her back to me.

With a scream, she fell back into the harness and clutched onto the rope.

"You are amazing, Liliana!" I yelled up at her.

"You can compliment me once I'm on the ground." She clung to the rope with both her hands. "Just don't let go."

As soon as her feet touched the ground, she opened her eyes and threw her hands around my neck. My pulse hit the roof. I didn't expect her to come this close to me. Her soft body pressed against mine; I dropped the rope and cautiously placed my hands around her waist.

She pushed back from my chest. "I've never been happier to be on solid ground."

Stepping out of my arms, she tucked a stray hair behind her ear. She licked her lips, and I couldn't focus my eyes anywhere but there.

I'd never met such an enchanting woman.

The sun neared its apex by the time I served lunch. I had climbed a couple of runs after Lili finished her first climb, but she refused to go on another trip up the cliff wall. We sat together in the bed of my pickup, eating sandwiches and watching the dirt spin into the air.

"Are you ready for my first question?" Lili sat next to me on the tailgate of my truck.

We kicked our legs back and forth.

"Yes, and I'm counting that as your first question." I lifted one corner of my mouth with a cheek full of sandwich.

"Hey, not fair." She threw a carrot at me. "But since this is the best peanut butter and jelly I've ever eaten, I'll give it to you. I only have one question anyway."

As a single dad, I was the king of PB&Js. The ratio of peanut butter to jelly had to be perfect.

"And your question is?"

Her bottom lip disappeared beneath her top teeth while she examined her sandwich.

"Will you explain the scar on your shoulder, and why you try to keep it hidden?" She pointed to my left shoulder. "Was it the reason you didn't take your shirt off while we painted?"

"Oh." My voice dwindled to silence.

How could I word my answer without completely scaring her off? Skeletons were better left buried, but scars remained. I rubbed my shoulder.

Lili spoke again as if she sensed my discomfort. "I didn't mean to be so nosy. Forget it."

"No, it's okay. It's ... bad memories, you know?" I took a breath. "It's a common story for a kid in the system from Southern California. The man who I view as my father, Jorge Rodriguez, had a mechanic's garage—"

"Which explains your skillset."

I nodded. "When Jorge died, he left everything he owned to me, but he didn't tell me that the local gangs expected him to pay them for their protection. When they came to collect his debt from me, I refused. I was self-centered and overconfident at the time. I thought I could take on anyone."

I stopped talking. I'd been a cocky kid in my twenties, mostly because I also belonged to one of those gangs. I thought they'd show some sense of loyalty, but they hadn't. How could I tell her about the death threats? The drive-by shootings? Most of all, about the day I was attacked? I could still smell, almost taste, my burnt flesh. I chose my words carefully. "One day, a bunch of them came with a branding iron. I got in a few good punches, but I didn't stand a chance. They held me down while their leader heated it with a propane torch. He shoved the glowing branding iron onto my shoulder."

I lifted my sleeve and exposed the distorted double S brand.

She gasped and touched her fingers to her mouth.

"Don't worry, I'm okay." I wrapped my arm around her, reacting before I thought through my action. At my touch, she went rigid, and I froze. Then, she leaned into me ever so slightly and it gave me courage. I rubbed at her shoulder, the whole time thinking, I shouldn't be here with her. I shouldn't have asked her on this non-date, and I sure as hell shouldn't have my arm around her. I couldn't stop myself.

"Did they ever come back?"

"Yes. He threatened to go after Cindy, my ex-wife. I played along until I found a way out. I sold the shop for much less than what it was worth and came here. To small-town Idaho." My sleeve slipped back over my scar. "And I changed my name to Richardson. I couldn't let my daughter grow up in that environment."

I took a bite of my sandwich. "There are things I did for them, things I'm ashamed of. I pray that someday I'll do enough good to right some of those wrongs."

In those days, the people wronged were criminals. They deserved what I gave them, but Michael and Lili's baby girl were innocent. They haunted me the most. "That's why I owe so much to Jorge. When he adopted me, he taught me his trade and, with the last years of his life, he saved mine."

The wind picked up one of the plastic baggies in the truck bed and whipped it out into the desert. I hopped down and grabbed it before it was lost forever. When I turned back to the tailgate, Lili looked at me.

Her lips parted slightly. Her eyebrows drew upward in—concern? Pity? But not an ounce of the judgement I would expect from someone in a profession like hers.

"Thank you for today." Her voice was almost lost to the wind. "I've never done anything like this."

As if nothing had passed between us, she went back to eating her sandwich, but something did happen to me. Like the cold rock-face of a cliff touched by the sun, I warmed from the inside out any time she looked at me. The late morning sun illuminated her face and highlighted her lips. More than anything, I wanted to kiss them, but I didn't.

Tossing the rest of my sandwich into my mouth, I chewed too fast, and choked it down. I shouldn't have brought her here. I shouldn't be having these thoughts, or the urge to pull her into my arms and kiss her senseless.

I hopped back up onto the tailgate and looped one arm around her. She leaned against my chest, fitting there naturally. One tip of her happiness-o-meter toward the green was worth risking becoming too attached.

Wasn't it?

# Chapter 13

## Liliana

Nearly all of the seven hundred residents of Clear Springs crowded in the shadows of large cottonwood trees,. Tractors cut across distant fields, and dust clouds rose behind them with the grain harvest in full swing. Rows of scattered grain stalks were sucked up and shoved into neatly packaged bales. I focused on the tractors as I followed Renee into the mass of people.

If only the pieces of my life could be shoved into place with one easy pass of a tractor. I laughed under my breath and stepped onto the bright green grass which contrasted with the gravel and dried weeds lining the park. My legs were still shaky from going rock climbing yesterday. I needed to work out more.

Vendors, bouncy houses, and food trucks added to the rush of activity at Trout Fest, the social event of the year. A large metal tub sat at the center of it all, filled with clear water and hundreds of fish. Juana's street taco aroma mixed with the fishy smell.

The sun warmed my face and the back of my neck as I weaved my way through the crowd. The closer we came to the pond, the fishier the air became. I held my hand over my nose and looked at the food trucks. If only their smells could follow me everywhere. My phone buzzed. A text from Tiff.

> *Any sign of the hot mechanic?*

> *Nope. Maybe he won't show. (Fingers crossed.)*

> *Oh, he's coming. This is the most activity your love life has seen since I've known you.*

> *He'll come for his daughter, not because he's interested in me.*

> *You keep telling yourself that. Remember, when he goes in for the kiss, open your mouth, and go with the flow.*

Blake. Kiss. Blood pulsed to my extremities at the possibility. I knew how to kiss. Okay, I might be a little rusty, but I didn't have anything to worry about with the way Blake had barely looked at my boobs the other day. The 'girls' had been right in front of his face, and his eyes didn't even linger. I shoved my phone back into my pocket.

My old high school volleyball coach, Mr. Southerland, splashed his hand in the water as Renee and I approached.

"Hey, Lili." Coach Southerland waved to me with the same efficient enthusiasm he used on the court.

His once thick, black hair had dwindled to nothing but a thin ring around the base of his skull. Sunlight glared off his dark-toned scalp and the thick-framed glasses on his nose. He was still as tall and thin as a bean pole.

I returned his greeting with a smile.

"Hello, Rex. Where's Wendy? She promised to give me her salsa recipe. My garden is bursting with tomatoes this year," Renee said.

Renee had also finally found time to garden. Throughout my childhood, she'd bought gardening magazines, and one year we'd even been brave enough to plant one. Only the beans had survived.

Coach pointed to the round outdoor amphitheater at the far end of the park. Much like a giant clam shell, white plaster lined the domed interior of the theater while gray-brown lava rock covered the exterior. The stage consisted of a slab of concrete. Large, speckled pink-and-green fish banners flapped in the wind against its railing.

"I'll be right back, Lili." Renee sped off toward Wendy, leaving me alone with Coach.

"Do you still have a wicked arm swing?"

I hadn't touched a volleyball since I'd graduated high school. "No."

"Shame. You're still one of the best right-side hitters I had come through the program. If you hadn't run off and gotten married, I would have gotten you a scholarship."

I kept my face plastered with an expression I hoped looked like pleasure, remembering why I'd moved away.

"Blake," Coach said, looking over my shoulder.

I turned around to find Blake approaching. A black backpack hung over his shoulder and Maddie, headphones securely in place, walked by his side with a large bag of cotton candy. I hugged my arms close to my chest, thinking of the kiss Tiff kept rooting for.

I hadn't been able to keep him out of my mind and found myself daydreaming of his arm slipping around my shoulder and holding me like he had on his tailgate. In my dreams, he'd pulled me in for a kiss.

That scared me.

"Hello, Mr. Rex." Maddie held her sticky hand in front of her like it was contaminated.

"Hi, Sweetie," Coach said to Maddie. Then he pointed at Blake and me. "You know, you two make a good-looking couple. Maybe you'll be crowned Trout King and Queen." Coach lifted his hand at another person passing by. "This year's Trout King and Queen get a sponsored night out from the Moose Lodge. All you have to do is catch the most trout."

He wanted me to climb into a trout pond and compete with the other unmarried people in this town? I looked down at my blue summer dress and red, Italian alligator leather heels. Hell no.

"I know what a fierce competitor you are, Lili. Don't let me down." Rex tipped his head to us, his bright white teeth stood out against his lips. "Got to go. Mayoral duties call." He bent closer to my ear. "I beat Williams by fifteen votes."

I bit my lip to keep from laughing. He took this town and its festival seriously. Maddie shoved a large bite of cotton candy in her mouth. The little girl glanced at her bag and then at me. She raised it to me.

I shook my head but softened my rejection with a small grin. Maddie hugged closer to her daddy's leg but still stayed by my side. The smell of the trout pond became overpowering, so I moved closer to the food trucks. Maddie tugged her father along with her as she followed me.

Blake gestured to the makeshift pond. "You going to do it?"

A dimple formed when he half-smiled at me. Men shouldn't be given dimples. It gave them an unfair advantage over us women. "No. You?"

"You're looking at the reigning Trout King." He stepped in front of me and took a bow.

I laughed.

Maddie giggled. "Can I go in the pond yet, Daddy?"

"Not yet. How about you run and play at the bouncy houses? They look like fun."

Maddie stepped toward the large yellow slide with kids hollering and running all around, her sticky hand still out in front of her, but shook her head and tucked herself behind her father.

"She has a hard time with kids her age." Blake patted her back and rubbed it in circles.

I nodded and stared at the chaos surrounding the bounce houses. "Can you blame her? I don't want to go near there either."

Maddie looked at me and offered me a shy smile.

A few yards away, Angelina Johnson, my closest friend from high school, waved at us, a street taco in the other hand. She'd dyed her hair platinum blonde and lost some weight, but I'd recognize her anywhere.

"Ohmygoodness, Blake, is that *you?* I was so excited you were at the 'Connection Mixer' last weekend." She stopped by Blake's side and took a bite of her taco. "Oh, hi Lili. Mom said you were back in town." She spoke around the food in her mouth.

"Angelina? How are you?"

"I'm good. I go by Angie now, by the way. I haven't seen you in forever." She stepped between Blake and me and gave me a hug.

I hugged her back.

"We used to be practically sisters," I explained.

"Yep," Angie continued. "Lili'd come over and spend the night all the time. She never did any of the farm chores, though. I think she's afraid of farm animals."

Blake laughed out loud, and the corner of my mouth tipped downward. A fear of cows and horses was not unheard of. Roosters? Those birds came straight from hell.

"Can I have everyone's attention?" Mayor Southerland spoke into a microphone on the stage. "It's time for this year's Trout Fest to begin."

A cheer rose from the crowd.

"We'd like to say thank you to Greg Randalls' family trout hatchery for donating such fine fish."

Loud applause sounded as Greg took off his cowboy hat and waved it in the air. I couldn't stifle my laugh. Nothing could be more country than this.

Wendy stepped to the microphone. "Kids between the ages of five and ten, please make your way to the trout pool. On the whistle, the trout catching will begin. Y'all know the drill from there. Remember, be safe and have fun."

With another cheer, the mayor and his wife stepped down from the stage. Renee stood right behind him still occasionally whispering to his wife. She glanced in my direction and waved.

"Daddy, I'm old enough to do it this year," Maddie reminded Blake, the bag of cotton candy swinging in her grip.

"You sure are, honey. Hand me your shirt and shorts, and I'll get you a good spot."

Maddie slipped off her grease-stained tennis shoes, then slid her headphones around her neck and looked at her hand like she didn't know what to do with it. Blake lowered the backpack and pulled out some wipes. He cleaned off her hand and helped her remove her shorts and shirt to reveal a navy blue and white polka-dotted swimming suit.

"Oh, Blake, your daughter is so cute," Angie said.

Maddie met my gaze and quirked her eyebrow before she shoved her headphones back over her ears and followed her father to the edge of the shiny metal trough. I chuckled and walked closer, braving the smell.

Maddie pressed her headphones tighter to her head in the middle of the chaos next to the pond.

The whistle sounded and the kids, assisted by their parents, clambered over the edge into the water. Maddie didn't go in right away. She stared at the other kids for a minute before she nodded at Blake. He lifted her into the pool, but unlike the other kids who were diving, and grabbing at wriggling fish, Maddie stood still, the water at her waste, her eyes wide.

"Try to get one, Mads." Blake pointed to the middle of the makeshift pool.

Placing my hands on the metal edge, I looked at the trout darting through the water. Each time Maddie got hit with water she flinched. She eventually relaxed and put her hand in the water, laughing any time a fish touched it.

Bug never got old enough to experience this. I let go of the edge of the trough.

Angie stood by Blake's side, still talking, but his focus centered on his daughter. When Maddie beamed, he beamed. When she grimaced, he grimaced. He was the same type of devoted father Michael had been.

I sucked in air through my nose. Blake was nothing like Michael. Michael had been the lean, tall, bookworm type, and Blake was anything but that.

The whistle sounded again. Kids spilled out of the pool and the next age group hopped in. Blake helped Maddie out of the pond and wrapped a towel around her shoulders. While Maddie talked about the way the fish tickled her legs, I walked to the base of a tree. Maddie grabbed Blake's hand and pulled him over to where I sat. Angie followed.

"Hey, I'll be right back. I'm going to grab some popcorn. You want something?" Angie paused on her way to the food vendors.

Blake shook his head. Angie lifted her eyebrows at me waiting for an answer.

"Will you get me one of Juana's tacos?" I asked. I hadn't eaten one since Michael and I moved back home after finishing our bachelor's.

Angie nodded once and walked away toward the popcorn vendor.

"Did you see me in the water, Lili?" Maddie asked as she put on her shorts and sat next to the tree, matching me with one knee bent and an arm draped over it.

Her bright eyes held the wonder of a new experience, as if she had dreamed of this moment for years and it had been more than what she expected, never mind that she hadn't caught a single fish.

"You did great, Maddie," I said over the whistle as it sounded again. "I didn't want to get in when I was your age."

"Did your mom make you?" Maddie asked.

"No, but my dad did." That was back when my life had been perfect and untouched by tragedy, but there was no going back, no matter how badly I wanted to.

"I'm sure you miss him," Blake said.

I missed my dad. My husband. My daughter. "Missed"—such a shallow word for the depth of feeling it evoked. We sat quietly watching the people pass by us. Maddie, tucked in her towel, leaned against the tree. Blake knew everyone there and got sucked into a few short conversations. I remembered what it'd been like living in this town. Part of me craved

WHAT HAPPENS IN IDAHO

to go back to the anonymity of the city, yet a growing part of me wanted to be seen.

Angie returned with her bag of popcorn and handed me my taco. I took a bite. The cilantro, grilled onions, and spicy pork tasted of home. The whistle sounded as kids climbed in and fish came out. I finished my taco. The teenagers hopped in for their turn.

"Oh," Angie threw some popcorn into her mouth. "It's almost time. I'm totally going to kick your butt, Lili. You may have caught more fish our junior year, but this time, I'm going to win."

"I'm not doing it."

"Why not?" Maddie hugged her towel around her. "Don't be afraid. It doesn't hurt when the fish bite."

"I'm not afraid of the fish." I brushed my ponytail off my shoulder.

"Then what are you afraid of? That I'll beat you?" Angie lifted one side of her lips, challenging me.

This grown-up version of Angelina wasn't going to goad me into jumping into a fishpond.

"And we'll finally know who deserves to be the real Dandelion Princess," Angie continued.

The Dandelion Princess—Angie and I had fought over a crown of weeds Angie's mom had made when we were around eleven years old. Nora offered to make another one, but the first one had been the best. We'd fought over the chain until it broke. With both of us in tears, Nora had made us race around the house for it. I had won. Until I'd moved to St. Louis, with any competition, we'd traded a crown of dandelions back and forth, except in the winter, when the dandelions didn't grow.

"We already know I am the Dandelion Princess. I don't need to prove anything." I stood and leaned my shoulder against the trunk of the tree. Maddie mimicked me.

"Can I be a Dandelion Princess, Daddy?" Maddie tugged on Blake's arm.

"Sure, honey." Blake helped her slip her arm into her sleeve. He tucked the damp towel back into the bag.

"Last I recall, I have the crown. You are currently the loser." Angie looked at me with smugness coating her face.

"It's time for the event you have all been waiting for." Mayor Southerland's voice echoed through the microphone cutting off my reply. "Will all the unmarried adults nineteen and up make their way to the pond?"

Renee chose to show up as I stomped toward the pond. I was the damned Dandelion Princess. I yanked off my alligator pumps. After handing Maddie her headphones, Blake followed, probably grinning at my back.

"I'll keep an eye on Maddie for you, Blake. Good luck, Lili." Renee stayed by the tree with Maddie just outside the crowd.

"May the best woman win." Angie took off her shoes and climbed in the pond.

I swung over the edge and dipped my feet in the not-so-clear water. I ignored how much fish feces and urine was likely in it at this point in the day. A large trout nibbled at my toe, and I squeaked. Blake slid into the pond beside me.

"What's the matter Lili? Are you scared of a little fish?" Angie taunted me.

Angie slid her hands into the water, caught a small trout and tossed it at me. It flopped against my chest before falling back into the makeshift pond.

It. Was. On. The dandelion crown, and the one with the large trout on it, were mine.

"Dude. Lil-dog. It's been forever." A man with an all too familiar face splashed his way over to me. "What's up?"

A rock had a higher IQ than Troy Matthews. His board shorts hung low, exposing the top of his plaid boxer shorts. A picture of a rhinoceros on his shirt sat beneath the words *Save the Chubby Unicorns*.

I'd dated him in high school to annoy Renee. I regretted it.

"Hi, Troy." I remained on the edge of the trough, not quite ready to enter the cesspool.

"You want to be my queen?" He flicked his shaggy hair out of his eyes. "I'm going to win this thing this year." He glared at Blake.

Blake ignored Troy and placed his hand on the small of my back, helping me the rest of the way into the pond. The bottom of my dress soaked up the trout water. "Thank you."

"Are you good?" Blake asked.

"I'm fine. Thanks. Any tips?"

"Yeah. Don't be afraid of the fish." He laughed.

I lumped fish into the same category as cows. I like to eat a fish filet, but I didn't like to be the one to catch and prepare it.

Less than a dozen people competed in the Clear Springs singles' market, which included Chuck and my ex-man-child, Troy. It didn't matter how many other people were in the competition, this was between me and Angie.

Mayor Southerland shouted into the microphone. "Wendy. Set the countdown to ten minutes."

The baseball score board lit up with ten minutes on the clock. With the glare of the sun, the numbers were hard to make out.

"On your mark," Mayor Southerland called. "Get set."

I bent my knees and focused on the fish, trying to make sense of their patterns. My muscles tensed, but I forced my arms to relax.

"*Go!*"

The whistle sounded and I dove after my first fish. I missed and slapped the water. Again and again I tried, but couldn't manage to catch one fetching fish. Angie stood with a trout in her hands and ran to her tub to drop it in.

With five minutes left, I had yet to catch a single one. Letting my hands hang in the water, I waited until a big one swam close, trying to remember how to do this. Chuck ran past me, splashing me with water, chasing a group of fish in my direction. This was my chance.

I closed my fingers around the cold slime of a rainbow trout. The fish floundered in my hands, but I wasn't going to let it out of my grasp. I pulled it close to my chest and ran to my bin.

One fish successfully deposited in my bucket. I threw my hands in the air celebrating my triumph, but then I peeked in Blake's trout bin. He had at least ten in his.

Three minutes. I used the same tactic on the next fish. I grabbed another trout, and another. I ran back and forth until my heart raced, and my breaths came in shallow gasps.

The buzzer sounded.

My soaked dress and arms glinted with silvery fish scales. I was going to scrub for hours in the shower when I got home. I counted my fish.

Five. Not too bad. Angie dumped her fish on the opposite side of the pond, and I was too proud to walk over there and count her collection.

This time Wendy took over the microphone. "Time is up put down your trout and come to the stage while the judges make their count."

Blake hopped out first and held his hand out to help me. I thought of the mud squishing between my fingers during the cow incident, the way he'd wiped the paint off my face, the feeling of his hard chest against mine when I'd hugged him rock climbing, and the concern on his face when I ran to my room to cry.

I knew I was at risk of falling head over heels for him.

Without taking his hand, I managed to scramble to the grass. Goosebumps stood on my arms. I looked at my shoes and at my wet feet covered in blades of grass. Cringing, I bent and slipped my heels on.

Blake peeked into my bin. "Pretty good."

"How many did you catch?" I asked.

"A few."

"Blake." Renee walked to him with a teary-eyed Maddie at her side. She held her headphones tight to her ears. "Maddie's had enough of this crowd. I told her I would take her into town to buy stuff for one of the stray kitties to make her feel better. Would you mind taking Lili home?"

"I'll go with you," I interrupted before Blake could respond.

"Nonsense. I might be a while and you'll want to shower." Renee waved her hand in front of me.

"No problem, Renee. I'll make sure she gets home," Blake said.

If I had a car, none of this would be an issue. Stupid cow.

With Angie behind me and Blake in front of me, I followed the line of wet singles to the stage while Rex and Wendy went to each bin and tallied the fish.

"Would you like a towel?" Blake unzipped his backpack.

"Oh, I would love one," Angie leaned past me to take the pink towel from Blake. "Aren't you thoughtful?"

Apparently, we were competing for more than the dandelion crown. Angie didn't understand. I would let her have Blake, but I wanted that towel.

Rex and Wendy walked to the microphone.

"This year's Trout King and Queen are," Wendy paused to add to the suspense. Her dishwater-blonde hair pulled into a tight bun. "Blake Richardson and Angie Johnson."

Angie threw her hands in the air and yelled, "I'm the real Dandelion Princess!"

Even though I'd lost, I laughed as the crowd cheered. Rex placed a crown with a stuffed rainbow trout on both Blake and Angie.

"And your Trout Prince and Princess are—" Wendy's voice rang out clear.

Wait. Since when was there a prince and princess?

"Troy Mathews and our recently returned, Dr. Liliana Chase."

"Woo!" Troy jabbed his fist in the air and came to my side.

He threw his arm around my shoulders while Rex put a crown with a much smaller fish on my head. He also handed me a gift card.

"This is good for one night only. Royalty has an obligation to go together. Don't forget to wear your crowns." Rex left me to go stand next to his wife.

Troy pulled me into a side hug. "Pick you up at eight."

His voice grated against my ear drum, and I shuddered. He released my shoulders and loped off the stage with his fisted hands raised above his head.

My gaze shifted from Troy to the gift card. One free night of unlimited bowling at Evergreen Bowl. A fish hat and bowling. Life couldn't get any classier.

# Chapter 14

## Liliana

B lake said he had one errand to run, and then he would take me home where I could wash the fish filth off me. He'd driven to Angie's house—my sanctuary as a kid—to get a check from her mom, Nora, for his Relay for Life Team.

Could this guy be any more like Captain America?

Large, useless antique farming equipment sat in piles along the Johnson's long driveway. The rusted hunks of metal almost concealed the bright-blue house with its old cedar shake roof. The house was an island in the center of a hundred acres of farmland surrounded by a sea of cookie-cutter houses.

I'd never forgotten the nights I'd spent at Nora's house. A place of comfort when I couldn't handle Renee's drinking, or when her insults turned from mildly annoying to abuse. Nora had never turned me away.

"They built the neighborhood around her house and land, huh?" I asked.

"Yes, they did. The Johnsons aren't too happy about it." Blake pulled his truck to the side of the paved road.

The pungent smell of fish filled the cab of the truck, the cardboard tree car freshener not quite able to overpower it. Heat wavered on the horizon, yet I shivered in my wet clothes. I picked fish scales off my hands and dropped them in a pile on my lap, refusing to get Blake's truck dirty. Not a speck of mud could be found in its interior. He must have had it detailed.

"I'm going to walk from here. Their driveway gets muddy after it rains. I just cleaned my truck." He half-smiled at me. "If you're all right with that? You can wait here—"

"Sure. I thought—"

"Unless you want to walk with me?" He focused out the window as he asked his question.

He'd been a little more reserved since our rock-climbing non-date and painting the house. Maybe I'd pushed too far asking about his scar, but while he seemed content to keep me at a distance, I craved to know more about him. The broken parts of me connected with his rough upbringing. Perhaps, one damaged soul could heal another.

"I was actually going to come with you. This was like my second home."

He opened his door, and I slid over the seats to follow him out, having learned that I would never be able to open his passenger side door.

A brief cloudburst poured down after we'd left Trout Fest. The last of the rain from the passing dark cloud dropped through the sunshine. The wind ebbed and flowed about us. Killdeer and Meadowlarks sang in the late afternoon heat.

I avoided puddles and the piles of horse manure, remembering the horse and buggy rides Angie's dad had taken us on down this lane. Sprinklers sounded in the field; their mist and the moist smell of the dirt transported me back in time. Noises from the neighborhood kids as they got home from the festival mingled with the distant sounds of chickens and cows. Country living did have some charm to it.

I paused at the barn and turned full circle. "This used to be so different. All these houses were fields. What happened to the farms?"

"Developers are paying top dollar for farmland." Blake stepped closer to me. "Commercial farms are making it hard for the family operations to stay afloat."

"I love this place. Change is hard." I bit my bottom lip and continued walking.

He stayed by my side. By all accounts, the neighborhood people would see a couple on an afternoon walk, but we weren't a couple. I took two steps to my right and distanced myself from Blake. We walked in silence until we reached the porch.

"Do you do this every year? The Relay for Life thing?" I clasped my hands in front of me and walked up the old wooden steps to the front entry.

"This will be my third year. I think." Blake knocked on the door.

Eleanor Johnson opened it. "Lili? Lili Bo Billy? Is it really you? Renee told me you were coming for a visit, but I didn't believe her. I said, 'Renee, dear, are you sure you haven't lost your marbles, Lili is much too busy bein' a doctor to come visitin' small-town folk like us.' But now, here you are in the flesh. If I didn't see it with my own eyes, I still wouldn't be believin' it."

Nora was close in age to Renee. More wrinkles lined her face than I remembered, but her eyes were as youthful as ever. She still dyed her short hair red, which clashed with her maroon apron with the local grocery store's logo imprinted on it, *At Nora's We're Family*. Eleanor hadn't even changed the color of lipstick she wore. Bright, vibrant red.

"Hi, Nora. You still own the grocery store?" I should have come here sooner.

"Of course. The store has become one of the family. Couldn't get rid of it if I tried. Hello, Blake." She finally acknowledged Blake's presence. She waved her hand in front of her nose. "I can tell where you two are comin' from. I had to man the store. You caught me on my break. Why don't you come in out of the heat while I write you the check? Don't get any fish scales on the furniture."

We followed her into the entryway and down the hall. I crossed into the living room. The same light-blue carpet with a fleur-de-lis pattern etched into it covered the floor. They'd gotten new tan suede couches to replace the old floral loveseat I'd slept on as a teenager on the nights Angie had refused to share her bed. I hadn't minded. That couch had been the most comfortable thing on the planet.

Blake sat and shifted his weight against the armrest of the love seat while I wandered to the wall with the Johnson's family pictures on it. They kept the old family pictures hanging with their current ones. I moved my finger along the wall until I came to my favorite picture, where Eleanor and Tony had more than Jared and Angie in the picture.

"They still have it hanging up." I pointed at the picture and looked at Blake. "I went to help the photographer, but they asked me to stand in the picture with them."

Blake came to my side and leaned in closer. "You look happy."

It'd been a bittersweet moment where I acted as half imposter, half daughter. Not saying anything, Blake placed his hand on my upper back and rubbed in a circle. I closed my eyes and savored his touch.

"Lili, dear." Eleanor stood in the doorway to the hall with a check in her hand. Blake's hand fell away from my back. "We've missed y'all so much. It's so nice to have you back in this house. Anthony would come out and tell you himself, but he's taking his nap."

I opened my mouth to say something but closed it again. How long had it been since I'd seen Nora or Tony? When was the last time I'd talked to them? In the hospital when I'd lost Michael and my baby girl, they'd held me as my world crumbled, while Renee sat in jail.

"I'm sorry. It's hard for me to come back."

Nora handed the check to Blake. "Well." She cleared her throat. "Nothing much changes here. We'll be here when you need us."

Yeah, except for the whole neighborhood of houses and a new handsome mechanic, everything was exactly the same.

Blake slipped the check into his damp pocket. "Thank you, Nora. Tell Tony I said hi."

"Sure thing. Lili, you best come by and spend some time with your Papa Tony or there'll be hell to pay."

I followed Blake to the front door and paused. "Yes, Ma'am," I said in my finest country drawl. I walked through the door Blake held open for me.

I squinted against the bright sunshine; the smell of damp earth still thick in the air. Blake walked close to my side, his hand occasionally brushing mine. We rounded a curve in the driveway. I could no longer see the Johnson's house, and the neighborhood houses were blocked by the corn field and a row of pine trees.

It was as if we were in a world of our own. The brief contact of his hand grounded me in the sea of loneliness I'd been drifting on for years. I closed my eyes and leaned into his touch.

He stopped walking and angled his face down to mine. Needing to be held by a man—to be kissed—to be wanted, I turned to him. The wind picked up, rustling the tall stalks of corn, and the sound of the large sprinkler on the pivot kept time with the beats of my heart. I lifted my chin, bringing my lips within inches of his.

Nervous, no, *afraid* I wouldn't be good at this anymore, I closed my eyes and took a deep breath. This was the biggest step I'd taken since the accident and opening to the vulnerability of potential attachment was like stepping to the edge of an endless chasm and jumping, not knowing what lay at the bottom. Reality hit me with a jolt—over the course of six days, my desire to let the spark between us envelope me had outweighed my fear.

His breath fluttered against my lips, he leaned closer to me, the warmth of his body tantalized my skin, still ripe with goosebumps from my damp clothes in the breeze.

Then he took a step back, and the air chilled in the shade of the corn without his presence. With his eyes still locked on mine, his boot landed in a pile of horse manure.

He cleared his throat and half laughed. "Do you think this smell is going to complement the fish thing I already have going for me?"

I didn't answer him.

Tucking my hands around my midsection, I moved to the corn, hoping he didn't notice my flushed cheeks. I swallowed around the lump in my throat. What in the hell had I tried to do? I loved Michael. I didn't need to be running around kissing guys I barely knew.

To top off my embarrassment, Blake didn't want to kiss me. I must have not understood the signals I thought he had intentionally sent me. The bracelet. The paint. The rock-climbing non-date which'd clearly been a date. The way he'd rubbed my back at Nora's, and with the way his hand kept brushing mine, I thought he'd been finding excuses to touch me.

I all but grabbed him and took advantage of him in this field, but he clearly had no interest in me. Tears stung my eyes. I'd promised myself I would never be with another man the day Michael died, yet I'd lost sight of that in one weak moment.

The whole way back to the truck, Blake gave me a wide berth, and I followed behind him, rejected, humiliated, and entirely guilty of betraying the memory of my husband.

# Chapter 15

## Blake

"Lili—" Not sure of what to say, my voice fell away with the sound of my truck engine.

A couple of tears ran down her cheek. I was lower than a turd on a toadstool. I shifted my truck into gear; so much for keeping my distance. Why did Lili have to be so tempting? I'd nearly kissed her. Luckily, I'd returned to my senses before my lips made contact.

What kind of a man lusted for a woman still grieving for her husband?

I wanted to comfort her, apologize, or tell her what an idiot I was, but I stayed silent, afraid I would make things worse. I faced the same challenges when my daughter cried. Nothing I could do would fix a crying woman and it drove me crazy. The tears in her eyes had cleared by the time we drove out of the neighborhood.

I wiped the sweat off my forehead, leftover fish stench clinging to the palms of my hands. How easy it would have been to kiss her. What would it be like to have her body pressed against me, her warm lips moving against mine? My tires rolled off the road onto the gravel shoulder, and I swerved back into my lane.

She yanked on the seat belt, but it locked twice before she was able to slip it over her shoulder and successfully latch it. She struggled to roll down the manual window.

I drove under the speed limit and occasionally glanced in her direction. "Look, Lili—"

Only managing to get the window down a crack, she slammed her hand against the door. My truck had done nothing to make her upset. I was the one who deserved to be punished.

"You know what, I don't get you. You say you're just a mechanic, yet you volunteer as a fireman or an EMT or whatever and run around the county on a mission to rid the world of cancer." Her voice wasn't loud, but it was as venomous as a rattler.

"I like to help people." I pressed my foot down harder on the accelerator.

She tore her hand away from the window handle.

"Do you even care about cancer, or is this one way you make yourself feel better about your life?"

No wonder she'd didn't have a boyfriend. Michael had to be a saint. I laughed. "Wow, you don't pull any punches when you're pissed."

I looked from the road to her. She folded her arms and glared at me.

"I don't even want to be here, in this truck, in this town with you, anyway." She threw her hands in the air and gestured out the window. "But Renee and your daughter had different ideas."

I no longer found her anger entertaining. "Leave Maddie out of this."

"Why? Because she's being raised in a mechanic's shop? Do you know how many ways she could get injured in that environment? I bet her mother wouldn't let her run around covered in grease."

Frustrating woman sensed my weakness like an expert boxer and didn't ease up. I slammed on the brakes and pulled over into the tall weeds along the side of the road, bringing the truck to a stop.

Cindy would have landed Maddie in the hospital, either from neglect or her impatience with Maddie's tantrums—or straight up abuse.

"You have no idea what her mother was like." I kept my voice low, but my control was slipping. One minute she'd been trying to kiss me, the next she was yelling at me and insulting my parenting. Selfish. That was what she was. It was about time someone told her. "You are so damn selfish." I killed the engine.

I leaned over to reach inside the glove compartment, and my face was inches from her. She shifted to the door and jiggled the handle, her knees blocking the glove compartment. She grimaced and closed her eyes.

I backed away from her. "Look, I'm just trying to get in the glove box to answer your question."

Lili moved out of my way, and I opened the glove box to retrieve a wallet-sized picture. I dropped it in her lap and sat back behind the steering wheel. I didn't have to look at the picture to know what image was on it—the cutest strawberry-blonde three-year-old girl with a grin that warmed your heart.

"This is Marlene. She was Maddie's best friend." I shoved my hand through my hair.

She studied the picture a moment longer before she spoke. "Was ...?"

"She was diagnosed with an incurable brain tumor while they were in pre-school together. Her home life wasn't good, she was autistic, and her parents didn't know how to deal with it, so she came and lived with us for a while before she was hospitalized."

"Did Maddie—I mean—was she okay?"

"Eventually. For a time, we had a small hope Marlene's cancer wasn't as incurable as the doctors had said, but—" I slumped my shoulders unable to finish the sentence.

*Do you even care about cancer?* Her question played again in my mind. Why did I spend so much time doing Relay for Life every year? I thought of Marlene, her curiosity, and her beautiful blue eyes. In the end, I couldn't do anything to save her.

"Yes. I do, in fact, care about cancer. I care since sometimes, no one else will," I said.

The truck's engine popped while it cooled down.

She shifted on my suede seat. "What happened to Marlene? I mean when did—"

"She die?" I finished. "Shortly after she turned four. She passed two years ago, almost to the day."

I moved to face her. She closed her eyes and let the tiny picture fall into her lap. Maybe I'd pushed her too hard, shoved her into the deep end without a floatie. Two years and losing Marlene still hurt. Since her death, Maddie had never made another friend or even played with another kid her age.

"Blake. I ... I'm sorry," Lili stammered. Tears welled in her eyes, but I turned away from her and stared out the window.

"I'm so sorry," she said again. "About what I said about Maddie. I just—"

I took a deep breath. Grief, the kind of pain that never really left, marked her. I owned a portion of her anguish, so I did my best to let it go. "It's all right."

I started the truck again and didn't say a word to her the entire way to Renee's house. I got out and opened her door. Lili slid off the seat, and her feet touched the ground.

Fish odor clung to her, and her ponytail sagged at the tip. Silver fish scales glistened on her dress, but she was still attractive in the most aggravating way, more so than she had been that morning all done up.

I shook my head, recalling the way she'd hugged those fish and carried them like she was going to tuck them in bed, and the clamp on my heart eased. "Are you planning on going on the date tonight, with Angie and Troy?"

"No. I don't think so." She shook her head. "You?"

I blew air out my nose and scrubbed a hand down the side of my face. I couldn't break tradition. It was the price of being king.

"Yes, I'll probably go. I can't stand up Angie It'd crush her."

I got back into my truck. Her trout princess crown sat crumpled next to the passenger-side door.

"Don't forget to wear this." I picked up the crown and tossed it out the window to her. "You should think about coming tonight. It'd be a lot more fun with you there. I might even look forward to it." The words cut their way through my dry throat. Honestly, if she didn't come, I'd probably be more relaxed.

She caught the crown. "I'll think about it."

I left her standing in the driveway, strangling the stuffed trout in her grip.

# Chapter 16

## Liliana

I leaned against the old wooden door of the bathroom, buried my face in my hands, and gagged. Nothing was worse than the stench of fish. Grabbing a rag, I turned on the sink and scrubbed at my face.

Why had I said those things about his wife and daughter? With a past like mine, I should be the most sensitive person, yet, I'd been callous, mean, and petty, all because he'd rejected me.

During residency and into my fellowship, my attending surgeons had psychologically flayed me, forcing me to learn how to be competent at my worst. They'd inadvertently taught me the art of torture. Sensing some-one's weakness and knowing where to push to cause maximum damage to a person's psyche wasn't a skill I'd intended to gain in my medical training, yet in one of my most vulnerable moments, I'd lashed out in anger, trying to make Blake taste of the agony his dismissal embedded in me.

It had backfired.

Turning on the bathwater, I adjusted the temperature to as hot as my skin could tolerate. I opened the cabinet under the sink and picked up the aromatherapy bubble bath labeled *Stress Relief*.

Something clattered to the bottom of the cabinet and a glint of metal caught my eye. I bent and picked up a Chevy car key—the key to the Malibu. So, my mother had stashed it. I didn't have to play her games anymore, at least not with transportation.

I left the key where it lay and moved to the bathtub, pouring the liquid into the water.

Bubbles formed, cresting the top of the tub, and I shut off the faucet. I took off my clothes and lowered myself into the water, breathing in eucalyptus and spearmint.

I squeezed my eyes shut and pushed the tips of my fingers to my forehead. Was I jealous of his daughter being alive and well? Yes. That was also why I avoided the pediatric floor, parks, and play places. I couldn't handle the direct evidence that other people had managed to keep their children healthy while my Bug ... I took a breath and opened my eyes.

As it turned out, Blake had watched a little girl die in a hospital bed—a girl he'd cared for. Sinking lower in the tub, I wished I could disappear.

Life support monitors had beeped in the background of my Bug's room until I'd stopped them. They'd left it up to me. The doctors had put the choice into my hands to give up all hope. When the beeping stopped, no other room in the world had been so silent. I'd half-believed my daughter's chest would rise and fall without the machine, hoping for a miracle. Two hours later, with no signs of life, I accepted that my miracle wouldn't come.

I pictured Maddie's little friend lying in a hospital bed, but the little girl morphed into my Bug. Gauze covered the side of her face. An endotracheal tube taped to her lips. Her eyes closed as if she could wake up at any moment, throw her arms around my neck, and say, 'Goo morning, Mommy' like she used to.

I lowered further into the warm water, my nose dipping beneath its surface. I stayed there until it became painful. How easy would it be to let myself sink—aspirate water, fill my lungs, and never have to face another day?

*Breathe*, my body screamed at me.

I lifted my nose above the water and forced air into my lungs, one painful breath at a time.

Michael once told me that he loved the light I carried with me. As cliché as it sounded, he told me that any time I entered a room, it brightened. When he died, my light went out, and I had no desire to get it back.

It wasn't all right, this person I'd become. The doctor. The surgeon. This wasn't me. How had I become so bitter and cynical toward the world and everyone in it? The cold porcelain rim of the clawfoot bathtub eased the ache at the base of my skull. Would it be possible to show Blake the way I used to be before day zero?

I scrubbed my hair and body twice, conditioned and rinsed. I stepped out of the tub and wrapped a towel around me.

Boots and an old skirt from my senior year of high school still sat in my closet. I put on the skirt and my green button-up shirt. The band of the skirt was slightly loose, but it still worked.

I braided my hair, put on mascara, and pinched my cheeks to add color, still not sure what I'd say to Troy when he came to take me on our one-sided date. To go or not to go, that was the question.

The stairs creaked under the pressure of my foot as I made my way downstairs.

"Hello?" Renee hollered. "Lili, is that you?"

Who else would it be? "Yeah, it's me."

I turned the corner into the living room where my mother sat on the couch with pictures spread all over. Toile curtains reduced the evening sunlight coming through the windows.

"I remember that skirt. You wore it for senior pictures," Renee said.

"Yep. I can't believe it still fits."

"It looks great on you. You going to go on the trout date tonight?"

"I haven't decided."

Renee frowned. "I don't blame you. Of all the men in this town who could have won, it had to be Troy Matthews."

I laughed and leaned over the arm of the couch to look at the faces grinning up at me. Pictures of my various birthdays with cakes alight before my ever-blowing face, of me on my first bike ride with helmet and elbow pads in place, and one of Renee and me laughing as we spread out a picnic blanket.

I picked up the picnic picture. I'd been eleven or twelve, and Renee's arms were wrapped around me from behind. She wore the same toothy grin I did. She'd asked someone to take the picture with the disposable camera she'd stashed in her purse.

I distinctly remembered that particular picnic. It was one of a handful of times that Renee had been sober and able to take me out during the day.

"We were really happy sometimes, weren't we?"

"Yes, we were." Renee smoothed the crinkled corner on the picture she held.

The pictures of my father were neatly organized into a pile on Renee's lap. I didn't have to look through the well-worn pictures to know what they'd show.

My father cheesing it up with his arm around my four-year-old shoulders as I held the first fish I'd caught. My family at the zoo with the hippos in the background. And, my favorite, the picture of my father in uniform with my little hand in his, Lieutenant Commander Thomas K. Hutchinson written on the back. I'd kept these pictures in my nightstand drawer and looked at them every night before bed.

The man who came to the door on that awful spring day had told me that I should be proud of my father. He'd sacrificed his life for America. At the time, I hadn't fully understood sacrifice, freedom, patriotism, or duty, but I'd understood death and gone forever.

"How did you go on when Daddy died?"

Renee lifted her eyes off the pictures. "I had you to take care of." She took a breath and shifted on the couch. "But nights were the hardest. The distractions of the day were over, and it was just me."

I frowned. "Why didn't you talk to me about him more?"

"You were young and trying to deal with the loss of your father in the best way you could, and I couldn't burden you with my feelings." Renee cleared her throat. "Besides, I have a piece of my Thomas in his beautiful daughter."

"I wish—" I began, but the ringing of the doorbell interrupted me. Ugh. Troy Matthews had arrived.

"Oh, that must be your date." Renee shook her head and stood to answer the door. "You better make up your mind quick." She pulled the door open.

"Mrs. Hutch!" Troy yelled, as tall, shaggy-haired, and immature as he had been in high school.

Renee looked at me and made a face.

I laughed.

"You ready to bounce, Lil-dog?" Troy asked, stepping past Renee, uninvited, into the house. "I borrowed my dad's 'Vette so we can roll in style."

"Well ..." I thought of Blake stuck between Troy and Angie all night and closed my mouth on the excuse I was about to give Troy. I grabbed my trout hat off the chair where I'd dropped it after coming inside. "I think I am."

I walked past Troy to the lawn and started picking dandelions.

# Chapter 17

## Blake

Evening settled around the parking lot of Evergreen Bowl. The setting sun pulled some of the warmth out of the air, bringing relief from the heat of the summer day. I sat next to Angie on a park bench, right of the front entrance. A mosquito buzzed in my ear, and I swatted at it. For the moment, Angie had stopped talking.

My eyes traveled over the woman next to me. Her outfit was nice. Leopard print leggings with a simple black top but, once again, she'd put on too much makeup for my taste. She wore her trout crown, and her blonde hair hung around her face in ringlets. My crown sat in my lap.

"Oh, don't you hate those darn mosquitoes?" Angie asked.

"Yeah. They're bad this year."

"I've heard there have been three cases of the West Nile Virus in this valley. They're like little death gnats. Spreading disease from one place to another. I guess it could be worse, one of my aunts went to South America and caught Yellow Fever. She nearly died—"

Angie continued describing the illness her aunt contracted before she'd been able to travel back to the States. I took another moment to check over my appearance. My cowboy boots were polished, the poop cleaned off them. They went well with my dark blue jeans and my best pearl-snapped shirt which hung over my black belt. Maddie had helped me pick out my clothes. To her, I was a large Ken doll.

Would Lili show up? I hoped she would—and hoped she wouldn't.

I tugged on the sleeve covering the edge of my scar. What did she think of me, since she knew about my past? She'd been all sweet and caring back by the rock, but that was before we almost kissed, and I'd made a complete fool of myself.

When I met Cindy, I'd been confident with women, but I'd also been naïve, immature, and in a tough spot doing things I regretted to this day, some of which I wished I could wipe off my slate.

"—so, do you like it here in Southern Idaho, mosquitoes and all?"

Angie leaned into me when she asked the question and I scooted to the edge of the bench. If she moved any closer, I would be standing.

"Yes." Angie wanted more than my short answer, but I couldn't focus on the conversation. A bundle of snakes twisted in my stomach.

Here I sat, next to a woman I only wanted to be friends with, waiting for the possible arrival of the one who wouldn't leave my thoughts. A grasshopper shifted in the gravel at my feet, a bright green dot in the evening light, completely out of place in the gray world.

How often had I felt like this? I was out of place, uncomfortable in a world where I spoke the same language but couldn't understand a thing. Angie picked at the peeling paint on the bench. The sound of screeching tires pulled my gaze to the red Corvette. It sprayed dust and gravel as it zoomed through the parking lot.

Angie popped off the bench. "That's his dad's Corvette. It's pretty, isn't it?"

Sure. It was a beautiful machine, but my muscles tensed as the brakes on the Z06 locked and the back end swung to a stop. Cars driven by jerkoffs like Troy landed in my shop at least every other month, their front dashes covered in dried blood. I waved at the dirt swirling around the convertible.

"Hey, Angie." Troy waved to her and removed his sunglasses. He jumped over the side of the convertible.

Angie nodded at Troy and moved to the passenger side of Troy's dad's car. "Lili. Did you bring the dandelion crown?"

That was the first time I allowed myself to look at Lili. She'd come—trout crown and all. Tension that I hadn't noticed I'd been carrying eased from my upper back.

Lili nodded and hobbled out of the car with a strand of dandelions hooked together in her hand. Her white, knee-length skirt emphasized her thin waist, and her brown boots accentuated her well-toned legs. Legs that I could easily imagine wrapped around my abdomen as I pressed her against a wall and—

I held my breath and released it slowly.

I was up a creek without a paddle.

Angie laughed and took the crown from Lili. "Just so long as we remember who the Dandelion Princess is." She slipped the yellow weeds over her trout crown.

"Hey dudes," Troy called from the entrance. His stuffed trout stuck sideways on his head. "Our lane is ready. The place is packed tonight."

"Well, I can't believe we are on a date together." Angie gestured around the full parking lot, but not a person could be found. She shrugged. "Isn't it funny how destiny works?"

I didn't believe in destiny. You made your own future. On the other hand, had it not been for Angie goading Lili into entering the competition, I wouldn't be standing next to her.

I slipped my crown on my head and offered my arm to Angie. She latched onto it and sidled up next to me. With my free hand, I opened the door for Lili. "Shall we?"

With a brief nod, she walked past me into the dark interior of the bowling alley. I followed her in with Angie still attached to my arm.

In the few days I'd known Lili, I'd made her cry twice. I'd count tonight as a success if her eyes remained dry.

The fluorescent lighting in the bowling alley highlighted the imperfections of the purple carpet with neon green, yellow, and orange accents. I looked around at the full room.

Everyone turned and cheered; the trout royalty had arrived. Open beer bottles and lit cigarettes in ash trays blended into an odor of alcohol-laced secondhand smoke. A lane had been decorated with silvery fish with bows wrapped around each seat.

The crowd calmed as we walked to the counter. The background noise of the alley consisted of rolling balls, falling pins, and the twang of a country singer coming out of the jukebox in the corner of the room.

"Oh, man." Angie waved her hand in front of her face. "It's so hot in here. Blake, aren't you dying? I honestly think the summers here are getting hotter. It's as if the sun is getting closer every year. You know, I watched that one movie where there's a big solar flare and everyone dies. Ever since then, I have wondered, on the hot days especially, if that's how everyone on Earth was really going to die. The world has to end one way or another—"

Lili locked eyes with me, communicating without words. Hers danced along with the rhythm of Angie's chatter. Troy already had his shoes and his bowling ball picked out. Lili handed the cashier the gift card we'd all won; as king, I got a free beer on top of the unlimited bowling. I pulled out my card and slid it on the counter as Angie continued to talk non-stop.

"—these shoes do nothing for your figure, and the color scheme. But maybe it's so people don't want to steal them. My Uncle Bubba loves to steal everything in sight. He's the one with the club foot so we don't understand why he chose to start stealing because he always gets caught—"

With Angie's dialogue in the background and Troy's over-eagerness to bowl, I didn't have much of a chance to say anything to Lili. I didn't have a chance to apologize. Our eyes met once again as Angie continued describing Uncle Bubba's misshapen foot.

"—anyway, so his toes are not as bad anymore, but I'm still glad his foot did not get passed onto me, my nephew wasn't so lucky, he— Oh!" Angie abruptly paused in her dialogue. "I see the ball I want. Be right back."

It was instantly quieter, even with the drone of the background noise.

Lili leaned over and laced up her shoes, giving me a perfect view of her cleavage. I only allowed myself a quick peek.

"She's always loved to talk," she said.

"Yeah." I couldn't think of anything else to say, so I smiled like a dumbass.

"Listen." She ducked her head. I had to lean toward her to hear. "I didn't mean what I said earlier about Maddie. She's a wonderful girl."

"Thank you. She's my entire world."

Angie walked over to me. She clicked her artificial nails on a black bowling ball sitting on the shelf next to us. "Someone took the ball I wanted. Can you come and help me?"

"Sure." I stood and followed Angie's swinging hips. I grabbed the nearest ten-pound ball and held it out to her. "How about this one?"

I looked over Angie's shoulder at Troy approaching Lili. He sat next to her and slid his arm around her waist. I frowned.

Angie shook her head and set the black ball down. "I have a lucky ball." She wandered away from me to go find it. I selected a ball for myself and got back to our lane in time to hear Troy try out a pick-up line.

"Hey, Lil'dog. Check it out." Troy put one arm around Lili's shoulders and pulled her into his chest. With the other hand he pointed to the farthest wall in the bowling alley. "See the wall over there, the three hundred club? Read the third name down."

I stayed out of Troy's line of vision.

"David Carlson?" Lili asked.

"Uhh, no read the—one, two, three, four—Oh, the—uh—fourth name down," Troy said.

"Troy, you got into the three-hundred club in high school. I'm as impressed now as I was then." Lili tried to push away from him.

"Pretty cool, huh?" Troy ran his fingers along Lili's bare bicep.

Seriously, how had this guy graduated? Even still, how had he ever dated Lili? I walked to them and shouted over the music close to Troy's ear. "Are we ready to play?"

I put my bowling ball on the conveyor belt, and Lili scooted out from Troy's grasp.

*Thank you*, she mouthed.

"I found the pink one. I had to pay the kid ten bucks for it, but I got it." Angie breathed heavily when she came up behind me.

"You're right, pink suits you better."

A blush crept into Angie's cheeks. She fiddled with her crown and carefully adjusted the dandelions. I'd meant to state fact—Angie was a bright color type of person. I didn't mean to make her believe I felt something for her other than friendship.

Angie sat next to Lili and patted the seat next to her. With the whole town watching, I sat next to my trout queen.

Troy started the game with three strikes, but I was close behind him with two strikes and a spare. Thanks to Wednesday night family bowling with Maddie, I'd gotten good. Angie followed with twenty-one and Lili came in dead last with a pitiful score of ten. Lili still appeared to be having fun, and, with every gutter ball, her face brightened.

Something about Lili had changed tonight. She was still reserved, a bit withdrawn, but not as angry. Three of the four trout crowns sat in a pile on one of the plastic chairs, but Angie kept hers on. As much as possible, I manipulated mine and Angie's position to keep Troy separate from Lili.

The more I stood in his way, the more determined he seemed to beat me at bowling, but the more he tried, the worse he got. The five beers he'd drunk couldn't have been helping his game.

By the last frame, Lili had fallen even further behind, finishing with a score of fifty-two. Angie finished with one hundred twelve points, and Troy with two hundred and twelve. I took first place. A personal best of two hundred fifty-three points. Troy folded his arms and glared at me.

Poor guy. I outplayed him in the one thing he was good at. "Since I won, how about I buy everyone drinks?"

"All right, man." Troy's scowl lessened. "I'll have a Coors." He held up his current beer and loped away.

"Me too. Only make mine a Light. Trying to cut calories," Angie said.

As far as I could tell, Angie had all the right kind of curves. Why would she be dieting? "I don't see why you need to worry about calories." Once again, fact.

Angie's face lit up. She ran her fingernails along my forearm until she reached my hand and interlaced her fingers with mine.

"Wha—" Angie squeezed my hand, and my voice cracked like a teenager heading into puberty. "What about you Lili? What would you like to drink?"

"I'll have a Coke, one *sugary* Coke." Lili bit her lips and raised her eyebrows at Angie, who responded with a frown.

I nodded and hid my laugh behind a cough.

Angie pulled me to the concession counter. "I'll help you bring the drinks to the table. You know I am quite handy when it comes to carrying drinks. I paid my way through college working as a waitress and boy do those customers love their—"

"You went to college?" I interrupted. It was the only way to have a conversation with her, and I was genuinely interested. "What was your major?"

"You are looking at a proud nursing school graduate. Well, almost graduate. I'm nearly there. I should be at home studying for finals, but Carpe Diem. Am I right?"

Troy went to the jukebox with a whole piggy bank of quarters. Some unknown rapper's voice replaced the twang of country in the background when Troy sat by Lili. I tapped my fingers on the bar and nodded to a few acquaintances from town while Angie talked it up with Sam, the bartender.

As casually as I could, I watched Lili. Troy still sat near her with his lips far too close to her ear. When Troy slapped his hand down on Lili's upper thigh, I was ready to put an end to the date, but Angie, with her impeccable timing, grabbed my arm.

"Hold on. You can't leave without the drinks."

Angie's fingers were wet with the Coke when she set the drinks on the table. She leaned closer while she licked it off her fingers. I cleared my throat and looked away—it was no wonder I'd avoided dating for as long as I had. I moved to a safe distance and pulled out a chair for her.

Left without the support of my shoulder, she jerked forward as she caught her balance. "Thank you."

Surprisingly, Troy sat far away from Lili now. I looked from Troy to Lili and back again. Lili smiled and shrugged. I followed her Coca-Cola glass from the table to her lips. The simple movement was much more impactful on my senses than Angie's finger-licking had been.

I took a sip of my beer and focused on the worn gold laminate on the table.

"You okay, Troy? You look a little sick," Angie said.

"No, I ... I'm cool," he slurred.

Angie nursed her Coors Light. "I was thinking we could play another couple of games then maybe drive to the canyon and go on a nice romantic walk once we're done."

Angie shimmied up next to me and, not so subtly, pulled down the front of her blouse, giving me a full view of her cavernous cleavage. I couldn't survive another game of bowling, let alone a walk along the canyon. I avoided staring at her chest.

"I have to go to the bathroom," Angie said abruptly and straightened her shirt, pushing away from the table. "Lili, come with me."

The two women jousted with their eyes and brows. A whole conversation passed between them without one word being said. This was why women remained in a realm where I would never understand them.

After their brief exchange, Lili stood. "All right." She followed Angie to the bathroom.

# Chapter 18

## Liliana

The water-damaged door closed behind us. I squeezed against the sink while Angie moved against the wall opposite me.

"Why did you need me to follow you in here?" I asked.

"I have tried every play in the book to get Blake to pay attention to me, to get him to stop looking at you, and I have failed." Angie pushed me to the side and pulled lipstick out of a hidden pocket from her leggings. She wiped it across her lips and pressed them together.

"I still don't understand why that required a trip to the bathroom." A dirty bathroom with a discolored puddle in front of the toilet. I kept my arms and hands tucked to my waist and didn't touch anything.

Angie flapped her lips together. "Are you really this clueless? Blake is totally into you. He won't stop looking at you. Oh, he tries to hide it, but I have caught him more than once with his eyes stuck on you."

"No." If he wanted more than a friendship from me than he would have kissed me when I'd thrown myself at him. "You're wrong. He's just a friend."

Angie adjusted her bra and tugged at her shirt. "I have friends and trust me, he wants to get into bed with you."

The temperature in the bathroom must have risen ten degrees, at least for me. "Really?"

"At the shoe counter, the whole time we were bowling, at the bar, and when I pulled my shirt so low he almost got a shot of my nipples, he was eyeing you."

Okay, so maybe he did like me more than I thought. He'd kept Troy away from me all night, and one time, I caught him glancing at my butt as I bent to pick up my bowling ball.

If all this was true and Angie had noticed, too, then why didn't he want to kiss me? "What am I supposed to do about it?"

Angie turned from the mirror to me. "You're going to go out there and make an excuse to get Blake out of this bowling alley. Without Troy. Without me."

My mouth went slack, and I stared at her. I could tell she really liked Blake. Yet, here she was, urging me to leave with him. "Why are you telling me to do this?"

Water droplets clicked into the drain in the quiet. "My heart broke for you when you lost Michael and your baby girl."

My throat closed off. I couldn't swallow. I couldn't breathe. I'd cut out Angie right along with the rest of this town after the accident. It'd affected her too.

Angie put her hand on my shoulder. "It's okay to be happy. Michael would want that for you." She smoothed a hand over her hair. "I kinda want to have some fun with Troy anyway. He can be a blast. And someone will need to drive him home anyway."

I took deep, slow breaths and blinked away the tears in my eyes. Somehow, hearing Michael's name wasn't as painful as it had been a few days ago.

141

"You have a real chance to be happy again with a guy like Blake. Even if it is a vacation fling. Go for it. Be brave." With one last dab of lipstick, Angie left me alone in the bathroom.

Could I be brave? No. Yes. Maybe? I paced in the small bathroom avoiding the puddle. I'd give it one more shot. For Angie. But if he shut me down again, I was done trying.

# Chapter 19

## Blake

Angie walked out of the bathroom alone. Where was Lili? Was she sick? Did Angie and her have some chick fight in the bathroom, and she was knocked out on the floor? I narrowed my eyes at Angie. She gave me a thumbs up and shot me a wink. What did that mean?

Lili came out of the bathroom and walked to our table. I relaxed. But I didn't let my guard down. Something was up.

"How about it, Blake? Don't you think a walk along the canyon rim is the perfect way to end the night?" Angie asked in a staged voice. She didn't look at me, but at Lili. What in the world was going on? And what had they talked about in the bathroom?

Troy leaned onto the table and ignored the conversation.

"Umm—well, Angie that does sound like fun, I promised to be somewhere else tonight." My eyes shifted from Angie to Lili and back again.

"You see," Lili put in a little late, "we promised to help Renee harvest her green beans." She looked past me at Angie and shrugged.

What was going on here? Green beans? That was the first thing that'd come to her mind? I could think of one hundred other excuses besides green beans.

Angie blew out a puff of air. "Really, Lili? Green beans? You're terrible at this."

Lili covered her face in her hands, and Troy perked up a little.

I had to do something. "It's the perfect time to pick beans." My mind churned fast to patch up Lili's sad alibi. "In the day it's hot, and Renee doesn't do well in the heat, so she harvests at night."

Angie took a drink from her beer. "But won't it be too dark?" Angie laughed and kept looking at Lili.

Lili straightened her back. "Oh, Renee bought those bright lights construction workers use at night so we could keep up the garden. I know it's unconventional."

Wow, she was a bad liar.

"Well, all right, then I guess we could go and pick beans tonight. I mean we'll still be under the stars." Angie lifted her eyes almost in a challenge to Lili.

"That's *it*," Troy shouted from his corner where he'd been drinking his Coors in silence. "I've had enough. You can't take both girls, it isn't fair. If I can't have Lili, then I'll arm wrestle you for Angie."

"Arm wrestle?" I leaned away from Troy. No one arm wrestled over girls. Fistfights sure, but arm wrestling?

Angie ducked her head but couldn't hide her laugh, and a little Coke sprayed from Lili's mouth. Troy's shouted challenge got a couple of drunken cheers from other bowlers. Between frames they'd cricked their necks, eager for two men to fight for girls in the most country way possible.

"Angie, you are so hot I need to put on suntan lotion just to be next to you." Troy puffed up his chest and tensed his muscles in anticipation of the upcoming confrontation, his movements disjointed.

Angie's cheeks turned pink. She shared a look with Lili. Humor. Entertainment. Maybe she was a little flattered. Angie deserved better than this guy. What if Maddie ever dated someone like Troy? Bile burned the back of my throat, and I prayed it would never happen.

"So, what do you say?" Troy's voice rose over the music.

"Okay," I said it more of a question than an acceptance, but Troy lowered himself in front of me and dropped his elbow on the table.

Lili sat opposite me. "Good luck." She saluted me with her Coke and laughed.

A couple of bowlers cheered again from their lanes as I placed my elbow in front of Troy's. I swallowed. Instant sweat beaded on my forehead. Why did this drunken idiot have to get the attention of a whole roomful of people I knew?

I gripped Troy's clammy palm. Red-faced and sweaty, it took all of Troy's strength to keep his arm a mere quarter inch from the game-ending table. I enjoyed losing about as much as a pin being shoved through my fingernail, but I'd do it for Lili. As Troy began to lose strength and conviction, I eased my grip and allowed him to slam my hand down on the table.

Troy jumped up and threw his arm in the air in victory, and I saluted him with my beer. Beaming from all the attention, Angie rushed to Troy's side.

"I'd do anything for you, baby." Troy crushed Angie against him and gave her a solid kiss. Lili and I slipped away without either of our dates noticing.

# Chapter 20

## Liliana

"I can't believe you went along with my green beans thing." I walked up the steps to Renee's house and sat on the porch swing. My sides hurt with laughter. I rubbed my abdomen. I didn't even know if Renee had green beans in her garden this year. The one year we'd attempted a garden, the beans were the only plants to live long enough to get somewhat of a harvest. I had picked them all.

"Harvesting beans at ten o'clock at night? What was I supposed to say?" Blake lifted his shoulders and took a seat next to me.

"I don't know." I wiped tears of laughter from my eyes. "And you arm-wrestled my date."

"I'm glad you enjoyed it. Just so you know, I let him win."

"Sure, you did. I bet I could beat you."

I kept my tone light, but I could hardly forget the image of his biceps straining against the short sleeves of his shirt. What would it be like to have those arms wrapped around me? I couldn't keep the not-too-distant memory of my attempted kiss out of my mind. Of his warm breath touching my lips right before he pulled away.

"You're right, you do have abnormally strong arms," he teased.

"Huh?" My thoughts still circled his lips.

"You said you could beat me—"

"Oh, yeah." I half attempted a laugh.

"Next time we go on a date, I think we'll have to get rid of the extras."

Alone? Again? With him and his biceps? Heat blossomed in my cheeks. Thankfully, the night air brushed against them, helping to cool my face.

In eighth grade, holding hands had been such a huge thing. You held hands and, boom, you were an insta-couple. Holding hands didn't mean anything these days. Not to adults. To prove this to myself, I reached across the white vinyl bench seat and rested my hand on his.

His eyebrows lifted at my touch, but he turned his hand palm facing up and closed his fingers around mine. Currents of warmth, coming from his hand spreading into mine, coursed through my body. I licked my lips and breathed in slowly, trying to calm my pulse. My mind might belong to a thirty-four-year-old, but my body responded to handholding like a fifteen-year-old.

"What did you say to Troy that made him stay away from you like you had a bad case of head lice?" He squeezed my hand and kept his eyes focused into the night.

I laughed. "Oh, I told him I wasn't interested." I'd be happy if I never saw Troy again, but he was relatively harmless.

"Sure." Disbelief etched his one-word response. "And that made him turn as white as a ghost?"

Troy had tried a horrible pick-up line on me. The one starting with—your clothes look pretty good on you—and ended with—but they would look even better on my floor.

"All right, I may have threatened to kick his testicles into his inguinal canals."

Blake burst out laughing. "Into where? Ouch."

"It's the passage your testicles drop from when you go through puberty."

Blake cringed. "Ow."

This was the most I'd laughed in years. I couldn't get enough of it.

His thumb traced the lines in my palm, fanning my need to be closer to him. After he'd turned me down this afternoon, I should do the smart thing and keep my distance. Besides, in a week, I'd be back in St. Louis. A relationship with Blake wasn't possible or practical, no matter what Angie said. For once in my life, I didn't want to think about practicality or possibility.

Be brave, Angie had said. I scooted across the bench and laid my head on his shoulder. He sat there for a couple of minutes, but then pointed past me to two glasses of lemonade sitting on the patio table. Condensation beaded along the outside and formed puddles around the bottom of the glass. Straws and little umbrellas rested in the chilled liquid; proof that Renee had been watching.

He reached across me, his chest touching mine for the barest of moments, and selected one of the drinks. He sat back onto the porch swing, took a drink, and paused before he swallowed. Apparently, Renee's culinary talents extended to her lemonade.

He was as skittish as an intern on their first day of residency.

I tried not to overanalyze his actions. True, women had an enlarged Corpus Callosum, but it didn't mean I had to be subject to its whims, always connecting an action with an emotion. Sometimes I wished I could shut it off.

"Listen." Blake rested his elbows on his knees with his fingers interlaced around the glass.

I waited but he didn't continue. "Yes?"

He took a deep breath. "I have to work at the fire station and things at the shop are piling up, but I would like to spend more time with you. Would that be all right?"

"What would we be doing together? Working on cars?" I didn't point out that we were already together, and that he was wasting his breath when he could be doing something better with his time.

"I was thinking of doing something else, like," he slid closer to me until our thighs touched, "horseshoes, or badminton. You know? A couple of yard games."

The tension eased from my shoulders. "I think I can find time for a good game of badminton."

He leaned his head closer to mine. With his lips within an inch of my ear, he whispered, "Then I couldn't be happier."

Goosebumps tingled down my neck and throughout my back. I glanced past Blake, toward the house, unsure of how to proceed.

I motioned to the still full lemonade in his hand. "Sorry. My mom can be overbearing."

"You don't have to apologize for Renee. She's like family."

I picked up the remaining lemonade, sniffed it and set it down.

Like family. Renee and I hadn't been family for quite some time. The distance between us had been growing since Dad died, and the accident killed whatever ties I'd had with Renee or this town. For over a decade, our relationship had been marked only by ignored phone calls and one sad visit.

"I know this is none of my business. But Renee told me that she wasn't a good mother to you. I think it's her biggest regret—"

I cut him off. "If you are trying to fix things between Renee and me, then you should stop now."

I shifted farther away from him. Without the heat of him next to me, the cold air caused a shiver to race through my body.

"I'm sorry." Blake rested his back against the swing and set it to motion as he pushed his feet against the concrete porch. "What did she do to ruin your relationship?"

Oh, to answer that question would take all night. I rested my elbows on my knees. My shoulders slumped forward. I couldn't bring myself to speak. How could I tear down the woman who meant so much to Blake? He had asked, and if I didn't give him some sort of answer, he would fill in the blanks with something worse.

"She wasn't mean unless she drank." I kept my voice quiet. "And she drank a lot. She never beat me, but she was verbally and mentally abusive."

The breeze strengthened and I shivered. Blake set his lemonade on the table and wrapped his arm around my shoulders. I leaned onto his arm, accepting his support, enjoying the motion of the swing.

"I don't even recognize the person she is now. I have memories of her, before my dad died, but it got real ugly through middle school. I don't know if she remembers how she spoke to me, and I guess I got tired of being the caretaker. That's why I married young."

"I'm sorry," he repeated.

Great. I'd ruined the woman he admired. I carried enough guilt—I couldn't handle any more.

"Just so you know," I spoke with a levity I didn't feel, "I only dated Troy to make Renee mad."

His chest shook when he chuckled. "I was wondering."

"I did anything to drive Renee crazy. Anything to get her attention, I suppose." Renee was the root cause of the worst day in my life. "Last time I was here, she wanted to set me up on a date. We got in an argument, and I left." I toyed with the umbrella on the cup next to me. "I was fine without her in my life as a little girl, and I'm fine without her now."

"I'm not saying your mother is perfect, but the woman you described isn't the woman I know." He rubbed my shoulder. "She's sober now and is trying to earn your respect. You don't know how lucky you are."

"Did you ever meet your mother? I mean, you said you grew up in the system." I stuttered. Why had I asked about his mother? *Way to kill the night, Lili.*

"I never knew her." He spoke as if we were discussing the weather; matter of fact, no emotion. "From what Jorge could gather, after she gave birth to me, she didn't hesitate to put me up for a closed adoption. She could have fought for an open adoption. Jorge was good with it. She chose to have nothing to do with me. When I was in elementary school, I wasn't put in the best homes. I used to dream of my mom coming for me, but it never happened. So, if I had the opportunity to have a mother like Renee, I'd jump at the chance."

I couldn't stop thinking of a little boy with bright blue eyes searching for his mother, waiting for her to come and get him.

"If it hadn't been for Jorge, I don't know where I would be today. Probably in prison." He stretched and removed his arm from my shoulders. "Besides, I've always heard mother knows best. Didn't Renee want you to meet me?"

"Well, yes."

He tucked a stray strand of hair behind my ear, and I closed my eyes. "And has being with me been all that bad?"

He moved his hand to cover mine. I opened my eyes and stared at our hands. He leaned close to me again and tilted my chin up. His gaze darted from my eyes to my lips. I tensed. Would he finally give in to this pull between us?

"Why didn't you want to meet me?" His breath fluttered against my cheek.

I thought about telling him the real reason I could never forgive my mother. About how my mother was the catalyst of the accident. Without her, Michael and my little girl wouldn't have been on the street. I opened my mouth to tell him everything, starting with day zero of my new life, but my throat tightened, blocking the words so close to having a voice.

"I wasn't ready to start dating."

"Are you ready now?"

"I'm not sure."

He lifted my hands to his lips and kissed the back of both. My eyes widened as I stared at where his lips had touched my hands. My stomach somersaulted. Was I ready? Up to now we'd flirted and played games with each other, but none of it could be construed as serious. If I let this progress, it would all become very real.

The porch swing swayed with his movement as he leaned closer to me. "I had a great time tonight." His breath tickled my cheek. "Thank you for coming."

He moved toward me like he was going to close the gap between our mouths but turned and kissed my cheek instead. The swing moved back and forth as he stood and walked down the porch steps to his truck. The chill in the night raised goosebumps on my arms without his warmth next to me.

"Good luck harvesting the beans," he called out his window. "And tell Renee thanks for the drinks."

I laughed and waved goodbye as he drove out of the driveway. My skirt flapped against my bare legs in the cool breeze, but I waited until his taillights had disappeared in the distance before I went inside.

As I'd predicted, Renee sat on the living room couch. My mind was so focused on processing what had just happened, I only caught every other word of Renee's questions. She stopped speaking and looked at me expectantly, so I said the first thing that popped into my head.

"We went bowling." I placed my hand to my cheek where his lips had touched me. It still buzzed from the contact and the skin on the back of my hand tingled.

"You all right?" Renee's question came out light and airy with her barely contained glee.

I ducked my head. "I'm fine. I am going to bed, so I can ... think."

"That's where I always go to think, but you may want to get some sleep as well." Her words followed me up the stairs.

Once I reached my room, I pulled out my cell phone. Tiff answered on the first ring. "I can't talk long. I'm on a shift. How'd it go?"

"He kissed me."

"Oh my gosh!" Tiff squealed into the phone. "Details. Now."

"Relax, he pecked me on the cheek on the porch swing in the moon-light—"

"Eeeee!" Tiff cut in with another squeal. "This is so great, Lili."

"I just ... I can't ... I can't stop smiling."

"It's about damn time. Next time don't let him get off without laying one full on your mouth. Hold on," Tiff said. "I'm on the phone, Amy.

Yeah. Okay. I'll be right there." Her voice muffled. "Med student needs help. Gotta go. But you better give me a play by play. Love yuz."

"Love ya too. Bye, Tiff."

I set my phone on the nightstand and went to the bathroom. I brushed my teeth, finished the rest of my nightly routine, and lay in bed. For hours, I rehashed the day. Blake was as unexpected as a snowy day in July. I could almost imagine myself waking up next to him, making breakfast for him and Maddie, but the possibility of opening myself to that kind of loss again terrified me.

I wasn't ready for commitment yet, but at least I could have some fun with him before I returned to my world of scalpels and sick people.

My eyelids grew heavy around two-thirty, but then the front door to the house opened and flicked closed. All sleepiness left me.

I bolted upright and crept to the window. No strange vehicle had parked in the driveway. Instead of the masked thief I expected, Renee walked into the front yard. Bathed in moonlight, she wore sweatpants and a T-shirt and moved toward the Mustang. Fully alert now, I rushed down the stairs and out to the front porch.

I made it to the swing as Renee pulled out of the driveway with her headlights off. Once on the road, the lights of the Mustang flipped on. In my slippers, I sprinted to the bathroom, grabbed the key, and ran to the old Malibu in the back. I climbed in the car, started the engine, and pulled out of the driveway, following the beacon of the Mustang's taillights.

# Chapter 21

## Liliana

**M**y clammy hands slipped on the steering wheel as I rounded a corner. I gripped it tighter. If not for the full moon, driving without headlights on country roads would be impossible. And if the Mustang ever escaped my vision, I'd be lost.

My stomach dropped as the taillights disappeared around another turn. I went through a list of things Renee could be doing at this time at night.

Dealing drugs?

Visiting a friend?

A tryst with her lover?

*That's it!*

My mother was having an affair with some hot farmer. Perhaps Renee's eagerness this evening had been a mask for her anxiety about the potential of getting caught, which was why she'd waited until two a.m. to go on her tryst.

Was she in love with her mysterious sex partner? Renee had only dated a handful of men since Dad had died. All of them had been losers she picked up at the bar. Hopefully, this one was better than the others.

But what if she chose to marry her lover? Then I'd be forced to come back for the wedding. Renee would insist that Blake be my plus one, with his vibrant blue eyes framed in dark lashes, and his square jaw perpetually covered in a light stubble. I sucked in air through my nose. *Calm down.* My thoughts were getting out of hand.

Renee could just be out on a late-night drive and avoided shining the headlights in my bedroom window.

My mind latched onto the fanciful idea of a lover even as the probable truth burned in my thoughts. My visit had caused her to relapse. She was on her way to buy booze.

"Get a hold of yourself," I whispered in the empty car.

The bumper of the Mustang steadily grew closer. Taking my foot off the gas, I hit the brake and gnawed on my lower lip. Renee decelerated to thirty miles, then twenty miles per hour until she pulled the Mustang off the side of the road and brought it to a standstill.

I held my breath, and the sound of my heart thudded in my ears. Maneuvering the Malibu to the other side of the road, I parked as close as I dared, behind an overgrown willow tree on the edge of someone's lawn. Through its wispy branches, the driver's side of the Mustang was visible.

A large cornfield went on for miles beyond the willow, and a never-ending field of some sort of grain sat to my left. Anyone could get lost here. I might be able to find my way home in daylight, but at night I'd float on an endless sea of farmland until I ran out of gas.

Honing my eyes in on the driver's side of the Mustang, I watched Renee's silhouette lean out the window and place something in a weather-worn mailbox. As quickly as she had pulled off the road, Renee sped away from the drop point.

"What is she doing?"

Ten minutes passed. Fifteen. Then twenty. I turned on the headlights and inched my car forward. I rolled down the window, pulled to a stop and tugged on the metal tab. Opening the rusty mailbox was like looking into Pandora's box. I placed my hand in the dark void and pulled out the single manila envelope.

I flipped the golden yellow envelope from front to back. Nothing made this envelope stand out above any other. No writing. I double-checked my rear-view as I pried at the seal. It didn't take long for it to pop open and reveal the contents of the package.

*Money.* Hundreds of dollars were arranged in bundles wrapped in rubber bands and stacked neatly into rows. I counted the number of hundreds in each of the bundles and then counted the bundles—twice. Renee had dumped *five thousand* dollars in a random, deserted mailbox. A mailbox about to fall over.

I crumpled the bills in my grip while my heart plummeted to the soles of my feet. Insinuations whirled around my mind. The envelope slipped out of my fingers and dropped to the ground, spilling its contents on the way down. Renee didn't have any money. She would never—no, *couldn't* do something like this. Yet, the evidence laid in a pile on my lap and spilled onto the floor mat.

Shock eased out of my muscles, and I rushed to shove the money back into the envelope. I didn't want to be anywhere near this spot in case a car did happen to drive by. I closed the envelope and shoved it back into the mailbox. Sure, Renee had quit drinking and found religion, but now she had an even bigger demon.

The Malibu's tires left the pavement and crunched onto a gravel road. The gravel disappeared in front of me, and I slammed on the brakes, skidding around a sharp corner. I had no desire to launch into another field. The seat belt tightened against my chest as the car spun to a stop. Light filtered through the dust billowing around my car, much like the never-ending questions swirled in my mind. Not one of which I could answer.

# Chapter 22

## Liliana

The dim lighting in the church still caused my eyes to ache. Wanting nothing more than to close my lids over them and fall asleep, I mouthed the hymn the congregation sang. I shot a glare at Renee for, number one, keeping me up so late and, number two, forcing me to get out of bed this morning to make it to the church by nine. For forty-five minutes I'd driven in the darkness, completely lost before I'd found my way back home last night. And at four o'clock in the morning I'd fallen into a restless sleep.

For the remainder of the night, my dreams had been filled with all my embarrassing childhood memories, like going to school in clothes too small or with stains or holes in them, the prissy rich kids looking at me with disgust, or all the times I'd hidden my feet since my scrounged church shoes had been two sizes too big.

My jaw clenched, and I stopped attempting to sing. I'd called and texted Tiff twice. She'd worked the night shift and wouldn't be awake until this afternoon.

Renee had always made room in her budget for booze. Had she been leaving thousands of dollars in mailboxes then as well? Through my few hours of no sleep, I still hadn't figured out what my mother had done to get her hands on such a wad of cash.

I turned my dry eyes to Renee, the root of all my problems. She appeared oblivious to my bad mood as she stared intently at the podium, where someone rambled on about prayer or some such religious jargon.

I snapped my head forward before she turned and caught me staring again. No matter how hard I acted normal, I couldn't forget that my mom had left five thousand dollars in a mailbox. The service closed with a prayer. I stood with Renee and followed her through the throng of churchgoers.

"Renee!" an older woman shouted and waved at us.

I stopped short of the exit and waited impatiently.

"Hello, Irene." Renee's voice was polite.

It grated on my ears. How could my mother be so chipper going on a night with little sleep? People were built to sleep. I sagged against the doorjamb, tempted to lay down on the floor even if it meant I'd get trampled.

"Land sakes, I didn't think I would catch up to you in time." Irene stopped to gather her breath. "Why were you all in such a hurry anyway? Usually, you like to mingle a little bit before you leave."

Renee gestured to me before responding. "My daughter isn't feeling the best, and I was trying to get her home as soon as possible."

"What's that, dear? Need to speak up." Irene put a finger to her ear and turned up her hearing aide. The faint squeal of the device filled the air.

"Lili's sick," Renee yelled. The crowd around us quieted and all looked at me.

I stood straight, hating being the target of all their stares. With the shadows under my eyes and with my pale skin, I might as well have been sick. Thankfully, they stopped gawking and went back to their conversations.

"Oh, well, she's not alone." Irene leaned closer as if she were imparting a great secret. "Blake said Maddie had some intestinal problems today, so they stayed home."

I hated to admit that I'd searched for Blake in the congregation this morning. My scowl deepened. I'd become attached much too soon.

"I wondered where they were when I saw you come in without them. Your pew looked empty." Renee pushed the loops of her bag back onto her left shoulder.

Wow. Renee had gone churchy. In her bag, Renee had not only her Bible, but she also had books for teaching Sunday School for children. No doubt she studied all the material, with her Amens and talk of heaven and hell.

"Yes, it's nice having a family to sit with now my kids have grown." Irene fidgeted with the huge bifocals on her face. "Well, I do have a purpose for stopping you—"

I leaned back against the door frame and faked a cough.

Irene looked at me and continued. "Um—Chuck and Pedro told me several times you're needed at the shop. They said it was an emergency. I'll tell them Lili is sick, and you had to go home."

Relief seeped through the dull ache in my head. Home to bed.

"I think Lili can handle stopping for a few minutes." Renee patted my shoulder.

"You little dear, pay no mind to those silly boys with your daughter being ill and all."

Irene made me feel like we were both back in grade school. She was right, of course. Listen to Irene, my mind whined at Renee.

"But I want to. Thanks for telling me." Renee swept out of the building.

My telekinesis didn't work.

I followed Renee to the Mustang and got in. As we drove down Main Street, I avoided looking at the vacant lot where the old farmhouse I'd purchased with Michael once stood. After I'd sold it, my home bounced on and off the market until it was condemned. One of the few letters Renee had written informed me of the demolition. I only remember feeling numb while reading about the foundation failing and the current owners cashing out on their insurance policy.

She parked at Blake's Place, and I tucked another uncomfortable drive under my belt.

"You can come in if you like, but I shouldn't be very long if you want to wait in the car." Renee stepped out of the Mustang.

"I'll come with you."

As much as I wanted to sit in the car and take a quick nap, I wasn't about to let Renee out of my sight. She might give away another grand to Chuck and Pedro.

Chuck's voice echoed through the doorway to the garage as we walked in. "Just reach in there and grab it, or are you afraid you will get your hands too dirty?"

Renee gestured to keep quiet. She walked into the adjoining room. I pressed my lips together and followed close behind her.

"At least I know my hands are clean and don't smell like ass like yours do," Pedro replied from underneath the hood of an oversized truck.

"What are you talkin' about? My hands are always minty fresh." Chuck grunted, and a wrench clanked to the floor.

"Rubbin' them on car air fresheners doesn't mean they're clean. Besides, it makes you smell like minty ass." Pedro reached for the fallen wrench, his Spanish accent growing thicker.

"Hey, personally, I like the smell of minty ass. It has a nice zing to it."

Renee burst into laughter, and I couldn't stop the upward curve of my lips. Chuck pulled himself out from under the driver's side door, and Pedro bumped his head on the hood as he jolted, his black mustache barely discernible from the grease on his face.

"I'll never get tired of you two boys, no matter how old I get. I swear you should put together a stand-up comedy routine." Laughter tinged Renee's voice.

"Naw." Chuck flicked his hand, always the spokesman for the pair. "Pedro'd pee his pants before we ever got on any stage."

"Whatever, it'd be you who'd be pukin' behind the curtain," Pedro retorted and pulled at his mustache. "Then you'd smell like minty butt puke," he added softly, which sent Renee into another round of laughter.

Before Chuck could reply, Renee waved her hands to stop him. "I can't take anymore. Irene said you had some emergency."

Chuck and Pedro looked uncomfortably at each other and glanced at me.

"Well," Chuck said. "We were hopin' you'd come alone."

I blew air out my mouth. More secrets, just what I needed. "Whatever you want to tell her, you can tell me too."

"Lili ..." Renee hedged. The slight lowering of her voice was as solid as a brick wall. "Why don't you go wait out back in the shade while I talk with these boys?"

I didn't have the energy to fight her, so I left the garage to find a haven in the heat of the day. My eyes burned in the sunlight, but I couldn't get my legs to walk the distance to the car and retrieve my sunglasses.

The breeze filtered through the leaves. Cottonwood trees stood like sentinels around the well-manicured yard, stretching upward to block the burning rays of the sun. Flowers of every type and color abounded in the weed-free flower beds and surrounded the gazebo attached to the wrap-around porch. A waterfall fountain trickled into a goldfish-filled pond sitting behind a swing set which exceeded any child's fantasy.

It was beautiful.

Two distant figures played around the swing set. Branches from a large, swaying willow tree occasionally hid them from my view. I walked toward Blake and Maddie, not sure I wanted to know what they were doing.

"Land ho! Take the treasure to the starboard side so we can bring it ashore," Maddie said.

"Aye, aye captain," Blake replied, in his best imitation of a pirate.

Behind the safety of the cascading willow branches, I laughed softly. I watched Blake pick up a small jewelry box and carefully walk down the slide. The two of them had on ridiculous clothing. Maddie wore a white shirt with tight black pants and cowboy boots rising over the hem of the pants. She also sported a patch over her right eye and a wooden sword hanging over her left hip, tied on with one of her father's neckties.

For once, the headphones weren't on her head or hanging around her neck.

Blake had on the same basic clothes as Maddie, cowboy boots and all, but instead of a patch he wore an old straw hat, and instead of a sword, the butt end of a toy dagger stuck out of one of his cowboy boots.

"Wait a minute, Daddy." Maddie's words paused Blake's descent. "You forgot to walk the plank. That's my favorite part."

"But we've already made it to shore." Blake walked back up to where his daughter stood.

"Please, Daddy, will you, please? We could pretend we didn't land yet, and that you were mut ... mutian—"

"Mutinous," Blake finished.

"Yes, and as Captain, I won't stand for any mutinanany."

"All right," Blake held his hands in front of him. "Do you want to shackle me?"

"Means handcuff, right?" At her father's nod, Maddie pulled his arms behind his back and pretended to bind them. "It is time you meet the fishies at the bottom of the sea. Tell them hi for me."

"No, please, Captain. I promise to be a better first mate."

"You should have done what I asked the first time." Maddie pushed her father to the edge of a homemade plank.

As he walked onto the board, Blake made eye contact with me through the thin branches of the willow tree. His eyes widened, and he stopped mid-stride. Maddie, who still hadn't seen me, continued to march with the point of her wooden sword leading the way. The tip of Maddie's sword dug into Blake's backside and pushed him off balance.

His arms flailed about him as if he were trying to find some support in the air, but his effort turned futile as one foot slipped off the edge of the slim board and the rest of his body followed. He landed on his back in the awaiting grass.

Maddie giggled and looked down at her father. "That's the best one you've done yet. Can you walk the plank again?"

I jogged to stand over Blake and make sure he was all right, but I laughed through my concern.

"Hey, Lili." Maddie flipped up the patch covering her eye. "You can play pirates with us if you want. We have to bury the treasure, and Daddy just walked the plank."

"I would love to play pirates, but I'm going to check on your daddy first." I turned to Blake, stifling my amusement. "Do you want me to check for broken bones?" One chuckle broke free.

Blake grabbed onto the swing set for support and groaned as he stood up before he answered. "I don't think you can do anything to help me unless you learned how to fix my pride in medical school."

I laughed. "Give it plenty of rest, though I know it'll be pretty difficult for you."

"Hey, I'm the epitome of humility." Blake put his hand on his chest.

"Sure, you are—"

Maddie tapped her foot on the board above me. "You guys aren't being very good pirates." She put her hands on her hips. "And we still have to bury the treasure." She grabbed the weathered, green and gold jewelry box from behind the plank and held it out in front of me.

*Pirates of the Caribbean* had been one of my favorite movies in high school. "All right, Captain, where be the spot ye want the treasure to be buried?" I asked in my best imitation of Jack Sparrow.

"You don't look like a pirate at all. Here, you can wear this." Maddie ripped off her black eye patch and threw it at me. I caught it and put it over my left eye.

"Take the treasure." Maddie handed me the jewelry box and jumped off the plank.

"Looks like you've had more practice at walking the plank, Captain Maddie, than your first mate," I said.

In my peripheral vision, Blake reached out for me. I squealed and tried to run before he captured my arm, but my reaction time was too slow. He pulled me close against his chest.

"She doesn't have a distraction like you to deal with," Blake whispered in my ear.

His whisper sent goosebumps racing down my neck. I couldn't think. Couldn't breathe normally. My flirting muscles had atrophied with over a decade of little to no exercise. What was I supposed to say back to him? He knocked my thoughts off course more times than I could count, almost like the synapses in my brain slowed down when he came near me.

Maddie ran to us. She pushed Blake. "Let her go you evil, mutinanimous pirate."

She waved her small wooden sword at her dad. I didn't have time to let my chills settle before I leaped back into the pretend world Maddie had created.

"You'll have to come and get her. I'll never let her go." Blake pushed me behind his back.

He pulled his plastic dagger out of his boot. I overexaggerated a gasp, and Maddie charged forward, swinging her sword at the toy dagger. She hit it three times before Blake dropped it and admitted defeat.

Maddie grabbed my hand and ran toward the safety of the willow tree. "Do you still have the treasure?"

I shook the box next to Maddie's ear. The treasure clattered around inside the small jewelry box. From many years of practice on Christmas mornings, I guessed that the contents of the box consisted of plastic beads and pocket change.

"Good. We'll bury it over there." Maddie pointed to the willow tree.

She took the treasure box from me and placed it between two large roots protruding out from the base of the tree. She wrapped her small hands around a patch of tall grass and pulled. Once the roots released their hold on the soil, Maddie lost her balance and fell back onto her bottom. I sat back on my haunches while she finished burying the treasure in grass. My legs cramped by the time Maddie declared the job was done.

"Now all we have to do is mark it, so we'll know where to find it." She slapped the remnants of the grass from her hands.

"Do you want to mark it with an X?" I stood and stretched out my legs.

I found Blake. He leaned against the swing set, looking handsome in his thrown-together pirate outfit.

"No. Too easy." Maddie hit her forehead with her right hand, leaving a smudge of dirt on her head the size of her palm. "Hey, I know what we could do. Let's mark it with a *Y*. Then other pirates will never find it."

I kept tight control over my lips as Maddie bent down to arrange the loose grass into the letter Y.

"Come on, Lili. We have to go." Maddie waved for me to follow her. "The evil Pirate Daddy is coming to steal our treasure."

Blake sauntered near the grass covering the jewelry box. "Hmmm ... I don't see any treasure here," Blake called out. "I see a Y, but no X that marks the spot."

In our hiding place, Maddie looked at me and covered her mouth to stifle a giggle. The heat of Maddie's body warmed the side of my leg. I turned from Maddie's sparkling eyes and rosy cheeks and scooted away from her until the soft summer breeze came between us.

Blake returned to his spot near the swing set.

"Yay." Maddie jumped up and squeezed close to me, eliminating the space I'd created. "We did it. The treasure is safe."

Maddie quieted. I followed her gaze; Chuck stood next to the back door of the mechanic's shop. "Oh, I forgot." Maddie turned to Blake. "Daddy, I have to go talk to Chuck and Pedro and Renee, okay?" Before he could answer, Maddie ran down the slight hill to the garage.

A kid could be present for the top-secret meeting, but I couldn't? I yanked the patch off, put my hands on my hips, and faced Blake. At least someone else was left out of the loop, and maybe he could help me solve the mystery of the cash-loaded mailbox.

"Can we talk?"

"Depends on what you want to say." He took a couple steps toward me, close enough his body heat prickled my skin. "And I believe we are already talking."

"Well, it's about Renee—" My cheeks flushed even though I had nothing to be ashamed of. Anyone would have done what I did, but I still felt like I'd intruded somehow.

"Don't worry about what they are discussing in there." Blake pointed to the shop. "You'll know soon—"

I reeled backward, distancing myself from him. "You know what they are talking about?" So much for two people being out of the loop.

Too many secrets surrounded me. I should go home and leave them in my rearview mirror. In St. Louis, no one bothered me, no one lied to me, or kept things from me. I was left alone, which is the way I wanted it. I'd buy myself a new fern, or maybe I'd get a cactus. They were harder to kill.

"Of course, I know what they're talking about." Blake rubbed the back of his neck. "I own the shop and anything going on in it has to be cleared through me first."

"So, I'm the only one left out?" I was back to being the fool. Blake stepped away from me and studied me with a quizzical look on his face. He waited silently for me to explain.

"First Renee doesn't tell me anything," I mumbled. "And now everyone else I care for in this town is—"

"You care for me?" Blake smiled and lifted my chin, so we were speaking eye to eye.

"That doesn't matter right now." I pulled my head away. I wasn't ready for this conversation yet. "I want to know what is going on."

He took a hold of both my hands and tugged me to him. Tucking a stray hair behind my ear, he cupped my cheek. "Oh, but to me, it's all that matters."

Warmth spread from the contact of his hand. It buzzed down my arms and up my legs. The deep timbre of his voice and the sincerity in it made me momentarily forget about my problems with Renee. He shifted toward me as if he was going to kiss my forehead but stopped. I took a breath and leaned against his chest. Hesitantly ... slowly, he wrapped his arms around me.

"I'm so happy you came to visit." His voice reverberated through his chest and reminded me of the night we met.

So much had happened in the week since then.

"Me too," I answered, surprised I really meant it.

He leaned back, placed his hands on my shoulders, and gave them a light squeeze. "Now, what did you want to ask me about your mother?"

"What is she talking about in there?"

"I promised I wouldn't tell."

I stepped out of his soft grip and threw my hands in the air. "I give up."

"You know, I care about you too." Blake winked at me.

"I'm going to go nuts." I marched away from him.

"That's not exactly how I planned on you reacting." Blake jogged and caught up to me. "Wait." He took my arm. "I'm sorry. I do want to know what you have to say. I would tell you everything, but some secrets are not mine to tell."

"I'm so stinking tired." I shook my head and rubbed my palm across my forehead. Blake traced his fingers along my upper arm. It eased my tension. "When you left last night, I couldn't sleep—"

"I was that good, was I?"

I slugged his shoulder. "Really? You're supposed to be resting your pride, remember?"

"I'm sorry, I'm sorry. I promise I won't say another word until you're done. You couldn't sleep and ..." He prompted with a smile in his voice.

He listened while I told him about following Renee. "I couldn't take the money and confront Renee. I mean, what if she was being blackmailed and I took the money, and her blackmailer killed her or something? There are so many questions I want to ask her. She's acting like she's a millionaire, yet we lived on crumbs. She doesn't have money to be giving away." I looked at Blake, waiting for answers. A response. Anything.

"Blackmailers don't kill the person they're blackmailing." He rubbed his chin.

After all I'd told him, he had nothing more to say. Why had I even come to him?

"Okay, so I could have taken the money, and her blackmailer would have revealed the secret she paid them to keep hidden. Is that better?" I looked away from him and watched a killdeer as it skittered down Blake's graveled path.

He studied me a while longer before he spoke. "You think your mother is poor?"

I opened my arms wide and faced him. "I grew up on cold hot dogs and Ramen noodles. It was a special night when I got to eat Rice-a-Roni and chicken. I cooked every meal. Renee had worked non-stop. We even bought my underwear second-hand. What else am I supposed to think?"

Could it be Renee had lied to me all my life? Blake seemed to think Renee was loaded, but why? If she had enough money to leave five-thousand-dollar gifts here and there, she would need more money than a lottery winner.

"You don't know anything about your mother, do you?" His eyes widened when he searched mine.

I broke eye-contact and stared at the ground. Wasn't that what I had tried to tell him earlier? "I know everything about her since we have heart to heart chats every night." Blake had spent more time with Renee than I had in my entire lifetime. He was the son Renee never had, a better child for her than I could ever be.

I'd been ashamed of the truth, but I may as well admit it to myself. "Is she in some sort of trouble?"

"I think I can help, but I need to show you something so you will understand what I'm about to tell you." He held out his hand to me.

I shook my head and backed up. I couldn't handle knowing I'd been neglected and starved as a girl for no reason at all.

Blake leveled a look at me. "You should learn to trust her a little." He kept his hand extended.

I had an ally now, and while I may not always trust Renee, I could trust Blake. I took his hand, interlaced my fingers in his, and followed him away from the mechanic's shop where Renee stood in the midst of one of her many secrets.

# Chapter 23

## Blake

I took Lili into my attached garage and moved to the third bay where my beauty sat, covered, and protected from UV light, dust, and rodents—mouse traps lay in a full circumference around her. She wasn't really mine, but I'd handled every part of her, twisted every bolt, torqued every nut. It was natural that I felt a bit of ownership.

I flipped on the light, unclipped the car cover and pulled the tarp off, exposing the gleaming orange paint. Rolling the tarp into a bundle and dropping it to the floor, I stood tall; this had been created by me. Making it perfect had become an obsession once Cindy had left.

Lili let out a soft intake of air. Who wouldn't be impressed by the perfection of the machine before us? The black racing stripes, the white-wall tires, original chrome wheels polished until they gleamed.

"I have no idea what type of car this is, but it's gorgeous." She traced her finger along the hood.

"This is my favorite car. It's a 1970 Hemi 'Cuda with—"

"A hemi whata?"

"A 1970 Plymouth Hemi Barracuda Coupe with a four-speed manual transmission and a 340 block, 426 c.i.d Hemi V-8 engine with dual quads under the hood."

Her face went blank, and she furrowed her eyebrows.

I pressed my mouth shut. I'd let my inner mechanic take the light again.

"Should I start taking notes? Today's topic in car mechanics 101, classic cars," she teased.

I laughed and dialed back the car information overload. "Basically, you wouldn't want to get in a race with this. It even has the look of a racing car with the spoiler on the trunk, and the sport hood. Any car enthusiast would itch to sit behind the wheel."

So, she wasn't into cars. Big deal. The simple fact she drove an Audi A8 meant she liked speed.

"Despite my lack of knowledge..." She bit her lower lip. Something I noticed she often did when she found herself in an uncomfortable situation, even when her lip had mud on it. "... I think this car is really special. I like a nice-looking classic car, but the only ones I am familiar with are the Mustangs and the 'Vettes. Now thanks to you I'll be able to recognize 'Cudas—"

"Hemi 'Cudas," I corrected. "Don't mix it up with the regular Plymouth Barracuda."

"*Hemi* 'Cudas. But you brought me here to show me something to do with Renee and the money."

"It's hers."

"What do you mean it's hers?"

"She owns it."

"That's impossible. Restoring a car to this condition would cost—"

"Seventy to eighty thousand dollars," I finished.

"*Eighty thousand dollars.* I don't see how—" she stuttered into silence.

"I can't explain the how, but I might be able to help with the why." I leaned against the car. "Your mother and I met while I was renovating my house. At the time, Maddie was three. I came home one afternoon and found my daughter locked in her room screaming. Cynthia—my ex—was supposed to be watching her."

"She left Maddie alone?"

I could hear it in her tone. How could anyone be that irresponsible? How could I have been dumb enough to marry her? I'd married Cindy *for* my daughter, so she would never feel the same abandonment that still haunted me.

"Yes." I scratched the side of my head. How much should I tell her? Should I use every detail to paint an accurate picture of Cindy, and how bad life had gotten for me? "Something had been wrong with Maddie's arm. Turned out, she had a spiral fracture and the doctor thought I'd abused her."

Lili let out a small gasp and covered her mouth with her fingertips. I supposed she knew exactly what the ER's response was to suspected abuse. I rested my hip against the driver's side window.

"They wouldn't let me take my daughter home with me. I had to battle for a week to get her back. In the middle of that mess, Cindy emptied our bank accounts, personal and business, and left me penniless."

The rest of the money from selling Jorge's garage, any savings I'd scraped together to give us a secure future, gone in an instant. I'd never hated anyone before, but I'd hated Cindy for what she'd done to her own child.

Lili walked close to me and touched my arm. "I'm so sorry."

I lifted one corner of my mouth and took hold of her fingers. "It's not your fault. Turned out losing the money was the evidence the courts needed to back up my story and get custody of Maddie. I would have paid a million times that if it meant having my baby girl."

I never wanted to go back there to those sleepless nights, where I spent every waking minute wondering when the bank would foreclose, planning for worst-case scenario for when me and my baby were homeless. "Still, without the money, I faced losing my business, a plot of land, and my half-finished house."

"What did you do?" She leaned her tight backside against the Hemi 'Cuda.

Her coconut scent mixed with the smells of my clean garage drove me crazy. She wet her lips with her tongue, and I lost my train of thought.

"Um—your mom found out about my situation and stepped in to help. I was angry, rejected, and ready to declare bankruptcy. She saved me from myself. Renee grossly overpaid me to restore the Hemi 'Cuda, the Mustang, and referred everyone she knew to my business. She saved my shop." I looked at her, proud of myself for only glancing at her lips once. "I was able to give Chuck and Pedro jobs. Blake's Place is the most popular mechanic's shop in the Magic Valley, but had it not been for your mother, it wouldn't exist."

Who knew where I would be or what I would have resorted to, to provide for my little girl. Lili didn't say anything. My story showed proof of her mother's wealth, but not where it had come from. I didn't have that answer for her. Minutes passed before Lili spoke again.

"Why do you keep the car here? I mean if it's Renee's, why doesn't she drive it or sell it?" She ran her fingers over the paint.

Another question I didn't have an answer to. "She told me to sell it, to keep the money for the shop, and she'd keep the Mustang. The Hemi 'Cuda isn't mine, so I couldn't bring myself to do it." In my mind's eye,

I could strip both cars down to the frame, since I'd scrubbed every inch of them free of rust and started to rebuild from there.

"You did this?" She tickled the orange paint with her fingertips. "Without any help?"

How I wanted to be the Hemi 'Cuda right now with her butt pressed against me and her hand tracing goosebumps on my skin.

"Yeah." My mind was no longer focused on the car.

A crease formed between her eyebrows. She licked her lips again and didn't say anything. I breathed in the smell of her shampoo, or whatever product it was that made her hair smell like tropical heaven. What would she do if I leaned down and kissed her?

Unable to resist the chemistry between us any longer, I shifted off the car and moved in front of her. She leaned more heavily onto the hood and looked up at me with wide eyes. I inched closer to her and placed my hands on her waist. Her gaze dropped to my hands, then centered on my lips, and I was sunk. I brushed my lips against hers in the barest contact. I met her eyes, questioning. She wrapped her fingers in my shirt and tugged me closer. It was all the answer I needed to crush my lips against hers.

# Chapter 24

## Liliana

A volcano erupted inside me, and molten lava spread from my core to my fingertips. I shifted my hand from his shirt to the back of his neck, adding pressure to my touch—demanding more.

He responded and lifted one of my legs to wrap it around him. I fell back against the hood of his car, adding more tilt to my world, already off its axis. His leg slid between mine as he pressed into me, his lips becoming more insistent. I touched his biceps, his chest, the scruff on his cheek. This was real, and I couldn't get enough of him.

Tasting the outdoors and a hint of cinnamon on his breath, I grew dizzy, and I broke contact to take in some air. His breath came out in gusts against my mouth as he ran his hand along the side of my body from my thigh up to my chest, settling there, exploring every inch of me he could, sending my body spiraling. I rested my shoulders on the cool metal of the pristine car and pulled him to me.

He didn't resist, pressing his lips to mine again. Looping his hand behind my head, he interlaced his fingers through my hair and tilted my head upward to gain access to my neck. He brushed his lips along the curve of my throat and made his way to my ear, nibbling on its lobe.

"You are so amazing," he breathed, before claiming my mouth once again.

I responded with a feverish desire I didn't know had existed before he'd ignited it, as if this part of me had remained dormant until I'd found him. Our bodies fit together, my curves meeting his in the right places. How had I lived without him for so long?

My nerves burned everywhere he touched, and I ached for more. He tipped his forehead to mine as I wrapped my legs around his waist, and he lifted me into his arms. Spinning me away from the car, he stepped back until his butt angled against the hood. My legs slid down the length of him until my toes touched the floor, giving me leverage to press him against the windshield. My fingers brushed against the wipers to the smooth, clear surface. The full length of my body rested on his. He kissed my jaw and traced my collarbone with his lips.

I sucked in a deep breath, elevating my soft chest to his scruffy chin, and let the air ease from my lungs. Lifting my eyelids, I met his gaze, his pupils almost as wide as his irises, and gently caressed his lips with mine. I kept just within reach, taunting him to raise his head off the glass and press his hands to the base of my skull, tangling his fingers in my hair.

The click of a doorknob registered in my brain, and I pushed off Blake.

"Daddy?" Maddie asked as she walked in. "I saw you come in here with Lili."

Blake stood and smoothed his shirt.

"Lili, your hair's all messy and why was Daddy on the car?" She raised her eyebrows and gasped. "Are you doing tango?"

"No," Blake and I said at the same time.

She rocked on her heels, a slow smile spreading across her face. "Benny. That's what I want to name my baby brother when he comes."

# Chapter 25

## Liliana

Steam from my chicken noodle soup and grilled cheese sandwiches wafted into my face. I rubbed my eyes and yawned. My tired mind couldn't think of anything else but the kiss, the way his legs pressed between mine as his lips shifted across my skin—

"What's on your mind? You've been kind of quiet all day." Renee opened the door for conversation.

A hot and heavy make-out session with a mechanic on his race car. "Hm?" I opened my mouth and closed it again. The ring of my cell phone saved me. "It might be someone from work." I ran into the dining room and tugged my phone out of my purse. Tiffany's face flashed on my screen.

"I need details. On a scale of one to ten how hot was the kiss?" Her familiar voice, her caring face, calmed me.

I bit my lip. I'd texted Tiffany a lip emoji followed by a mind blown. "Twelve point six."

Tiffany squealed. "Do you understand what a big deal this is? You haven't kissed a guy since med school and that one was only a peck. Is he there with you right now?"

If only I could have stayed on the hood of his car with him the rest of the afternoon. I touched my lips remembering the feel of his skin beneath them. It'd actually happened. Like always, the unpleasantries of life had invaded and shoved me onward.

"Uh, Tiff?"

"Yeah."

"Can I call you back later? I have so much to fill you in on, but I can't talk right now."

"Aw," Tiff whined like a disappointed child. "Can you at least tell him hi for me?"

"Sure." The tension in my voice relaxed. "But it's just a fun vacay fling."

"You can underplay it all you want, Lili. This is huge. You haven't dated—"

"I've been on dates." One to the pizza place on the corner. Two, went and got coffee. Three, hospital cafeteria lunch date—

"You hardly touched any of the guys I set you up with. Half the time you didn't even sit next to them. Those dates don't count."

"Whatever." I'd been able to keep men who'd been interested in me at a distance. Blake was different.

"Are you okay?"

"Yeah. I need to talk with Renee."

"Oh. One of *those* talks. Well, give me a ring later if you need me."

"Sounds good."

"All right, but don't keep me in suspense too long about this guy. You might just find me on your mother's doorstep. See ya."

I stared at the screen until it went black and turned my phone on silent before I walked back into the kitchen and sat at the table.

"I followed you last night," I said, getting right to the heart of the issue.

"I guessed as much."

"How?"

I'd been invisible. No headlights. No turn signals. I kept at the appropriate distance and followed the rules of pursuing a vehicle without being spotted from all the spy movies I'd watched.

"I didn't figure it out until today. You have never been good at hiding your feelings, dear. You get that from your father."

"Well?"

"Well, what?"

"What do you mean *well what*? What the hell were you doing putting five thousand dollars in a mailbox? And whose mailbox was it *anyway*?"

Renee set her sandwich down before she answered. "It was Vivian and Jack's mailbox. Viv wouldn't be able to afford the medicine for Jack and still make her mortgage payments, so I thought I would help out a bit. You don't know Viv and Jack. Last year he was diagnosed with leukemia. The treatments are expensive. Viv's a good woman—raising a kid all on her own. I thought they could use a little money to pay their deductible."

"You define 'a little help' as *five thousand dollars?*"

"Yes."

Her small and short answer pushed my patience over the edge. "Why the mailbox, then? Why didn't you go hand it to her?"

"Have you ever given anyone money?"

"No."

"You should try it and see how far you get. Believe me, it doesn't work. People don't like charity when they are looking their benefactor in the face." Renee paused and shook her head. "A long time ago I found it was much easier to remain anonymous when giving away money."

"You've done this before?"

"Yes." Renee acted as if everyone had a habit of leaving cash in mailboxes.

"Let me get this straight. When I was wearing shoes too big and socks with holes in them, you were putting thousands of dollars in mailboxes?" My voice raised to the point of cracking.

"Oh, heavens no. Back then I did anything to survive and keep our house from getting foreclosed. Do you think I enjoyed working three jobs?"

"For all I know, you were out doing who knows what while you said you were working. Besides, the paycheck for at least one of those jobs went straight to Jack Daniels." I put a hand to my temple. "I'm sorry. I have no idea what to believe."

"How many times do I need to tell you? I don't drink anymore. I know I tried to quit when you had M—"

"Don't." I cut her off with a sharp hand movement. "Don't go there."

Renee took a breath and went on. "I never once lied to you when you were growing up. We had very little money. I never would have made you grow up like that had I known that it could have been different."

"What do you mean? It could have been different."

"When your father died, he had a life insurance policy—"

"That you didn't know about?" I scoffed and folded my arms across my chest.

"*Yes.*" She laid her hands out in front of me and crumpled back into her chair. The wrinkles on her face stood out as did the bags under her eyes. "He took it out a week before he left on his last job, without telling me."

"When he died, his lawyer, or somebody, would have told you about it." I leaned my elbows on the table, my growling stomach forgotten, my food lukewarm.

"He didn't involve a lawyer." A distant look overshadowed her eyes. She turned her head and pushed around bits of crumbs on the table. "I thought he quit when we moved here—when you were born-but he was taking side jobs as a civilian contractor for Triple Canopy based out of Reston, VA. The last one must have worried him, which would explain the policy."

"So, how did you find out about the money?"

"Papers I didn't have the heart to go through when Thomas died, and then they got lost. I found them a few years back."

"A few *years*? You've got to be kidding me." I slumped back into my chair. Renee could have tried more ways than one to get in contact with me. If the phone didn't work, she could have sent me a letter, or visited me. She had several years to tell me about this, yet she'd waited until last week to be persistent enough to get me here.

"If you give me a chance, I'll explain everything." Renee ran her hand through her short hair. "You remember your Uncle Joe?" At my flat look she went on, "No? When you first arrived, I told you your father's gift wasn't ready yet. Well, I may have stretched the truth a bit—"

"A bad habit of yours," I cut her off.

"We all have our flaws." Renee absently swirled her spoon around in her soup. "I told you that Uncle Joe wasn't your dad's brother in the blood sense. They were in the same special-ops unit before they took the job at Triple Canopy. In life, they were as inseparable as I'm sure they are in death."

I took a deep breath. Patience, Lili. "I'm sorry you lost a friend, I truly am, but if he's dead, why did you even bring him into this?"

"Without his wife, we wouldn't have been able to prove anything." She wiped her hands on a paper towel and looked directly at me. "He went with your father, and they took out the life insurance together. I fought for a solid year to have the policy paid in full. After all, Thomas never defaulted on a payment before he died."

"How many payments did he make?"

"Two." Renee breathed in through her nose and let air out her mouth. "You can imagine their resistance to paying out two one-million-dollar policies when they'd only been paid a couple hundred dollars."

"Did you say *one million*?"

"Yes. I got a hold of Suzanna, and she showed them all of Joe's papers, threatened to sue, and they became way more cooperative. I've invested some of it, and I've done well in the stock market."

The stock market? Investments? Who was this woman?

"The other policy is for you. It's in a trust. Accruing interest."

"You mean I have a million dollars sitting in an account for me?" That would pay off my medical school loans.

"A little more. Yes."

I looked around the room; there was nothing lavish. Aside from the kitchen, everything was the same as it had been when I'd last been here, down to the cheap cotton clothes Renee wore. Renee had always been frugal, but anyone would buy a few things for themselves if they fell into that much cash.

"What the hell, Renee? You've known about this for years and you couldn't find a way to get ahold of me before?" Heat flushed into my face and burned into my glare.

"Don't look at me like that." Renee slapped her hand on the table. "I called you three times a day for months after you left. You didn't have the decency to answer one phone call." She held her index finger in front of my nose. "You hurt me, and my hurt turned to anger. I figured you'd get your money as soon as you stopped being stubborn."

"You didn't leave a single message. Not one text. Look what happened when you did. I'm here." I threw my hands wide.

"I had to get myself in a healthy place before I saw you again."

I dropped my face into my hands and rubbed my temples. Renee was wealthy. I had a million-dollar trust fund. This stuff didn't happen in real life.

This couldn't be real.

So many aspects of our lives could have been different. No struggles to pay the mortgage. No worrying about paying for gas and groceries or going without food for days at a time with my only meals coming from the school.

She would have blown it all on booze anyway. I shifted from doubt to confusion back to anger, but it wasn't until I started laughing while my eyes filled with tears that Renee showed her concern. She reached out and touched my shoulder.

I jerked away from her touch as if she'd shocked me. "Why *did* you make me come home for this? You could have sent a letter with a check."

"I wanted to see you. To tell you this in person. You never returned my calls—"

"You want to get into this now, Renee?" I braced my hands on the table and met her eye for eye.

"Stop with this Renee bullshit!" Renee yelled. "I am your *mother*."

"Being called mother isn't something you automatically get when you birth a child. It's an earned title!" I shouted back at her. "You should have tried harder to be my mother after Daddy died. Maybe the reason I never called or visited is I had to raise myself. You had the chance to be a mom, *my* mom. I cooked, I cleaned, and once I started high school, I even made the money."

"That's not fair, Lili—" Renee put her hands out in front of her.

"You were a drunk, lazy and unhappy, and you took it out on me." The words wouldn't stop pouring out of my mouth. They'd been building up for years.

With each one of my words, Renee's spine stiffened a fraction more as if each one was an arrow piercing her side. "Yes, I was different back then, but I did what I had to do to keep food on the table. 'When life drops a pile of cow manure in your lap—'"

"Yeah, yeah, I know, 'use it to fertilize the flowers,'" I finished for her. I couldn't count the number of times Renee had used this saying. It was a bunch of hogwash. "Did you use my paychecks in high school to fertilize your flowers too?"

Renee's lips tightened into a frown. "The money you made went to pay for your school expenses." She ran her hands through her hair.

"Right, 'school expenses.'" I air quoted. "I wasn't aware the school asked for liquor on the supply list."

"Come on, Lili. Give me a chance to—"

"A chance to what? Ruin my life some more?" I brushed the tears off my cheeks. "You should keep the money, and don't give me a holier than thou routine. Forget the prayers at dinner. I know who you really are."

Renee leaned closer to me and held up her three fingers. "I worked three minimum wage jobs. Even still, without the money from your paychecks, I wouldn't have been able to pay the mortgage."

"Teenagers are not supposed to pay their parents' house payments."

"I wish I could change the way you were raised, but I can't. I worked as many hours as I could—"

"Then why didn't you get more education and find a worthwhile job?"

Renee rubbed the back of her neck. "I didn't have the money to pay for it."

"Don't give me that. I put myself through college and medical school with no help from you." If she'd wanted me bad enough, she would have fought harder to be there for me. "You were depressed and ignored me. You couldn't get out of your hole."

"*You're right.*" Renee sank into her chair like a deflated balloon. All at once she looked much older than her sixty years. "But at least I've changed. I'm done drinking. I even went to a therapist for a while. What are you doing to make yourself better?"

A bucket of frigid water doused the fire feeding my anger. I sat up straight with my spine rigid. How many years had I pushed away Renee? I'd surrounded myself with a cocoon of safety. Let no one in. Love no one.

Renee gave her love freely to the whole town … but not to me. "Now, you bounce around the countryside like Robin Hood?"

"I had lost everything, Lili—even you. I turned to religion to remain sane, then I met Blake and Maddie. I found out that I could do a lot of good with the money. I could serve God by serving His children."

"God," I scoffed.

"God is not the enemy. He can't stop the natural consequences of life. Everyone has to die. Sometimes He needs someone with Him sooner rather than later."

"So, God saved you, huh?" Renee was an honest-to-goodness living angel, and yet I couldn't stand to be around her right now.

"Besides, you and I aren't much different—"

"I am nothing like you. When my world fell apart, I didn't give up and try to drink myself to death—"

"How many times do I have to say it? *I don't drink anymore.*" Renee stretched her hands out wide in front of her.

"*Now*, you don't drink anymore, but it's too late! I needed you then."

"You have your fancy degree, and you succeeded much better than I did, are you happy?"

I shifted away from her and bumped my elbow on the table. Renee's question hit hard. *Was* I happy?

"Face it. You drown yourself in work the same way that I drowned myself in alcohol. You keep everyone at a distance to keep yourself from being hurt again." Renee fiddled with her soup spoon. It clinked against the glass bowl. "You went to medical school to escape; you went to avoid anything that would remind you of your family. You went so that you wouldn't have to feel anything. But, you have to come back to me sometime." Renee took a breath and continued, "I miss you. You're the only family I have."

Seconds ticked by on the clock as neither of us spoke. Happiness didn't exist. It was a fairytale that parents told their kids at night. True happiness was fleeting at best, especially with all the calamities, accidents, twisted perverts, evil, and abuse in the world.

I'd seen it all come through the ER and into my trauma bay. Why did Renee expect me to possess something impossible to obtain?

All these years, I told myself that I wouldn't fail like Renee had. I would stay strong and not let myself fall to pieces. Could Renee be right? Were we the same?

Renee's ragged breaths resonated in the quiet room for a few minutes before I could say the words I had been meaning to say for years. "You weren't there for me the one day I needed you most. They're gone, like Daddy, because of you."

Fresh tears coursed down Renee's face, but I ignored them and walked out of the house. In less than five minutes, I had the Malibu on the country roads crusted with dirt from the harvest. I drove without destination. Not sure of where I was going, my awareness of time slipped as I lost myself in my thoughts.

With Michael gone, I had no choice but to find my own way. Two weeks after the funeral I'd taken the MCAT, and the following June, I was in medical school. I never looked back. Never took the time to process. Never took the time to grieve. The day I lost them, I had no control, no knowledge about how to save them, and I couldn't let that happen again. Medical school made sense. I was good at it. It distracted me from the ever-present ache of loss. I would never be put in the same situation again, watching someone I loved die without knowing how to save them.

I often wondered, if I'd been a doctor then, would things have turned out differently? Would I have been able to save them?

Somewhere in the middle of med school, I'd become almost vengeful. I wanted to humiliate Renee, to show her that loss didn't mean giving up. Now that I'd completed all my goals, I lost the ability to drive in the final punch. I'd succeeded. I was a doctor, a trauma surgeon, close to making more money than I'd ever dreamed, yet I was empty. How long had it been since I'd felt alive?

If Michael were with me today, would he be proud of me? Would he love this cold, reserved person I'd become?

I pulled to a stop and turned off the car's engine. The low fuel light on the dash faded as the car's life sputtered out. The sound of the creek, cows, and crickets filled the night air. Wispy willow tree branches created flickering shadows in the moonlight. A vague awareness of my surroundings penetrated through my melancholy. I'd driven to the one place I could find help. I'd guided the car to Blake.

# Chapter 26

## Liliana

Light from inside trickled onto the porch in front of me. The tightening in my chest eased. He wore plaid pajama pants and a loose Blake's Place T-shirt.

"Hey, what's up?" Blake closed his eyes and put his hand on his face. "I ... I mean, come in."

I pulled my purse strap onto my shoulder and walked inside. "I hope you don't mind. I didn't mean to barge in like this."

"Ouch!" He swung his hand in the air. "No. I don't mind at all."

"What did you do? Are you okay?" I stepped close to him, my senses coming alive at his presence.

He leaned down, his mouth hovering over mine. "I shut my thumb in the door," he said, his breath fluttering against my skin.

Closing the miniscule gap between us, his lips slanted over mine. His hands found the small of my back and pressed me against him. My body sculpted to his. Numbness eased inside me, replaced by a fire beginning in my core, igniting my otherwise lifeless feelings. Hungry for more, I draped my arms over his shoulders and rubbed the base of his neck.

Much to my disappointment, he broke contact. He rested his forehead on mine, his breathing heavy. "I couldn't wait to do that again."

Speechless, all I could do was move my head up and down in agreement.

He took my hand and led me inside to the couch. Without his warmth next to me the deadening chills shuddered over me, anesthetizing my remaining passion. Reality hurtled back into my world.

The soft leather squeaked when I sat. A large fireplace dominated the center of the wall opposite me, its river-rock chimney rising to the ceiling above the dark, ornate wooden mantel at its center.

A candle flame flickered in its jar, adding the scent of lavender to the room. An oversized window to the left framed a view of Blake's backyard bathed in moonlight. The austere brown and blue shades in this room implied a very masculine domain. I set my purse on his end table, placed my hands in my lap, and picked at a dry cuticle.

Why had I come here?

Blake walked over to the candle and blew it out. "Lavender helps Maddie sleep," he explained, as if embarrassed by the purple candle on the mantle.

On cue, Maddie wailed from upstairs. Her cries cut through the quiet in the room and continued to gather in strength.

"Would you excuse me for a moment?" Blake started toward the stairs.

"I can go, if you—"

"*No.*" Blake paused on his way up the stairs. "I forgot her song, and she needs her blanket. It'll only take a minute to calm her down."

Tapping my hands on my thighs, I sat while I waited for Maddie's screams to subside.

Forget it. I shouldn't have come here.

I stood and strode to the front door. The metal doorknob warmed in my grip, but I didn't open it. I walked back into the living room, past the couch, and followed Blake up the stairs. Maddie's cries grew louder the closer I got to her slightly ajar door.

Only a dim nightlight lit the room. Blake sang an out-of-tune version of *Twinkle Little Star* as he rubbed a hand along Maddie's face and tucked her blanket around her shoulders. Her screams calmed even as she covered her ears.

The scene pulled at my memory of another time when I watched Michael with my baby girl. Blake, with his calloused hands, was gentle like Michael. I closed my eyes and took a breath. I had no place here.

I walked down the stairs and headed for the door.

"Lili, wait," Blake called from behind me. "Maddie is okay now. Why don't you come sit?"

"It's fine, really. I didn't mean to interrupt—"

"Don't worry." Blake glanced up the stairs and back up to my face. "I have to follow the same routine every night. Maddie's on the spectrum."

"Maddie is an amazing girl. She's brilliant." I remembered enough from my pediatric rotation in medical school and had observed Maddie long enough to determine that she met the DSM-5 diagnostic criteria to be on the autism spectrum.

"Yeah. She's pretty amazing." One side of his mouth lifted. He sat on the couch and patted the seat next to him. A clock on the mantle ticked in the quiet. "What brought you here tonight?" Mischief glinted in his eyes, adding to his lopsided grin, like a naughty boy about to snitch from the cookie jar. "Booty call?"

Clearly, he was joking, but if he could read my thoughts—see how many times I'd imagined taking off his clothes, kissing every inch of his toned body... "You wish." I laughed and sat next to him, resting my elbows on my knees. "I asked Renee about the money."

"How'd that go?" Blake shifted. He crossed and uncrossed his ankles.

"She told me she had a million dollars—well, we have a million dollars each, and I left." Maybe, eventually, I'd get used to associating Renee with the word million, but not yet.

"Did you say a *million* dollars, times two?" He straightened and planted both feet on the ground.

I leaned back. "Wait, I thought you knew."

"I knew she had a lot of money, but she never gave me the specifics. Renee's not one to talk about herself."

"I did have to weasel it out of her."

"So ...," Blake pushed.

"So, Renee isn't poor like I always thought. I drove myself through medical school to show her that even though I ... suffered through a traumatic event, I could still provide for myself." I would never measure up to the woman Renee had become. A week ago, I would have thought the opposite.

"What's the big deal? So, your mom's worth a cool mil."

"*What's the big deal?*" I threw my hands in the air. "The big deal is, she lied to me; she hid her fortune from me. I was starved as a kid for food and attention, and I find out that it could have been different, well, not really, but it could have been possible. I worked so hard—you don't understand. I ... I just—" I stuttered and paused. "What's wrong with me, Blake? How could my controlling, manipulative mother turn into a living saint, while I became like—well, like this?"

He didn't respond right away. He rubbed his jawline like a psychiatrist analyzing his patient. I should have called Tiffany. "Well, aren't you going to say anything?"

"Like what?"

I held out my arms. "I don't know. You could say, 'Lili, you didn't turn out so bad,' or 'Renee's not a saint,' or 'get the hell out of my house, you crazy woman.' Something."

A low chuckle rumbled in his chest. He placed his fingers under my chin and lifted my head to meet his eyes. "Whatever drove a wedge between you and your mother made you the woman you are today." He let go of my chin and fell back into the cushions. "And you are an incredible person."

Placing his hands on either side of my face, he kissed me again, his lips soft. Gentle. Taking his time. Awakening my desires. Making me want to forget everything. My past. My job. The drama with Renee.

He pulled back. "One I can't resist." Tracing his thumbs along my jawline, he met my gaze.

Looking into his sincere eyes, my first line of defenses crumbled. I took a deep breath. Should I tell him about the wedge? Day zero of my new life? Trust this man I'd barely met? He sat there, waiting with patience for me to speak.

I could leave and go back to St. Louis, but my once-busy life didn't appeal to me in this moment.

"Want some coffee? Decaf? Or some hot chocolate?"

I leaned my cheek into his palm and took a breath. "Decaf would be great. With a little cream and sugar."

He stood with a nod and walked to the kitchen. He turned the water faucet on, and the sounds of the trickle of the coffee maker echoed to me. I rubbed under my eyes and groaned at the black mascara flakes on my thumb. I straightened my shirt, ran my fingers through my hair, and wiped at my ruined makeup.

Ten minutes later, he returned to my side and offered me a mug.

"I thought you'd like French Roast."

"Thanks."

I held it and took a sip. The vanilla-flavored, nutty coffee tracked a warm path inside me while the heat seeping through the ceramic cup thawed my fingers. Too much trauma and too much anger lay in wait for me to skip down memory lane, but I wanted somebody to understand me. Somebody to know everything.

I squeezed the mug tight to keep my hands from trembling. "My husband, Michael, he—"

The weight pressing down on my chest threatened to break my ribs. How was I supposed to tell Blake about something I'd kept locked away for so long?

I put a hand to my forehead and breathed in and out. My mug clattered when I set it on the end table. I remembered the afternoon of October fifth with clear definition. It began with a lost cap to a green marker. Coloring pages littered the table. I searched for it. At the time, I thought my Bug had been watching *The Little Mermaid* in the living room.

"I'd finished cleaning the kitchen when my daughter came to me covered in lipstick." I let out a short laugh before my lips quivered downward. "I went from cleaning one mess to another, like any other day. Luckily, I only found lipstick on the television screen."

I stopped. I didn't allow my mind to remain on this day. Ever. The pain became real and stabbed me. I pulled at a loose thread on Blake's couch, almost losing my courage to continue. He put his coffee on the end table and sat unmoving.

"I was a nervous wreck that day, anyway." I lifted my eyes to Blake. "Michael had been fighting for a promotion at his new job. At first, when he came home, he made me believe that he hadn't gotten it."

"Sounds like we would have been friends." Blake spoke soft, his voice cracking.

"When I saw the roses though, I knew. He beat out four other people for his promotion." I bit my lower lip. "I put the roses in a plastic pitcher and asked him if he had picked up the rolls from the bakery on the corner. Martha's Bakery made the best rolls. They closed down a year or two after Michael and ..." My chin quivered, and I cleared my throat. "Anyway, I'd promised my friend I'd bring them to our celebratory dinner."

Michael had gone to the grocery store near his work to buy the roses and bought generic rolls. To my ever-living regret, I'd made him go to the bakery on the corner for fresh ones. Of course, Michael had cracked some joke about grocery store rolls and celibacy. But he'd still agreed to go to Martha's. Why hadn't he told me no?

"Renee called my cell phone. She was supposed to babysit Bug. Michael answered it. She was drunk at the Tractor's Bar and Grille. I didn't want to go get her, so Michael told me to go shower and call our list of back-up babysitters while he went to buy the rolls and pick up Renee."

I hadn't been able to contact Renee for an entire day following the accident. I'd tried. Later, I'd found out that Renee had passed out at the bar and spent the night in the jail. She'd yelled at me until I cried when she finally picked up the phone. By that time Michael was gone, and my Bug was brain dead.

"Before he left, my daughter latched onto his leg and begged to go with him. She'd put on her pink tutu and one of his ties." My daughter's voice echoed through time. *I go too, Daddy?* So many regrets. So many answers I'd change if I could relive that day. "They left, with her hand in his."

Blake slid closer to me and rested his hand on my shoulder, his touch light. My chin quivered, and though I ached with loss, my eyes remained dry.

"I was about ready to climb in the shower when I remembered the rewards card. I threw a robe over my bra and underwear and ran outside. Michael and Bug were across the street. I shouted at him and waved the card in the air."

I'd been one stamp away from a free bagel sandwich. "Michael let go of Bug's hand and took a few steps away from her. She tiptoed along the curb, like a ballerina. That's when I heard the first crash. A pop. A faded green Bronco ricocheted off a parked car and veered toward Bug. I screamed, and Michael ran. He got to Bug just in time for the bumper of the truck to smash into him."

I closed my eyes and saw them get hit. The impact threw their bodies forward and then the green Bronco sped over them. The driver of the Bronco had moved away from Southern Idaho a few months after the accident. She'd sent me an apology letter, but I couldn't be angry at her or hold her accountable for their deaths. Not when I was the reason my family had been on the road.

"The cops told me that the brakes failed. She couldn't slow down or stop." The chill in the air. The crispy, dead leaves on the ground. The spray from a broken fire hydrant. All details I would never forget. "Michael lay next to Bug. I fell to my knees next to their bodies. I held my baby against my chest. Michael started coughing blood, and I didn't know what to do."

Blake dropped his hand from my shoulder. He sat as still as a statue next to me.

"I didn't move. I rocked Bug back and forth. I never let go of Michael's hand even when the paramedics got there and took Bug from me."

I'd whispered to Bug, *Mommy is here. Mommy is here. Mommy is here.* In the end, my Bug and Michael left me, but I was still here, empty and alone.

My tears began to fall.

# Chapter 27

## Blake

I sat next to Lili on the couch, too afraid to move, make a sound, or do anything else. I watched her take gulps of air as she steadied herself to continue her story. It was made of nightmares.

My insides felt like they'd been jack-hammered with a knife. All the moisture fled my mouth and filled my eyes. She thought it was her fault when I was the one who'd had the power to prevent the accident. Words failed me.

I let my breath hiss through my teeth. As the father of a dramatic little girl, I'd learned how to comfort her and make her 'owies' better. Not this kind of hurt, though. I hoped that Maddie would never have to suffer through something like this. I put my arms around Lili's shoulders. At my touch, she shifted closer to me and began to speak again.

"I loved them so much, and I couldn't do anything to help them." Lili continued to stare at nothing as she spoke. "If only I knew then what I know now." Lili took big gulping breaths and let her grief come out in deep sobs. "I wasn't strong enough to keep them here with me."

I ached for her. How could I ever make this better, or figure out how to soothe her? Fear sliced through my chest. How could I ever tell her now? I did nothing except sit, listen, and hold her, like the coward I was with my heart stuck in a bench vice. And with each passing minute, the vice grew tighter.

"I can't keep living like there is an empty hole in my chest." She stopped again as her sorrow overtook her.

My mind replayed an imagined scene based on Lili's reality, only it was me holding Madeline as her life left her. A lump clogged my throat. I wouldn't have survived.

She calmed her sobs and wiped her eyes. "I went to the hospital in the ambulance. Michael crashed, his heart stopped, and ... he was gone."

She looked up at me. I tucked a stray lock of hair behind her ear and cradled her cheek in my hand. If only I could take this pain away. If only I could go back and comb over the green Bronco one more time before any of this happened.

"Bug was on life support for two weeks. I was there every day by her side, singing her lullaby. In my heart, I believed she'd be okay, but it didn't happen." Lili rubbed her shoulders and shivered.

I drew her back to me and my warmth. "Shhh." I turned her head to my chest and rubbed her hair. "I'm here."

"I had to decide to take her off life support." Her voice cracked. "It seemed impossible that something so full of life could be gone. She had always been on the go, running, riding her tricycle, dancing ... I hadn't been able to keep up with laundry, and my husband died in mismatched socks."

She pulled away from my chest and blinked at her tears, her eyes clouded with memories of the past. "If Renee hadn't forgotten about babysitting, they wouldn't have been out on the street. I wouldn't have rushed out to give him my card, and—"

"You can't do this to yourself. There is no way you could have known what would happen."

If only I hadn't let the Bronco leave the shop. I squeezed my eyes shut. Why did she have to blame herself?

"At the funeral, everything was all wrong. My little girl had the wrong shoes on. I know she would have wanted to wear her red boots, but she had on her black church shoes. They parted Michael's hair. He never parted his hair. It was all I could think about the whole time, she had the wrong shoes, and he had the wrong hairstyle." She turned her watery eyes to me. "One accident, one bad decision, and they were gone, but I don't understand why."

I cleared my throat. Each time I opened my mouth to tell her, I couldn't find the right words. "This isn't your fault." My lame attempt at a confession ended prematurely. How could I tell her of my responsibility while at the same time cursing myself and Maddie to a life without Lili?

She continued as if I hadn't spoken. "After they had left to get the rolls, I remember thinking how nice it was to be alone." She rested against my chest. "But now I'm so tired of being alone. So tired."

The same threat of loneliness hovered over me, an ache to be with someone who meant the world to me. Lili was the first woman who could fit into my life, but the Bronco stood between us. She'd be leaving. All roads of this relationship came to a dead end. "It's okay, Lili. You're not alone anymore."

Lili didn't respond. As a father I connected with her grief: she cried for the loss of a husband, for the life her daughter would never lead. She cried for the first day of school, for the first boyfriend, the first kiss, and the wedding day her baby girl would never get to experience. I held her tight. The whole time, I saw the green Bronco drive out of the shop, the same one that hit Lili's family.

Her cries eventually subsided, and her exhausted body relaxed against mine. For a while, I held her in my arms on the couch. I couldn't sit here listening to her heartache any longer without her knowing my connection to the worst day of her life.

"It's my fault." I choked on the words. "The green Bronco—the brakes failed, and I may have missed something."

She didn't stir against me, and I dipped my head toward her. Her chest lifted in deep, even breaths—she was asleep. I released a shaky sigh, almost grateful that she didn't hear my confession, and brushed her hair back from her cheek.

When Cindy had left me, I was rejected and alone, but my pain had been nothing compared to what Lili had gone through. She'd watched her family die right in front of her eyes. How could anyone be strong enough to live through that?

I looked at her face, still beautiful despite being blotchy and red. I saw her face every time I closed my eyes. For the first time in my life, I was truly falling in love. This wasn't the infatuation I'd experienced with Cindy. It ran much deeper.

*Shit.*

I rubbed my hand through my hair and kissed the top of Lili's head. I should have listened to Chuck.

*Dammit.*

I'd tried to stay away from her, but I couldn't resist the pull drawing me to her from the beginning. Tears edged the bottom of my eyelids, and I blinked them away. I'd found the woman of my dreams, and I was sure to lose her.

I'd move to St. Louis, or she could find a job here, if she wanted to. I'd do anything to be with her. After I told her everything, what would she do? If she abandoned us like Cindy, what would be left of me?

Jorge always told me I felt too much, too strong, too soon. His words came back to me. *It's like you jump off a cliff only to realize that instead of water at the bottom, there's a den of rattlesnakes. Won't you ever learn to stop jumping?*

My teenage, cocky reply had been, *I guess I better learn how to fly.*

I memorized Lili's sleeping face. Her worry lines relaxed. She looked peaceful and so beautiful. Well, Jorge, I still hadn't learned. I'd better start growing some wings. Bronco or no, I'd figure out a way to tell her, convince her to see, it wasn't on purpose. I had to fight for this woman.

I was about to jump again.

# Chapter 28

## Liliana

My eyes rebelled as I pulled my eyelids open. A blurry, peach-brown shape bounced within inches of my face. My world cleared with a blink. Maddie's breath brushed against my cheek like a moth's wing against a light bulb. Her hair stuck at odd angles underneath her black headphones. She wore a blue Tinkerbell nightgown.

Blood rushed to my cheeks. Last night. Sobbing. Blake's couch. *Blake.* I buried my face in the pillow. I must have soaked his shirt in tears. Ugh.

The scent of his woodsy soap on the pillow filled my lungs.

"Daddy, she's waking up."

Maddie's loud whisper cut through my head like a scalpel through skin covered in iodine. The pulsing pain in my head thrummed along with my heartbeat. Crying hangovers were very much comparable to real ones, except without the fun of the night before. I buried my face further in the pillow. Where were my ruby red slippers to click together and take me home?

"Hurry, *Daddy.* Everything has to be ready before she gets out of bed!" Maddie yelled. "Wait here, Lili. Don't move," she said on her way out of the bedroom, her tone as solemn as an undertaker.

What on earth was going on?

WHAT HAPPENS IN IDAHO

I peeked out from under the pillow. Taking deep breaths helped ease the pain from my head. A small stone fireplace centered on the wall across from the bed, a single blue leather, wing-backed chair sat next to the fireplace, with a bearskin hanging over its back. Its claws stretched downward as if the bear were still alive and waiting for its prey. I shivered and pressed my fingers to my temples, rubbing in circles. I would definitely not be sitting in that chair. Mud clung to a pair of worn work boots sitting in front of a closet, and there were crumbs of dirt scattered on the variegated carpet.

"Okay, Lili!" Maddie yelled from outside the room. "You can come out."

I got out of bed, smoothed my rumpled clothes, and tiptoed into the hallway. It was empty. A couple of family pictures hung on the walls. I touched the glass covering a picture of Maddie on Blake's back captured mid-giggle while Blake looked over his shoulder at her. My ribs squeezed tight. Once upon a time, I'd orbited around this level of happiness. This time, I was an outsider looking in through the thin layer glass at it, my reflection overlaying Blake and Maddie's joyful visages.

"We're in here."

Following Maddie's voice, I walked into the kitchen. Place settings of fine China sat in front of three of the four chairs. Three cups of flowering weeds were placed in a line in the middle of the table. The largest arrangement rested in the center with dandelions wilting over the edge of the vase gathered by small hands specifically to please me. Tension ebbed from my tight abdomen. I let out the breath I'd been holding and forgot about my headache.

"Daddy, you can say it now." Maddie's whisper could have been heard in the next room, but Blake didn't respond to it.

His mouth gaped open slightly as he stared at me. The touch of his gaze seared my skin from the top of my head to the bottom of my feet. I must look awful with bed-head and puffy eyes. What if I had drool marks down the sides of my face?

Maddie nudged her father with her elbow, and he finally responded.

The second he looked away, I finger-brushed my hair, ran my tongue along the base of my lip, and rubbed at my chin.

"Breakfast is served." He pulled my chair out for me with a bow, and I laughed as I sat.

Maddie darted into the kitchen and returned with a plateful of waffles. "Daddy made you breakfast. It's waffle Monday."

"I thought it was waffle Wednesdays," I said.

"Huh? Today is Monday and we have waffles on Mondays." Maddie looked at me as if I was from an alien planet.

Monday was waffle day and dinner at Renee's house. Got it. What other routines existed in this house?

Maddie ate her breakfast without taking her eyes off me. I shifted in my chair. Waffles, perfectly cooked bacon, a man, and a little girl were sitting across from me. This was a perfect re-enactment of my nightmare. I sucked in and nearly choked on my last bite of waffle.

"You okay?" Blake asked. I nodded and sipped my orange juice.

I took a deep breath and managed not to cough. What was I going to do about Blake? He was a man who made me breakfast and let me sleep in his bed after I'd cried on his shoulder. I set my orange juice down. Handsome. Smart. Caring. Not a bad choice for a vacay fling—or for a longer relationship. If only I could take him back to St. Louis.

I straightened in my chair. Did I want him to be more of a permanent fixture in my life? More than one week down and less than a week to go until my car was fixed and I'd be out of here, maybe never to return.

My first few days, I couldn't wait to watch this town disappear in my review mirror, but this slow country lifestyle had grown on me. It'd become the eye of my own personal storm. I started to notice things that I'd taken for granted growing up, like the scenery of the distant mountains, the quiet, no streetlights glaring into windows at night, the sounds of the birds and sprinkler pivots running.

Blake and Maddie stood and started clearing the table. I joined them against their protests.

True, I'd never liked farm animals, but I'd be willing to share space with them in this town as long as I had Blake and his daughter with her dandelion bouquet and waffle Mondays. My job at Barnes-Jewish was all I'd ever dreamed about for so long. Now I had it. Could I simply give it all up?

The hospital here might have a spot for a trauma surgeon. One application, an interview, and a few credentials later, I'd have a job. I might be able to have a real relationship with Renee for the first time since Dad died.

I squeezed my eyes shut. *Slow down.* I'd just met this guy. Was I willing to rewrite my life for him? To love meant to lose, to lose meant to hurt, and I promised myself I'd never feel pain like that again.

"Oh, I almost forgot." Maddie dumped her load of dishes in the sink. "Dad, is it okay if we go to work a little later today? I want to play with my new puppets. I'm sure Chuck and Pedro can handle everything until we get there."

Blake saluted her. "You got it, boss."

"Thanks." She walked out of the kitchen and her feet sounded on the stairs.

"Don't take too long, I have to be at the shop before ten!" Blake yelled and then turned to me. "I can do these later." He gestured at the sink full of dishes. "You want to sit down in the living room?"

"Sure."

I followed him and chose to sit in the chair next to the large window where the morning sun covered me in warmth. Blake sat on the couch kitty-corner from me. Left alone with him, I set my hands in my lap, then down at my side, and then rested them on my knees. I hadn't allowed myself to feel an emotional connection this deep with a man who wasn't Michael. New territory loomed in front of me, and I wasn't sure if I was brave enough to take the first step. After all, this was temporary, a Band-Aid that'd make me feel better—until I had to rip it off.

"Does Maddie always act like a little CEO of Blake's Place?" I began to smile, but then remembered I hadn't brushed my teeth since yesterday morning. I ran my tongue over them. My purse still sat on his end table, and I dug through it for a mint.

Blake let out a soft chuckle. "Most of the time." He scrubbed his hand through his hair and stretched his legs out in front of him. "She's always been smart for her age and a little different than the other kids." He cleared his throat. "Do you have any plans today?"

I popped the mint in my mouth and caught myself staring at his lips. A shadow of stubble framed his jaw. My eyes shifted away from him to the window. If I didn't look at him, then maybe I wouldn't think about the bedroom and the scruff on his chin tickling my bare skin.

"I don't have much to do today." I looked back at him when he didn't respond to my comment, unless his sideways tilt of his mouth counted

212

as a response. If only I could read his thoughts. I understood how my mother felt any time a conversation fell silent. I squirmed. Why did I feel like a kettle filled with steam and no way to let it out?

"By the way," I started again. "Thank you for last night. I mean—thank you for listening."

"You're welcome."

Releasing a shaky breath, I relaxed back in the chair. He didn't offer any unwanted advice or say he understood. He'd listened to me and that was all I needed.

Noise clattered down the stairwell. Maddie managed to maneuver down the stairs carrying her puppets and a cardboard stage. The puppets dragged behind her and bounced down each step.

She ran to her father. "Daddy, would it be okay if I leave the puppets out while I work today? I want to practice with them later."

"As long as you promise to clean them up when you are done."

She nodded. "I'm going to work now. Chuck promised to show me how he installed the water pump in Lili's car."

Maddie laid out her puppet strings in a nice straight line, walked over to me, and placed a hand on my shoulder. Warmth seeped from her hand through my T-shirt and into my deltoid. I froze.

"I hope you have a good day, Lili," she said in all seriousness.

She walked out of the house. Blake stood at the window until she entered the garage.

"Wow, she is a sweet girl."

"Yeah, she forces me to sit through some interesting puppet shows, but she's sweet." Blake laughed.

I wanted nothing more than to bask in the peace filling his home for the rest of the day, so I got up to leave. "I'd better go, it's past nine already, and you said you had a lot of work to catch up on."

"Yeah, I guess I do." He didn't move.

"Come on, get up." I laughed and pulled him to his feet.

He didn't let go of my hand when I walked to the front door. His hand warmed my chilled fingers. He opened the door and stepped outside with me onto the front porch.

We stood on the porch for a few minutes, our hands intertwined. I traced where my hands began and his ended with my gaze as he rubbed his thumb along my palm. Pleasing shivers followed in its wake. If only I could stay here all morning. "Renee is probably worried about me. I didn't tell her where I was going last night, I just left."

"Don't worry. I called her."

Oh. Hell. He called her. Please tell me he didn't tell her I spent the night here. "Did she sound worried?"

"Not after I told her where you were."

"You told her I slept over at your *house*?" My voice raised to a near screech. Renee equated sharing the same living quarters with marriage. In Renee's mind, Blake would be more than a friend. She already treated him as a son, so it wouldn't be much of a leap to have him as a son-in-law.

"What was I supposed to tell her?"

"I don't know, you could tell her anything you wanted to, as long as it didn't involve you and me under the same roof. Now Renee thinks we have—" Been intimate? Shared a bed? I couldn't bring myself to say had sex. "Slept together."

"You sound like sleeping with me would be torture."

"No, I'm sure it wouldn't, but if Renee thinks we're *intimate*, it'd confuse her." A blush crept into my cheeks, but I hid it by turning toward the car.

Blake pulled me back to him. He wrapped his arms around me and kissed my forehead.

"Don't worry, your mother doesn't think we slept together." He paused to brush a strand of hair away from my face. "You know, for a doctor, you sure have a hard time saying 'sex.'"

Our faces were so close that the heat of Blake's skin pulsed against mine. His soft, wintergreen-scented breath brushed across my forehead, making me even more bashful. "Only when it involves me."

"Well, I'll have to see if I can change that." Blake moved in for a kiss.

His lips hovered over mine until I closed the short distance, touching my lips to his.

Blake was gentle at first, but then, he became insistent. He moved me under the shade of the porch until my back pressed against the wooden planks of his house. I molded my body to his. The heat spreading through me had nothing to do with the morning sunlight. His lips moved from my mouth to my neck. I tilted my head, gasping in deep and steady breaths.

Tingling sensations flowed from anywhere his lips teased my skin. Like the stroke of a flickering flame, each touch melted the encasement of ice around my heart until nothing but warmth cascaded over me in waves.

No secrets or hidden truths stood between us. I'd shared my darkest day with him, shown him my brokenness, and it hadn't scared him off. One strategic move at a time, Blake had weaseled his way behind my defenses.

He returned his attentions to my mouth, and I responded, holding nothing back. Then, in one abrupt motion, he pulled away and pressed his forehead to mine.

"I've got to go to work," he said between breaths.

"Yeah." I nodded and pressed my lips to his.

He looped his hand underneath the back of my shirt, his fingertips tickling my bare skin. With every contact of our lips, we took one stride closer to my car.

Kiss.

Step.

Down his front porch steps.

Kiss.

Step.

He backed me up until my spine met the contours of the Malibu. I became bolder and left a trail of kisses to his ears, where I teased his earlobe. "Why is it?" He tilted his head to give me better access, his hand splayed across my bare abdomen. "We always end up against a car."

His deep laugh reverberated in his chest. "I guess that's what you get for hooking up with a mechanic."

# Chapter 29

## Liliana

The sun dipped behind the grove of Russian olive trees that followed the creek, bordering fields of corn. All the white and blue canopied tents burned amber, the hue of the sunset. Our town's Relay for Life was in full swing, the opening ceremonies had begun promptly at five p.m. with the same flare as Trout Fest. It was now closing in on eight thirty. Blake had run home to get Maddie her jacket and blanket for the night ahead, leaving my mother and I alone.

I set a bowl of apples and another one filled with granola bars on the white plastic table. I wiped at the sweat beading on my forehead. The sun couldn't go down soon enough. Other Relay for Life teams busied themselves with similar tasks. Coach—no—*Mayor* Southerland walked by in a short-sleeved, pink button-up shirt and smiled at me. I waved at him in return. An image of Michael in his pale pink shirt on the day of our picnic flashed through my mind. The accompanying sharp, painful longing followed right behind.

I steadied myself against the edge of the table.

These vivid memories happened more frequently the longer I stayed here. A child swinging at the park, a coloring book, the mayor's pink shirt—seemingly random simple sights triggered them. Part of me loved remembering the things that I'd thought were lost, but a greater part of me longed to be free of the sharp pain lodged in my chest.

Blake and I had been inseparable throughout the past week. I did my best to hide these moments of weakness, not wanting him to psychoanalyze me or feel any more pity.

We were good together. We watched shows at night cuddled up on the couch, Maddie with her feet tucked under her in her own chair after hiking mountain trails all day. We went on the swings at the park, swam at the local hot springs—I woke up each morning excited for the adventure Blake would take me on once he got off work. I didn't ever go to bed until one or two a.m.

Maddie didn't even notice my slight hesitations when she was around. Once again, I couldn't help but wonder what my Bug would have been like at six. Would she have been an outdoorsy, artsy kid like Maddie, or more into dolls and princesses? Would her favorite color still have been purple?

I slumped into a camp chair and shoved my thoughts to the back of my mind. Aside from a few trips to the grocery store, I'd been stuck on the high school football field all afternoon. The old gravel track, sandwiched between two weathered sets of bleachers, buzzed with constant activity, yet I was an outsider.

I didn't fit here, but after Blake, once I went back to St. Louis, I wouldn't belong there anymore, either. This didn't mean I loved him. I'd only known him for two weeks, and love couldn't possibly take root in that amount of time, but this showed me another side to life, the not-lonely side. In two days, my car would be repaired, and I'd leave.

A cow mooed in a distant pasture. At this point, I'd even miss the cows when I went back home.

The wind rustled the tent and hinted at the promise of a cool evening. I looped my arm over the camp chair until my fingertips touched the soft carpet of the green grass. Grass didn't grow like this in the Midwest. At least, not at my apartment complex. Bare spots and weeds were a constant plague.

"Are you tired, Lili?" Renee opened another camp chair next to me and sat in it.

"It feels good to sit down."

"Well, I think we have most everything set for tonight."

This was how it had been with Renee since our argument: passing pleasantries, but not talking about anything with depth or meaning.

"Would you like a Dr. Pepper?" Renee held the maroon can out to me.

I wrinkled my nose. "You drink that stuff?"

"I've come to appreciate the good doctor."

I laughed. "I prefer Coke."

"Oh, so you prefer the taste of garbage."

"Whatever, Coke is not garbage. Dr. Pepper is a sorry imitation of Coke."

Renee held up her Dr. Pepper on display, like in a *Fansville* commercial. "Not with its twenty-three individual and unique flavors."

"That taste like ass."

We both burst out laughing. Renee fished a Coke out of the cooler and handed it to me.

"I'm sorry about what I said the other day—when we fought." I rolled the can in my hand and played with the droplets running together on the red tin.

Renee took a breath. "I've made some big mistakes, and we aren't going to automatically get past them." She stared at the people bustling around, getting ready for the event. "My hope is we can build a relationship one brick at a time, little by little."

"I'll try, Ren—Mom. That's all I can give."

She put a hand to her mouth and her eyes crinkled at the corners. "Hearing you call me 'mom' is enough."

Even doing this small thing was difficult for me, but her reaction made it easier. One brick at a time, not all at once. I could do that.

I slipped the unopened can of Coke into the cupholder of the chair, saving it for later. Blake's old blue truck pulled into the parking lot. After muttering a brief explanation to Renee, I jogged across the field and over the gravel track into the parking lot. Maddie ran to me and wrapped her arms around my waist.

"Guess what?" She tipped her head up at me, her headphones in place.

"What?"

Maddie stepped back and took a micro-breath before she spoke. "I can't tell, it's a surprise."

Blake exchanged a look with his daughter.

"I'll give you a piece of gum if you tell me." I winked at Maddie.

She stepped away from me and slapped her hand over her mouth. "Uh-uh. I can't tell you. I promised," she mumbled through her fingers.

"Well then, I guess I'll be really surprised tonight." She'd probably made a macaroni necklace for me, or she'd figured out how to make a dandelion crown. We'd been working to perfect that skill yesterday.

Blake reached for my hand, and I took his without hesitation. The stares from the entire town burned a hole in my back as Blake, Maddie, and I crossed through the middle of the football field. When the three of us reached the tent, Maddie hung back with Renee while Blake and I continued to the track.

The gravel crunched beneath my feet as we started our long night. I looked up at the sky. Although clouds obstructed most of it, a few early stars peeked out from behind their masses.

"I love the Idaho sky." I returned my gaze to Blake's face. "Nothing compares to a western sky on a clear night. St. Louis doesn't even come close." I gripped his hand with mine.

"Why did you choose St. Louis? I mean, why not somewhere closer to home?" Blake put his free hand in his pocket.

"Well, at the time, the distance was good. It was also the first medical school to get back to me with an acceptance, and I took it."

Nothing from my old apartment had come with me. I'd saved some pictures and a few tokens I couldn't bear to part with, but even those I'd put in the storage room in the basement of my building. I'd arrived in Missouri with one suitcase and a pillow, and within a week I'd moved into the apartment I still lived in.

Blake nodded. "Was medical school as hard as they say?"

"Yes and no. Some classes and rotations were more demanding than I expected, but those are the classes I liked the most. Residency and fellowship were worse. But the more my training demanded, the less time I had to—"

"Remember them."

He didn't say it in a pitiful way, he stated fact. Conversations buzzed around us, but we continued to crunch our way around the track in silence. Occasionally, someone would yell a greeting at us, and we would wave or shout something back.

"You want to go make out behind the bleachers?" His eyes were full of boyish mischief.

I threw my head back and laughed. I hadn't expected him to say that. "Really?"

"I've never been more serious." The smirk on his face implied otherwise.

"Here I thought having a six-year-old daughter would make you more mature."

"I know. There should be some application you have to fill out before they let you be a parent. I never would have made it in."

I laughed again and shivered. I hadn't thought of bringing a jacket. A typical August day in Missouri only varied in temperature by a few degrees. It'd be ninety degrees in the morning, maybe ninety-eight in the afternoon, and ninety degrees in the evening. Always hot. In Idaho, summer evenings cooled off to fall temperatures.

Blake took off his jacket and placed it over my shoulders. My smile flattened at his grimace as he pulled the hand I hadn't been holding out of his jacket.

I shoved my arms in his sleeves and breathed in his smell. "Thanks." Without asking, I pulled his other hand into mine so I could inspect it. Mottled bruises and a deep gash marred his knuckles.

"How'd you do this?" I motioned toward his wound as I met his eyes.

"My hand slipped while I was working on your car, and I punched your engine block."

Another reminder that this brief period of happiness was about to come to an end.

"Your knuckles are swollen." I tugged him toward the tent. "You need to put ice on them."

A brief shiver shook his shoulders, but he didn't ask for his jacket back.

Once we reached the tent, Chuck, Pedro, Maddie, and my mother swapped places with us. They walked toward Pedro's wife, who sat in the stands with the baby wrapped up in her arms, while her and Pedro's other four kids played tag on the edge of the track.

I forced Blake to sit in one of the camp chairs while I grabbed the first aid kit and took some ice from the cooler. I placed it on his knuckles. "You didn't have to punch my engine, you know. I'm sure it would have cooperated if you'd asked nicely."

Blake chuckled. "It won the fight anyway." He tucked my hair behind my ear and pulled my chin up as he lowered his lips to mine. "Thank you for taking care of me," he whispered against my lips.

Out of my periphery, I saw the group of town gossips—including Irene, Wendy, the mayor's wife, and Nora, along with three of my old elementary school teachers—eye us as they walked past. They didn't bother looking away when they spoke to each other animatedly.

I moved back from Blake and retrieved more ice, using the sleeve of his jacket to warm my frozen fingers. "You've probably heard so many rumors about me." I moved my gaze directly to the gaggle of older women.

Blake put his free hand on my shoulder and rubbed his thumb along my collar bone. "You don't have to worry. Nothing would change the way I feel about you. I love the person you are."

My heart skipped a beat; my hand froze. Did he say *love*? With my throat constricting until I couldn't take in a breath, I broke out into a cold sweat and stayed as still as a stone statue. "You love me?"

He paused. His face flushed, like it did any time he was uncomfortable. Then he straightened and met my eyes. "Yeah. At the very least, I'm falling in love with you." His eye contact didn't waver. There was no hesitation in his voice.

Oh. Hell. He did love me.

This was bad.

Shallow breaths shook in and out of my lungs, my head dizzy with the effort. What happened to my vacay fling with no commitments?

The ice fell out of my trembling hands and didn't make a sound when it landed on the grass. Blades clung to it, covering it as it continued to melt. Would I destroy Blake with this relationship? It was impossible for me to fall in love again. I promised myself. I couldn't—*wouldn't*—put myself through the fires of love again.

He saw a future with me, an impossible one. He didn't understand that I'd been down that road before, and it'd nearly killed me. I focused on the ice, and though there wasn't a visible difference, it was growing infinitesimally smaller.

Blake laughed. "Look, don't think about it." He took my hand with his uninjured one and stroked my cold fingers. "I want to kiss that disgusted look off your face before I get insulted."

"But I'm not—"

His lips pressed against mine again before I could finish. He coaxed me into a response, and I only held out a few seconds before my treacherous body did exactly what he wanted.

Blake pulled away. "You mind taking a walk with me?"

I ignored the goosebumps cascading down my body, focused on regulating my breathing, and nodded. "Aren't we supposed to be walking all night?"

He chuckled. "Yes, but this will be a special walk. I promise."

"Blake!" Chuck shouted as we started to walk toward the bleachers. "Come talk with me for a minute."

"Now?" Blake asked, his voice full of intent I didn't understand.

"Right now." Chuck gestured to the old bleachers and walked toward them without a backward glance.

"I better go see what he wants." Blake kissed my hand. "Wait here. I'll be right back."

I nodded, remaining stock still while my mind whirled. *He loves me.* No one was supposed to get hurt. *What am I supposed to do now?*

# Chapter 30

## Blake

"What are you thinking?" Chuck asked as soon as we were out of Lili's earshot.

"What?" I didn't look at him.

"I haven't seen you without Lili all night. You just told her you love her!"

"You heard that?"

"I heard Lili's reaction." Chuck shoved his hand through his hair. "Did you mean it?"

I didn't answer right away. Hell yes, I meant what I'd said, but it scared the piss out of me. She would be leaving in a matter of days, never to come back. She'd been clear about how much she hated small-town life, and though her relationship with Renee had improved, I didn't think it would be enough to get her to stay here. Would I be willing to give up the life I'd built here to be with her?

Yes.

No.

Maybe.

Daydreams of Lili staying with me had to come to an end, but I wanted to live in the fantasy a few days longer. Maddie had fallen in love

WHAT HAPPENS IN IDAHO

with her as well. She'd never been so animated or so connected to another person, aside from myself and maybe Renee. My stoic, logical daughter became alive and even joked around in Lili's presence.

All that would be taken away the moment this ended.

Chuck shook his head and closed his eyes. "I told you this was a bad idea. You never should have—"

"I know." I looked my friend in the eye. "I couldn't help it. I tried, but—"

"Blake. She's gonna leave." Chuck held his hands out in front of him. "Even in high school she couldn't wait to jet out of here. If she hadn't fallen in love with Michael, she would have left long before she actually did."

I paced behind the bleachers and stared at the chipped white paint. The weathered wood grayed even more in the light cast from the football stadium lights. "I know she's leaving. I always have, but maybe—"

"Maybe she'd choose to stay with you?" Chuck moved alongside me. "Are you listening to yourself? She's a doctor. She has a job in St. Louis. Her life is there."

"You're saying I can't enjoy this fun summer fling?"

"Flings don't involve the L-word." Chuck lowered his voice. "I've known you a long time. You don't do light, fun relationships. You always look for lasting ones. It's in your DNA." Chuck set his hand on my shoulder, and I stopped pacing. "What do you think will happen when she finds out?"

I examined the grass, the specks of gravel in it and the sky. Anything to avoid Chuck seeing the truth in my eyes.

"You're not planning on telling her, are you?" he asked.

I was only trying to do what was right for Lili. Michael would want her to be happy. Telling her would only bring her unnecessary sadness.

"You will never be able to forgive yourself until she knows. You were young. It wasn't your fault," Chuck said.

"You don't know that for sure. Maybe I could have prevented it."

"Like I've said a thousand times, I don't know a single mechanic who would have done anything different."

I scanned the bleachers, the ground, and Chuck. I couldn't focus. The grainy images from the newspaper clipping haunted me. "She won't see it that way."

"How do you know if you don't give her the chance? A relationship built on lies will never last." Chuck tucked his hands into his pockets.

"You're some sort of relationship expert? I can't count the number of women you've been with—"

"Tell Lili tonight. Don't let this go on any longer."

"Tell me what?" Lili stepped out from the shadow of the bleachers. "I'm sorry I didn't stay at the tent. Pedro came looking for Chuck, acting all dodgy. He told me to tell you he'd be waiting by the you-know-what."

Maddie. The surprise.

Chuck folded his arms and nodded his head toward Lili. This was my chance to unburden my soul and ruin any shred of happiness I'd found with her.

"Nothing." I dragged that one word out. I had to wait to tell her until the big reveal was over, for my daughter's sake.

Chuck's shoulders slumped at my words. Lili's hands dropped to her sides, and I walked over to her. She leaned into me slightly, and I caressed her hand.

*Hell.* I was going to miss her.

# Chapter 31

## Liliana

I had to jog to keep up with Blake's long strides. We made our way toward the home bleachers on the other side of the field. I slowed and tugged him to stay beside me. My lungs burned. "We could have made out under those bleachers, no need to go all the way to these ones." I gulped in air.

He flinched and laughed an abnormal, almost staged laugh. "We're almost there, and don't worry, we're not going to make out under the bleachers."

"Why are you talking so loud?" I caught sight of a car with a tarp draped over it, hiding behind the bleachers. "Renee didn't remodel another old car for me, did she?"

"Well, not technically."

"What do you mean by—"

"*Surprise!*"

Maddie, Renee, and Pedro, with all his kids around him, popped up from behind the car, and swept the cover off. Chuck came up behind Blake and me, not as enthusiastic as the others. Pedro's kids pointed and chattered with each other in Spanish.

The beam of the football lights illuminated the unveiled car. It was not any car. It was *my* car. If it hadn't been for the Audi symbol on the hood, I wouldn't have recognized it.

The car looked like my Audi, but at the same time, it didn't. There were no rust holes or dents. The entire body of the car was as smooth as glass. Brand new silver paint gleamed in the stadium lights. I clenched my teeth together as I walked to the trunk of my car and back around to the front.

"This engine is an Audi four-point two-liter V8 twin-turbo with a six-speed conversion. It will put out four hundred fifty horsepower and three hundred seventeen pound-feet of torque. I mean, with this engine you can accelerate zero to sixty miles per hour in four-point six seconds." Blake spoke with energy, completely unaware of what he had done to me.

The night I first saw this car, Michael and I had used grants from college to make a down payment on it. It'd been three years old when we'd found it, and out of our price range, but he insisted that we could find a way to pay for it. Michael had put the first dent on it when he opened the door and bumped into a shopping cart. I brushed my hand against the driver's side door. The dent didn't exist anymore.

With my hand covering my mouth, I looked into the back window. The floormat with the juice stain was gone, replaced by a brand-new one. The hole in my chest ripped wide open. Tears wet my eyes, and I choked them back.

"Do you like it?" Maddie asked. "I wanted to paint a pink lily on it, but they wouldn't let me."

"This—" My voice came out as a whisper. I barely heard Maddie and looked at Blake. "This, is what you have been working on?" I finished with more confidence.

Blake's smile faltered.

Renee stepped forward. "We thought you would like your car fixed up. After all, a surgeon shouldn't be driving a broken-down old car."

"This was the last car I bought with Michael," I shot back at Renee. "But of course, you wouldn't remember."

"Kids, run and find your mother." Pedro nudged his children toward the bleachers, and they quieted and jogged away.

"You don't like your surprise?" Maddie's chin quivered. She squeezed her headphones tight to her ears.

"I do, honey, but this car meant a lot to me the way it looked before."

"But now it has NOS," Pedro piped in. "Don't push the red button unless you are ready for the ride of your life." His accent marked his words.

"A NOS button?" I put my hand to my temple. "Like they put in race cars?"

"Just kidding," Pedro added. "It's just an overdrive button. You can pretend it's NOS." His voice got quieter with each word, sensing that I wasn't in a joking mood.

I shook my head and fell silent. Blake tried to pull me into his arms, but I pushed him back. I walked further into the parking lot, away from the circle of people I had been foolish enough to let into my life.

"Lili, hold up." Blake jogged to catch up to me.

Of course, he couldn't let me be alone. Up to this point, I'd managed to keep my anger inside.

"I'm sorry, I shouldn't have, I mean ...," he stuttered when he stopped in front of me. "If I would have known—"

"*Exactly.* You should have asked, and then I would have told you about the time I bought the car with my dead husband, and about the time we went on one road trip as a family in it. About the last time I drove to the park with my dead daughter. She spilled grape juice and stained the floor mat and now it's erased as if she never existed."

"I didn't think—"

"That's right, you didn't think. As if it makes it all better." I rubbed the last of my tears off my face.

"Come on, Lili. It's just a car. As it stood, after you wrecked it, it wouldn't have made it back to St. Louis. I'm surprised it made it here. You've been holding on to the past long enough." He threw his hands up in the air and stepped closer to me. "I can't compete with Michael! He's gone, and there's nothing that I can do to bring him or your daughter back."

His chest heaved up and down. I turned to walk away from him.

"I couldn't let you drive that car until everything was fixed." He stepped in front of me. "Lili, the green Bronco. I should have—I couldn't let you—"

His voice came out so quiet I almost didn't hear him. I paused. "What are you talking about?" I looked straight at him, but he didn't meet my eyes.

"The green Bronco. The brakes."

The Bronco with the radio still playing. The spray from the fire hydrant mixing with my family's blood. I shook my head and took a step back.

"About eleven years ago, Jorge found me a job with my Uncle Marcos in a small, southern Idaho town. He wanted Marcos to meet me and give me more options to get out of my current situation. I ended up moving back to California after working here for half a year. I couldn't abandon Jorge, and ..." Blake shook his head once and breathed in deep. "I'm the one who did the maintenance on the green Bronco a week before the accident. I swear on my life, I thought I checked the brake lines, but I could have missed something."

The green Bronco. Blood everywhere. Blake? This couldn't be happening. I clutched my stomach. The world pitched and spun around me.

People I'd known my whole life milled about us as they moved to their cars, completely unaware of the ground coming out from under me. If he had done his job, my family would still be alive. He knew this the whole time, but he pursued me anyway—tricked me into falling in love with him.

"Why—" Why did he come to live here? Why did he make me a part of his family? I swallowed and fought to breathe.

He pulled his wallet out of his pocket, opened it, and tugged out a worn piece of newspaper. He handed it to me. A black and white picture of Michael and Bug rested in my palm. Along the creases the words were illegible, but I knew what they said.

*A tragic accident occurred on Main Street in Clear Springs when the brakes on a green Bronco failed, and it slammed into two pedestrians, killing them both ...*

"I didn't mean to get so close to you. I tried to stay distant—"

"You should have told me." I crumpled the paper in a ball and threw it at his chest. It fell to the ground and blew away in the wind.

"Yes. You're right." Watery tears filled the base of his eyes, but I didn't care how bad he felt. "I'm sorry, Lili. I was afraid to tell you at first; then, I didn't want to hurt you."

Coward. Selfish bastard. He'd only been nice to me this whole time to make him feel better for what he'd done. He didn't love me. Love and lies couldn't co-exist.

"Lili, please look at me. If I could bring Michael—"

"I told you to never to say his name." I cut him off and met his gaze. Boiling heat rose up my neck and into my cheeks.

"I'm so sorry. Please forgive me." He held his hands out in front of him.

I hated him. His chin, his eyes, his body, *everything*. How could he do this to me? I brushed past him and walked to my car.

The keys sat in the cup holder. Renee stood next to Chuck, Pedro, and Maddie. Renee looked past me to Blake. She'd probably heard everything, and by the look on her face, she hadn't known the traitor Blake was.

I opened the shiny door to my car.

"Don't go." Maddie stepped forward, but I ignored her.

I slammed the door shut, turned the key in the ignition, and hit the gas. Blake stood with Maddie by his side at the edge of the parking lot, two tiny figures framed in my rearview mirror until I turned onto the main road and sped away.

The dark night closed in around me. I made it to the driveway of the house before I started to cry. Blake. I knew better. I'd let him in and trusted him. What a lovesick fool I'd been.

I'd let myself care for the man who had taken everything from me. He was responsible for the person I was: jaded, afraid, heart-broken, lost.

*Oh, Michael.* If only he was here to guide me. He'd been my rock, the only thing that kept me from collapsing. Yes, I was successful. I loved my work. To what end? I came home every day to an empty apartment. Tiff was hardly ever home.

All because of Blake and the brakes that had failed at precisely the wrong moment. What would I say to Blake when I saw him next? What would I do the next time I looked into his lying blue eyes? I couldn't see him again.

The fluorescent numbers on my dash lit the darkened interior of my car. One a.m. I was exhausted both emotionally and physically, and driving over twenty-four hours right now wasn't smart. I wouldn't be able to say goodbye to Angie or Nora or fulfil my promise to come visit Papa Tony, but leaving was the only choice I had. I took a deep breath before I climbed out.

My feet slipped to a stop at the bottom of the porch.

Tiffany stood up from the porch swing, a backpack and a carry-on bag at her feet. "I had a heck of a time finding a ride out to your mom's place at this time of—what's wrong?" she asked when the porch light reached my face.

I ran up the steps and fell sobbing into her arms.

# Chapter 32

## Blake

I stood in a pile of rubble and soupy garbage at the base of my half-full dumpster. My headlamp illuminated the pile of destroyed bags and loose garbage. Why had I been so stupid?

I should have told Lili right away and given up my fantasy to be with her. I tore into another black bag and searched through the contents. Banana peels and eggshells dropped at my feet, but I kicked them aside and kept looking.

I didn't know if the interior had been redone at the beginning of last week or in the past couple of days. Chuck and Pedro had worked non-stop on Lili's car. They'd spent time after hours on it, and when they'd left for home, I'd worked on it every night until three a.m. after I'd said goodnight to Lili. My sleep-deprived brain couldn't remember where I'd put the floor mats.

I leaned against the side of the dumpster. My mind replayed every moment of the past week. Lili, with a fish flopping against her chest. Lili, throwing her bowling ball with the worst form I'd ever seen. Lili, kissing me, running her hands all over my body. Lili. I slammed my fist against the metal dumpster. Pain throbbed in my hand and in my wrist, but I embraced it.

"What are you doing in the garbage, Daddy?"

I straightened and dropped a bag. Maddie clung to the side of the dumpster and shielded her eyes from the light. The top of her Tinkerbell pajamas rose above the metal edge.

"Why aren't you asleep?" I shut off my headlamp as the sky lightened with the first sign of the morning sun.

"I had to pee, and you weren't in your bed. Then I saw the light in the big garbage, so I came over to see if it was you, and I was right."

"What if I had been a bad guy?"

"Bad guys don't steal garbage." She shook her head, her lips in a straight line.

"I guess you're right." I chuckled. "You want to hop in here and help me?"

"Sure." She climbed higher.

I took off my gloves, but still grimaced when I touched her clean pajamas and pulled her over the edge. She plugged her nose and turned in a circle, her slippers crunching on the eggshells. I'd have to burn those slippers and get her new ones.

"So, what are we looking for?"

"Little squares of carpet. One has a grape juice stain on it."

She pulled a crinkled bag of Doritos out of the torn garbage sack at my feet and threw it into the pile of discarded junk I'd already sifted through.

"Is that why Lili got so mad at me and cried?" She jutted out her bottom lip and sniffed.

"Oh no, honey." I squatted to her level and pulled her close to me. "She was mad at Daddy for lots of other grown-up things, not at you."

She nodded. "Will these carpet things make her like you again?"

"I need them to say sorry. They mean a lot to her."

She dropped her head to her chest. "They're not in the garbage."

I paused as I put on my gloves, too cautious to be hopeful.

"I took them and put them in my playhouse in the swing set. I'm sorry."

"Maddie." I dropped my gloves and lifted my daughter above my head. "I love you." I kissed her cheek.

She placed her arms around my neck. "I thought I'd be in trouble."

I lifted her over the side of the dumpster and jumped out. "I'm just happy you came and told me, so I didn't have to spend the whole morning looking through all those garbage bags."

She ran to the swing set and came back to me with her arms full of Lili's floor mats. My smile widened. Hope wasn't lost. I could beg her forgiveness, grovel if I had to. She held out the squares of carpet to me. "You have to promise to wash with soap first before you give these back to Lili. You smell bad, like the trash can."

I laughed, went inside, and did as my daughter instructed. The sun had risen bright in the sky by the time I had Maddie scrubbed clean and tucked back into bed. I drove to Renee's. Maybe I hadn't lost the best thing that'd happened to me in years. If Lili would talk to me. I tucked the floor mats under one arm and jogged up the porch steps.

I smoothed my hair before I rang Renee's doorbell. Five minutes went by, and the door didn't open. I pushed on the doorbell again.

What was I doing here? She wouldn't speak to me ever again, but I had to try.

Ten minutes, and still no sounds. I sagged onto the porch swing. She wasn't ready for this, for me. I stood, set the mat in front of the door, and started down the stairs.

The door latch clicked.

I flipped around. Renee braced herself in the doorway, her eyes red and puffy. I'd never seen Renee cry before. My mind went to the worst possible case scenario.

I ran back up the steps and clutched Renee's shoulders. "Is Lili all right? What happened? Where is she?"

She shook her head. "It's too late. She's gone. I found her note."

Renee held up a white envelope and a crumpled piece of paper.

"What did she say?"

Renee dropped the envelope and smoothed the paper. "'*I'm going back to St. Louis. Please give me time. Lili.*'"

I leaned against the house for support; the soft white paint mocked me. The air was sucked from my body and a sharp pain stabbed through my heart. I understood this feeling all too well. She had deserted me.

"She left one for you too." Renee picked up the sealed envelope and handed it to me.

I tore it open, praying I had a chance, and I read.

**I'm sorry, I can't forgive you.**

A physical punch to the gut wouldn't have hurt me worse than those six simple words.

# Chapter 33

## Blake

Sparks from my welder flashed onto my head. The old weld on my muffler had cracked, making my truck louder than a jet engine. The gravel beneath me dug into my back. Heatwaves from the sun were only kept at bay by the shade from the car. The old, clean pipes of the undercarriage were a foot above my head.

A week of sleep, work, and repeat had passed since Lili left. Nothing changed day in and day out to make me look forward to the next. I hated myself for what I'd done to Lili, for the lies of omission that I'd forced on Renee. Renee had distanced herself from me and therefore, Maddie. I'd been the cause of her daughter leaving. As much as possible, I had stayed away from my employees and even my daughter.

I lifted my welding mask and examined my weld. A couple more layers and I'd be finished with this project, and I'd have to find something else to occupy my time. I rubbed my hand back and forth over the gravel, searching for my socket wrench, but my hand never touched the cold metal handle.

I relaxed back onto the ground. Lili was everywhere. In my thoughts. In my house. Outside in my backyard. I couldn't escape her.

I climbed out from under the truck. The wrench wasn't behind my tire or under my welder. How could I have lost it? I'd just used it.

A thin rope coiled at the base of my toolbox. A rope with a diamond pattern and—scales?

I yelled and jumped back. How the hell had a rattlesnake gotten into my truck bed?

I threw my welding helmet to the ground, grabbed my torch, and approached the truck. My mouth went dry, and I licked my lips as I leaned over the edge of my truck bed the second time. I sagged against the side of my truck—the snake had no head.

Who, in their right mind, would throw a dead rattler in my truck bed?

I marched to my garage and nearly pulled the door off its hinges when I opened it. "Chuck!"

"What'd I do this time?" Chuck grumbled from under the hood of some teenager's broken-down Ford Ranger.

"You're *fired*." I jabbed a finger at my new ex-employee.

"Awww, again? This is the third time this week."

"What kind of a prank was that?" I shoved my thumb at the door.

"What prank?" Chuck threw his hands in the air as if he were innocent, but I continued to glare at him. "Honest, I have no idea what you're talking about."

"Then explain to me why I found a dead rattlesnake in my pick-up bed. I damn near peed my pants when I reached in there."

"Oh—um—I killed the snake with a shovel. Then Maddie was coming so I threw it in the back of the truck. I must've forgotten about it."

"You must've," I said, not believing him in the least bit.

"At least I killed it. I could have left it for your daughter to find."

Without another word, I turned to go to my office before I did or said something I really regretted. At that precise moment, Maddie came in, dragging the headless snake behind her.

"Daddy. Look at this. I found it."

I winced and backed away from the body of the snake. Maddie ran closer to me and shoved the corpse in my face.

"Eeeaaauuuh." I shuddered and hopped away from the creepy, headless, scaly monster. "Maddie put that thing down and go wash your hands right now."

Chuck all out laughed at me. Pedro was behind Chuck doing no better keeping his laughter in check. I should fire them both.

"But Daddy, can I keep it?"

"See why I tossed it in your truck bed?" Chuck pointed at the snake carcass.

I glared at him. "A fat lot of good it did." I turned to my daughter. "No, you can't keep it. Go put it outside and wash your hands."

"Why, boss? You afraid of snakes?" Pedro's face was all innocence.

"Hell, no. I'm not afraid of snakes, but I sure don't want that in my house."

Chuck nudged Pedro and smiled. "Look, I think he's sweating."

"Chuck, didn't I fire you?" I growled.

"Daddy, you shouldn't be afraid. Hell, the head is even cut off."

"Madeline Cynthia Richardson, listen to me right now. And don't say hell."

"But you did."

"I know, but it was because Daddy was angry."

"Well, I'm angry too. It's not fair you can say hell and I can't."

"Put it outside!"

"Fine, but I'm going to say hell," Maddie muttered. "Hell. Hell. Hell. Hell. Hell. And dammit too." She walked out the door with the snake body still trailing behind her.

Chuck burst out laughing as soon as the door was closed. "Looks like you got a lot on your hands, boss."

Yes, I had a lot on my hands, and it had nothing to do with the snake. "Just get back to work. I want the Ranger out of here by morning."

"But I thought you fired me."

I ignored Chuck and walked out of the garage—only to return three hours later and lock myself in my office.

Everything had gone south after I'd caught up to Maddie. She'd already dragged the snake's corpse all over the house. I'd yelled. She'd wailed and shut herself in her room. I'd used a stick to get the dead snake out of the house, and I bleached anything the carcass had touched.

Then I'd scrubbed Maddie. Tears had wet her face more than the bath water. She'd shrieked her characteristic ear-shattering screams the whole time. The look of her red eyes, her face still swollen and splotchy from crying, haunted me. At dinner, we'd barely spoken, although Maddie had her usual calm back by then.

What was I going to do about the anger I carried with me? It wasn't diminishing as I'd hoped. If anything, it'd grown stronger since Lili's departure. Irene jumped whenever I entered the room and had started removing her hearing aids. My house must be loud if a hearing-impaired person found it unbearable. Chuck and Pedro stayed at the opposite end of the garage from me.

I grunted and ran my hands through my hair as I thought of what Irene said to me earlier. *You know, you were a lot nicer when Renee's daughter was here.*

She was right. Like a fool I thought I could be genuinely happy with Lili.

If only I'd stayed away from her.

If only I'd remained quiet.

If only I'd told her sooner.

If only I'd sent her a letter.

If only it hadn't happened.

I covered my ears, shut out my regrets, and leaned my elbows on my desk. My last option was to find a new home, away from Renee, Lili, and this town. Maddie would struggle with the change, but I couldn't figure out any other way.

A knock sounded on the door. I ignored it and dug into another stack of papers. The doorknob jiggled and the knock became persistent. I growled and walked to the door to unlock it.

Chuck shifted past me into my office. "Umm, Pedro went home for the night. The RV is ready for delivery. It's out in the parking lot, and we already drove the Ranger to the Southerland's."

"Good. You can go home now."

Renee stepped into the office and stood beside Chuck. "Well, we've come to talk to you. Call it an intervention."

My mouth sagged open before I schooled my features and pulled the door closed. I went behind my desk again, as if it gave me added protection for the upcoming conversation. This past week had been lonely for both me and my daughter without Renee, and she showed up at my office, out of the blue, for an intervention?

I didn't need one. I needed to go back two weeks and forget everything that'd happened. Then the dullness of my life wouldn't bother me. "I didn't think you liked me much these days."

"I thought you wanted space, and I had to get a few things figured out," Renee said.

"You're being too subtle with him." Chuck nodded at me and leaned against the door. "What Renee meant to say is you've been a real bitch to live with." He slowed down his words like I spoke another language.

"Have I?"

"I ain't never seen you act like this. If Lili meant so much to you, then go after her."

"She hates me, Chuck. With good reason." I leaned my hands on my desk.

"When will you stop blaming yourself?" he asked. "You really messed it up when you told her about the Bronco."

"What if I did make a mistake and I'm the reason they're dead?" I fell into my chair and slumped forward.

"If the police had found you liable, they would have arrested you." Chuck walked up next to me.

Renee stood with her shoulders back, her lips smooshed tightly together. I couldn't tell if it was from anger or concern. "Do you agree with him?" I asked her. After all, she hadn't spoken to me all week. She had every right to be as mad at me as Lili.

"I have come to the same conclusion as Chuck," Renee said. "I lived with this same guilt for years. It'll tear you apart if you let it." She held her hands in front of her. "You are no more responsible than I am. It was a horrible accident that no one could have predicted or prevented."

Try as I might to accept her words, I couldn't let go of the responsibility I had as a mechanic. If a car broke down after it left my shop, I'd do anything in my power to fix my mistake or find anything I might have missed, but some actions had permanent consequences.

Chuck spoke again, his voice apologetic. "Listen, I only told you to stay away from Lili because I was afraid—"

"And you were right," I cut him off. If only I could go back to the mud and the field and tell Lili straight off about my connection to her past.

"No. I was wrong." Chuck tapped his pointer finger hard on a stack of papers on my desk, causing may attention to snap back to him. "I have never seen you happier than when you were with her. You need her, and she needs you."

I ran a hand through my already frazzled hair. "I don't know how to move past this. You saw her reaction when I told her."

"Chuck's right. You could have done a better job explaining what happened." Renee folded her arms across her chest.

"It doesn't matter now." I glanced at Chuck to my right and Renee standing in front of my desk. "She left. I can't do anything about it."

Chuck narrowed his eyes, his stare scalding me. Dropping my gaze to the floor, I studied the patterns in the beige laminate.

"You really love her, don't you?" Chuck asked in a soft voice.

*Yes.* My mind screamed. Even though she left me on the edge of a parking lot like last week's garbage, I would still go after her if I thought there was even a little chance that she could love me, but Lili had made it clear—she could never forgive me. I answered Chuck with a short nod.

"She's not like Cindy. She's a girl worth chasing." The corner of Chuck's mouth lifted into a half-smile.

A fly hummed around my desk lamp, caught in the sudden silence. What did Chuck or Renee know? The last time I'd trusted their dating advice, I'd ended up in a torture chamber of endless strangers. I simply could never be with Lili. End of story.

"I'm not sayin' I'm an expert on women, but sometimes they leave so they can be chased." Chuck's voice was quiet.

I shook my head. "She left because I lied to her, and we butchered her car."

Chuck walked to the door and opened it as Renee moved away from my desk.

"How will you ever know if you don't try?" she asked. "Lili hasn't been this happy in over a decade. She loves you, whether she has the courage to admit it or not."

They both walked out of the room, leaving me alone with the fly and my buzzing thoughts. I focused on the mess on my desk. With a scowl, I grabbed a stack of papers and thumped it down in front of me. Black lettering jumbled on the page.

Damn Chuck. Damn Renee. Some intervention, putting their noses where they didn't belong. If I went after Lili and she said no, I'd be even worse off, having been rejected twice. I glanced at the floor mat that still sat on my filing cabinet. If she rejected me, at least I'd be able to apologize and give her back something she treasured.

"Hey, do me a favor!" I shouted out the door, knowing Chuck and Renee were both still there. My chair rolled away from me as I stood and walked over to the filing cabinet to grab the stained floor mat. "Keep an eye on the shop while I'm gone."

Chuck darted back into the office and his face split into a large grin. "You're going?"

"Yes."

Renee leaned back into the doorway and hugged Chuck. With too much left to do, but none of it as important as Lili, I followed them out of my office with the floor mat tucked securely under my arm.

In my bedroom, I threw clothes in a bag while I explained things to Irene. I didn't set the stained car mat down, afraid if I did, I'd lose my connection to Lili.

"I don't know how long I'll be gone, probably no longer than a week, but I'll give you a raise if you stay here and watch Maddie. She's in bed, isn't she? I'll go and say good-bye before I leave."

"Yes, and don't you worry about a raise. I'll be glad for some peace and quiet. You can be quite loud when you want to be, dear." Irene patted my hand.

"Sorry."

"I thought what's left of my poor old ears was going to break, but you are going after your girl, and everything will go back to being good."

"You're going to get her?" Maddie asked from the bedroom door, her headphones looped around her neck.

I groaned.

"Yes, but don't even think about coming." My words killed the question forming on her lips.

"Why not?" she whined.

Irene slipped out of the bedroom.

This would most likely end in failure, and I couldn't risk Maddie being crushed again. I shook my head. No. Better to play it safe than have her get her heart broken all over again.

"Can't I come ... *please*?"

"Sorry, honey. I'm not going to budge on this one so you may as well give up."

"Fine. Then I'm not talking to you for—*forever*. I hope you have a not nice trip." Maddie marched out of the room. Her bedroom door slammed above me.

Someday she would come to understand why I needed to protect her. Being unwanted followed you your whole life. I never could escape the feeling of being placed on a second-hand store shelf, waiting for anybody to love me enough to take me home with them.

This risk was worth the pain it might bring me. I needed Lili more than a fish needed water, more than cars needed fuel, more than a stupid stagnant pond needed stupid bacteria.

With the floor mat still gripped between my arm and my side, I double checked I had everything. I took the time to brush my teeth and use the bathroom, then I tugged the loops of my duffel over my shoulder and jogged to the fastest car I owned—the Hemi 'Cuda.

# Chapter 34

## Liliana

The stillness of my apartment assaulted my ears as I lay in bed waiting for my alarm to sound. The constant drip in my kitchen faucet, the pop of a floorboard, the air conditioning kicking on, even the quiet hum of my laptop kept me alert. For the past week I'd been surviving on little to no sleep.

I'd forced everything to go back to normal. It was the same, numb normal I'd perfected before Idaho, before Blake, but nothing worked the way it used to. He hovered in the corners of all my thoughts. The image of his smiling blue eyes would come to my mind first, followed by his dark hair, and full lips—then his constantly scruffy square jaw.

The tips of my fingers remembered the feel of his skin, and my body longed for him. At my weakest moments, I'd imagine him leaning in to kiss me, but then my anger would return.

I'd hovered between sleep and sobbing on the road trip back to St. Louis. I'd told Tiffany the whole story, from the first slip in the mud to the final flick of gravel in the parking lot. My friend had remained quiet, only muttering supportive comments here and there. I'd blubbered about the betrayal of the car.

To be fair, the Audi did drive smoother than it ever had, but I still hated the change. The gears didn't grind anymore, and the little change drawer had lost its rattle. It even smelled new.

Then I rehashed his confession. We'd driven through half of Wyoming in heavy silence. Tiff had repeated at least ten times in various ways about how sorry she was for encouraging me to spend time with Blake, but it wasn't her fault. Nobody would've been able to predict that the man I'd fallen for had been the one to rip the sun from my solar system. Nobody except the bastard himself.

The alarm on my phone chimed. I stared at the bright-lit face until the square shape of it burned into my retinas. Six a.m. One short hour, then I could go back to work with all its blessed distractions and avoid the vulnerability surrounding me during my down time.

Work was better than my apartment, but my co-workers treated me like a live bomb. My medical student cried nearly every time I talked to her. My colleagues only spoke to me when I asked them a direct question, and the nursing staff purposefully tortured me with unnecessary garbage.

Even Tiff avoided me at work. I shivered as my feet touched the rough Berber carpet. I hated this carpet and the leaky faucets and everything else.

"Tiffany's right," I grumbled.

How many times had Tiffany asked to move to another apartment? At least a dozen. As of this moment, we were moving into the overpriced condos bordering Forest Park. Then I wouldn't have to drive my car to work. I'd walk and spare myself the agony of sitting in my Audi.

I went down the hall to the bathroom and turned on the light, which automatically started the jet-engine exhaust fan. Another check for moving. I started the shower.

The hot water pelted against my skin, working as a soothing balm on the aches and pains from the trip across the country and long surgeries at the hospital. The familiar tension knots in my neck, shoulders, and lower back fought for attention. Everywhere ached. Everything hurt.

Steam evaporated while I toweled dry and slipped into my underwear. The air-conditioned chill of the apartment broke through the warm cocoon surrounding me as I darted into my bedroom and put on my scrubs. I dragged a brush through my wet hair.

Still dripping, I stepped into my slippers and grabbed the basket of dirty laundry I'd meant to wash yesterday. I trudged out the door and down to the basement where our washer and dryer resided. Having dumped the clothes in, I dropped the empty basket and squirted the soap and fabric softener into their appropriate cubbies. I thumped the lid down and pressed start. The washer hummed to life.

I leaned against it, the gentle motion shaking me back and forth. Every time I came down here, I stared at the storage closet door, at the padlock I'd clicked in place the first day I'd moved in. The splintering wooden door hadn't changed from when I had examined it last week. I hadn't opened it once, but the box I'd placed in the center of the cement floor remained etched into the wrinkles of my brain.

Shoving away from the washer, I walked to the door and fingered the lock. I steadied the tremor in my hands and twisted the black and white dial.

4-15-11.

Bug's birthday, exactly one month after mine. The lock clicked open. Metal rubbed against metal as I pulled it from the latch. I opened the door and tugged on the pull-string.

The old light bulb bathed the room in a yellow glow. Set in motion, the illumination of the solitary box varied as it swung. I stepped closer, crouched down, and ran a finger around all four corners as I blew on the top of the box. A cloud of dust puffed up into the air.

I carried it up to my apartment, set it on the counter, and stared at it with a steak knife in my hand, the tip pointing at the ceiling. I paced the kitchen. After grabbing a mug, I placed it under the spout of the Keurig, shoved a pod in, and started it. This took less than a minute. The box still waited.

I'd gone back and forth between throwing the box out the window and shoving it back downstairs a dozen times. Before I lost my nerve, in one bold motion, I sliced the tape down the center and folded the cardboard flaps back.

A familiar tight sensation squeezed my chest and forced tears into my eyes. On top of Michael's favorite plaid jacket lay four bright coloring pages. A bird, a fish, a car, and an umbrella. All random things Bug had asked me to print for her.

I touched the colorful marker scribbled over the images with no care for the lines. On a normal day, I would have thrown these away, but this time, they were sacred. The drawings floated onto my counter as I pulled Michael's jacket to my chest. A white envelope, the size of a card fell out of its pocket. I squatted and picked it up off the floor.

I opened it.

*Liliana, my eternal love,*
*You have made me the happiest man in the whole world!*
*I want you to know how much I love you. The years we've*
*been together have been the best I've ever known. I can't see*
*an end to this lifetime of happiness with you. Thank you*
*for accepting me for who I am, and for saying yes the day I*
*proposed to you on the park slide. You make me so happy. I*
*promise to do my best, in return, to fill our lives with smiles*
*and laughter every day.*
*Love, your husband,*
*Michael*

My fingertips shook against my lips. He must have written this the day he got his promotion—the day I lost him. Michael wanted a lifetime of smiles and laughter for me, but he was gone, and I couldn't bring him back. It was amazing, the permanent, ever-rippling effects one overlooked brake line could have.

Even though his scent had long since left the jacket, I held it up to my nose and breathed in until breathing became painful.

His death robbed me of my smile. Although Blake hadn't been the one behind the wheel of the Bronco, his negligence had as much to do with the accident as the driver. Sure, he was a volunteer firefighter, EMT, and collected donations to fight cancer, but all those rights didn't make his wrong disappear.

Since losing Michael and Bug, my life had been constant sorrow, learning, challenges, failures, and successes, but no laughter ... until Idaho.

I pulled the jacket away from my face and hugged it to my chest. In Clear Springs, I'd slept in, stayed out late, caught trout with my hands, slept in a man's bed ... I'd climbed the face of a cliff and savored the sweetness of a first kiss.

Blake had still lied to me the night I'd told him about day zero. He'd let me sob into his shirt, comforting me even though he was the root cause of everything.

Bold letters on the paper at the bottom of the box caught my eye. It sat under Michael's Darth Vader pen and Bug's teddy bear she'd carried with her everywhere.

## TWIN FALLS POLICE DEPARTMENT

I'd requested the police report, but I'd never had the courage to read it. It'd been shoved into the same spot I'd put everything else—packaged in a box, locked in a basement where it couldn't hurt me. Dropping the coat on the counter, I tucked the teddy bear into the crook of my arm and dug the paper out of the box. I skimmed it to find what I was looking for. The handwritten report was nearly illegible.

## CASE NUMBER: 004057

... *examination of the Ford Bronco involved in a car and pedestrian accident on 5 Oct this year. Damaged brake line resulting in catastrophic failure. Most likely sustained from off-roading earlier in the day ...*

My grip crumpled the paper as the ground under me tilted. I sagged against the counter and clutched Bug's teddy bear.

Blake wasn't responsible. The damage done to the brake line happened after he'd seen it in his shop. Shivers raised the hairs over my entire body.

This paper brought the life Michael had wanted for me—a life with Blake—within my grasp, but did I want to seize it?

The Keurig finished filling my cup, but I didn't touch it. The strong smell of French roast turned my stomach. He'd still kept the truth from me, at least, the truth he believed. How could I be with him? I'd made the right choice, even if my heart disagreed.

Strength returned to my legs, and I straightened. Blake had also lived with guilt for all these years. It was guilt that he shouldn't be feeling, and I was well acquainted with how it could mar your soul. I pulled out my phone to take a picture of the report and send it to him, but I paused and let my phone fall onto my counter.

I breathed in the musty smell of my baby's teddy bear. Images of her carrying this bear all over creation flooded my mind. The bear was still here, and she wasn't.

One tear slid down my cheek, followed by another. If only I could make an exchange. Here, God, take this teddy bear and plaid jacket in exchange for my family.

After I lost Michael and Bug, I'd become obsessed with the myth of Orpheus and Eurydice. Gifted with the magic of song, Orpheus used his power to go to the underworld and retrieve the love of his life. Why wasn't there something I could do to get my family back? Ultimately, Orpheus failed, and Eurydice spent eternity with Hades, but at least he had had something actionable to do.

Maybe I wouldn't fail. Maybe with a safety net, I wouldn't be so afraid to love someone else. Who was to say that in a few years, I wouldn't be holding a token of Blake's life? An inanimate object he'd treasured, carrying none of his vibrancy. I couldn't survive another round of this.

I folded the police report and crumpled it into the deep pocket of my scrub bottoms. Tiffany wandered into the kitchen, rubbing her eyes and adjusting her glasses.

"You are already showered and dressed?" Tiffany asked. "Sheesh. What time did you get up?"

"Six." My voice wavered.

Tiffany narrowed her gaze at me, focused on the jacket, the teddy bear, and then the box.

"You opened it?"

I nodded once.

"Oh, hon." She walked to me and wrapped her arms around me. "How are you feeling?"

"Why did he lie to me?" A now constant stream of tears poured down my cheeks. I had an endless supply.

"Who? Blake?" Tiff relaxed against the counter next to me. "I don't know."

Why did he insert himself into my life? Why did he make me fall in love with him? He could have stayed away. He could have let me be. "I don't understand."

"I've been thinking about it." Tiff paused and took a breath. "It was an accident. No matter how much you want to blame someone, it wasn't Blake's fault. It wasn't your mother's fault. It wasn't *your* fault."

I stiffened. "You're saying that if I sewed someone up with a leaky brachial artery, it would be considered an accident too?" I couldn't meet her gaze, the truth in the police report burning a hole in my pocket. "I'm pretty sure their family would sue the pants off of me after they died."

"And it would haunt you for the rest of your life, but it would still be an accident."

I remembered every patient I'd lost on the operating table. Each case imprinted on my mind as I second guessed my every move for months afterward. Blake had been weighed down like this for over a decade, and it truly wasn't his fault.

Tiff nudged my arm as I stared at the floor. "But if you want, I'll call and leave him a nasty voicemail and sign his phone number up for every scam on the internet."

I laughed and wiped my tears off my cheeks. "No, but thanks."

I folded Michael's jacket and put it back into the box. I reverently set the teddy bear on top of it.

"No matter what you need, I'm here. I want you to be happy."

Happiness—my friend believed in the fairytale too. The walls of our apartment closed in on me. My cup of coffee sat full at the base of the Keurig, but I didn't move to get it. I'd buy some at the hospital.

"I better get to work." I grabbed my keys off the hook, traded my slippers for my white sneakers, slipped on the same shoe Blake had tossed at me, and walked out the door.

# Chapter 35

## Blake

The rest stop's white brick beamed in the sun along the side of the interstate, a beacon of hope for my bladder. I sped past a milepost sign. Kearny, Nebraska, sixteen miles. A sharp pain radiated from the base of my back as I decelerated and maneuvered onto the ramp. Five-point harnesses and racing seats were not made for long road trips.

I maneuvered the 'Cuda into the parking spot facing the brown-roofed building. The landscape around the bathroom wasn't anything different than when I'd first entered Nebraska. Corn and more corn. Rolling hills covered in fields of ... corn. Though I only saw what I could through the beam of my headlights until just before seven when the sun began to rise. Now, at eight a.m. I couldn't hold my bladder at bay any longer. I climbed out of the car and shuffled to the men's restroom.

Once I'd rid myself of my last two Mountain Dews, I went to the vending machine and bought a Dr. Pepper. Condensation gathered on the outside of the cold soda bottle. I rolled it across my forehead while I stretched my legs.

The dense air around me filled my lungs; soon my body would look much like the bottle I had in my hand. Sweat dampened my shirt at only eight-fifteen in the morning thanks to the stifling Midwestern humidity.

I pulled my car door open, and a blast of air-conditioning hit me. I dropped my pop into a cup holder and retrieved my phone, my gaze lingering on the car mat sitting in the passenger seat. The mat and I had shared some riveting conversation over the course of the drive.

What was I doing, chasing after a woman who probably didn't want to be chased?

I rubbed a hand down my face and pulled up Google Maps, tracing my route to Kearny, a couple of hours shy of Lincoln. With the way I'd been driving, I would be able to reach Lincoln in an hour. Chuck had stuck a radar detector in my front windshield, and it'd already saved me at least three times. I guessed I would make it to St. Louis in seven hours, even though Google said it should take eight hours and thirty-six minutes.

A small cough from the backseat froze me in place.

I got out and flipped the driver's seat forward. In one swift movement, I had the blankets piled on the floor in my hands. All that was left was my sleepy-eyed, tangled-haired, head-phoned, stubborn daughter.

"Hi, Daddy." Maddie blinked and rubbed her eyes against the brightness of the sun. She put on what I liked to call her "angel face" and stretched like a cat while I continued to glare down at her.

I motioned for her to join me in the front of the car and tucked the floor mat behind the console, still within my reach. With only lap belts in the back seat, the front five-point harness would be the safest place for her in this car. She climbed out and gave me a shy smile.

"Is it okay if I go pee pee?"

"Hurry." I grunted and followed after her. "I'll be right outside if you need me."

Maddie potty danced her way through the open door. While she used the bathroom, I texted Irene, who, like me, thought Maddie'd been sleeping all night. Her last response was *Don't be too hard on her.*

Maddie was gone and back in under five minutes. I didn't even check if she had washed her hands as we tromped back to the Barracuda. After making sure she was buckled, I sat in the driver's seat, started the engine, and sped up the on ramp, keeping my speed within five miles of the speed limit.

Fifteen minutes passed. Still, I didn't speak. Twenty. Before it hit thirty minutes, she broke.

Silent treatment: one. Maddie: zero.

"I'm sorry, but I had to come, and you wouldn't let me, so I *had* to hide in the backseat."

I didn't trust myself to speak. My mind skimmed over the past twelve hours of massive speeding when my little girl had been unbuckled in the backseat. If something had happened while I'd been going one hundred plus miles an hour she wouldn't have lived.

A sickening feeling spread through me like gangrene. I took a deep breath. "You had to hide? You could have also waited back at home for me like I asked."

"Well, you're not the only one who needs to talk to Lili, you know?"

"What do you have to say to her that is important enough for you to lie to me?"

"I wanted to ask her why she left, and why she had to make you so angry."

"Couldn't you have written her a note?"

"You would have to help me with a note." She folded her arms across her chest and slumped against the seat. "Besides, I got mad at her too."

261

I blew out all the pent-up air in my lungs. Maddie didn't understand; Lili had every right to be mad at me. My anger was directed at myself, not Lili. I'd been so wrapped up in my own problems that I hadn't even considered my daughter's feelings.

"All right, if you ever do this again, then you will be grounded from the garage for a month. As it is, you've already lost two weeks."

"But Daddy—"

"Don't you *but Daddy* me." I stopped her protest. "Don't you understand how dangerous it is for you to lay in the back of the car without a seat belt? What if I'd gotten in an accident? The punishment is fair."

Maddie hung her head, looking like a true martyr.

"How did you manage to get in the car without me knowing anyway? And how'd you know I was going to take this car in the first place?"

"If I tell you, will you take off a week?" Maddie asked with her mouth in a stiff line.

"Nope."

"Fine, I'll tell you." She set her hands in her lap. "I took a rope from the shop and put it under my bed. You were being mean, and I thought I might have to escape to Renee's house."

"I was bad, huh?"

"You were madder than a grizzly bear with a hurt paw," she said with her tone even.

I laughed, as her phrase had Chuck written all over it. "Okay, I get it, and for what it's worth, I'm sorry."

"Really, really sorry?"

"Really, really, *really* sorry." I glanced over at her.

"Okay, I forgive you." Maddie looked out the window, a small smile softening her face.

"But you haven't told me the rest of the story about how you got into the backseat." I returned my focus to the road.

"Oh, yeah. Well, I knew you would take our fastest car. So, after I got down the rope—don't worry, I used the hand over hand like when you showed me—I went into the garage and used a long stick to get the keys off the wall."

"You planned this out pretty well."

"I saw someone do it on the TV. I even packed my backpack." She grinned.

"You have been watching too much television."

"If I promise not to watch any TV for a month, will you take off a week?" Maddie asked quickly.

"No." I laughed.

Maybe having her with me wasn't so terrible after all.

# Chapter 36

## Blake

As soon as I'd driven through Kansas City, a thunderstorm slowed me down even more. The rain pounded my car. My wipers swooshed as fast as they could, but they did little to help with visibility.

My Pandora station went to an ad when I passed a mile-post sign. Only forty-five more miles to St. Louis. I started to whistle along with the next song playing over Bluetooth. In an hour, I'd be with Lili. Probably longer with us coming into St. Louis at rush hour. But it'd just give me more time to figure out what to say to her. My muscles tensed at the mere thought of being in the same room with her.

This trip would end in one of two ways: either I would convince Lili to give me a second chance, to start the relationship right, and make things work somehow, or I'd leave, and go back to Idaho with the firm knowledge that she didn't care enough to forgive me.

I winced. That possibility stabbed straight through me. Even though leaving her would hurt, I would survive, but I had to know if even the slightest possibility existed for us. Any amount of happiness with Lili was worth fighting for.

Thunder cracked overhead and lightning lit the sky. Rain turned to hail.

Some drivers slowed to ridiculous speeds or parked under overpasses, while others sped by trying to get to their destinations before the storm worsened. A gust of wind nearly blew my Hemi 'Cuda off the road.

All of this was lost on Maddie. Her rapid-fire snores filled the passenger side of the car. Something about the hum of the motor and the motion of the car had always soothed her to sleep. Needless to say, she hadn't provided much entertainment for me during this last stretch of the drive.

Hopefully, she'd be awake enough to form a coherent sentence when we got there. I had the address to Lili's apartment, but my guess was she would be working. I plugged Barnes-Jewish Hospital into Google Maps.

I'd start with, *I'm sorry for keeping the truth from you.* Sorry I'd ruined her car. Sorry I didn't ask before I started the project in the first place.

What would I say to her next?

I'd go on to tell her how much she'd come to mean to me and to Maddie. I'd tell her that she was worth chasing, show her the car mats, and then grovel—pray she'd give me a sign, a reason to hope.

Then, she'd take the car mats and walk out of my life forever.

I wiped my sweaty palm on my jeans and leaned forward to swipe to a new station on my phone. Outside, the clouds took on a green hue. AC/DC's *Thunderstruck* rang throughout the car. It cracked along with the weather.

I sang to ease my tension.

"Daddy? What are you doing?" Maddie rubbed the sleep from her eyes.

"Singing, want to join me?" I continued singing and started to bob my head to the beat.

She pressed on her headphones. "You're a silly daddy. I only like it when you sing at bedtime."

Thunder boomed and shook the car. The hail grew to the size of small golf balls. I flinched anytime a piece deflected off the car. The storm had turned from something I could manage to drive through to absolute chaos.

Maddie gripped the armrest. "I'm scared."

I tightened my grip on the wheel. This storm scared the hell out of me too, but I couldn't show Maddie my fear. I imitated the whine of the lead singer's voice trying to distract from the loudness of the hail pummeling the car. "You sing."

She shook her head, but her grip on the armrest relaxed as I continued to sing more animatedly. I maintained a laser focus on the road. Maddie started humming, not in time with the music. Out of my peripheral vision, I saw her start to rock back and forth.

This was an enormous breakthrough. She'd never danced or hummed to music. I wanted to hug her tight and swing her around, but I couldn't.

"It's okay, Maddie." I kept my grip tight on the steering wheel and my eyes on the road. A speeding semi blew past us in the left lane and blasted the Hemi 'Cuda with a sheet of water as Maddie hummed in perfect pitch at the part of the song she knew.

I sang along with her humming until she calmed enough to let out a small laugh.

Cars pulled off on either side of the road and were barely visible in the slashing hail. If anyone lost sight of their lane, they'd plow into the parked vehicles. Stopping was too dangerous, so I pressed on, looking for the next exit.

Maddie's giggles turned into a scream as a sedan flew off the side of the freeway, flipping end over end until it slammed into the underpass. An SUV spun out of control to our left. It followed the same path as the sedan, finally flipping across the median and crashing into an oncoming car. At the same time, sirens began wailing in the city streets surrounding us.

I tried my hardest to stay out of the mess, but the Hemi 'Cuda was being pulled out of my control.

I jerked the wheel. "No!" I yelled at my car.

Brake lights lit up on the few cars the low visibility allowed me to see. A Cadillac Escalade slammed into the back of a Toyota sedan. The semitruck swerved into the lane in front of me and locked its brakes.

I glanced left—then right.

I had no avenue of escape. Fear as I had never felt before ate at me.

"Oh, sshhh—"

My daughter started screaming again.

A large funnel cloud descended from the sky. Its dark mass consumed the vehicles a hundred yards in front of me. I slammed on the brakes, willing the 'Cuda to stop before it hit the jack-knifed semitruck. Its trailer sat to the freeway.

"Come on. *Come on.*" The cars behind me made it impossible to reverse.

The rain had added enough water that no amount of braking or swerving would stop the inevitable. The semitrailer tipped onto two wheels, lifted by the wind. I was going to die. All thoughts turned to Maddie as the sky darkened further from the tornado and the semi tilting toward us.

"Maddie, get down."

*Please God*—my daughter.

Metal crunched together. My head slammed into the steering wheel as I careened into the semi. A chorus of screeching brakes and squealing tires followed our merged mass. My senses heightened and time slowed. Broken glass sounded like chimes of a demonic symphony, scattering everywhere. Hail and wind shocked me, splattered against my skin, as the 'Cuda's windshield shattered. The fatalistic music meshed with the shout of AC/DC, still playing on the radio.

But the only sound I focused on was my daughter's frightened cry.

*"Daddy!"*

I let go of the steering wheel and reached for her. My head jerked against something solid, and a black emptiness descended on me.

# Chapter 37

## Liliana

U rgent conversations and barked commands echoed from the room next door. I couldn't follow any of them. My trauma team prepped for another wave of patients about to overtake us. Life Flight and multiple ambulances were on their way. I closed my eyes and breathed in slowly, taking this moment of reprieve to sharpen and refocus my mind. Beds lined the halls of the emergency room and our trauma center.

A tornado had touched down along interstate sixty-four, and it wasn't tornado season. I hated these errant storms. They could take a good day and blow it to hell.

I opened my eyes. White was supposed to be a calming color—chosen to cause less stress, but it didn't work here. It reflected the tension inside of all of us in the room. We'd been through this hundreds of times before, but we didn't change jobs; we were addicted to the rush of saving lives. Adrenaline junkies, as Blake had said.

The helicopter's rotors thwacked outside, using the field in the park next door as a landing pad since multiple flights were coming in and out. Energy pulsed through me while I waited for the arrival of Life Flight's cargo. Every second counted.

When the doors burst open and shattered the quiet of the white room, I relaxed my shoulders and stretched my neck. The flight nurse shouted out the vital signs while another one kept pumping air into the patient's lungs. Usually, I gave my full attention to the flight nurse before I examined my patient, but I looked down at the little girl on the gurney, her small body only took up half of the bed.

I focused in on the child's chest watching for it to rise and fall, while I scanned for possible hemorrhaging. This wasn't the patient they'd called ahead about. The unconscious, middle-aged female with a head wound, possible pneumo, and a fractured leg.

The flight nurse yelled over the noise of the room as another gurney was rushed inside into the room next door. "The patient has probable internal bleeding in her abdomen near her left kidney—"

"Wait. Why wasn't this child taken to the Children's Hospital?"

"Three school buses were hit by the tornado. Field trip. She was diverted here when we arrived." The nurse continued his evaluation, but his voice became muffled. I stared at the patient's long, black, tattered pigtail so similar to Maddie's. I shook my head trying to refocus. Maddie was nowhere near here.

"Compound fracture in her right arm," the nurse continued.

I still couldn't bring myself to look away from the bloodied face—too familiar. The left side of the child's face was bruised and swollen, making her left eyelids stand out like two pink ridges resting on a jagged cut running along her cheekbone.

My gaze shifted to the sharp, white bone sticking out of her arm an odd angle with pink flesh clinging to it. Bone chips clumped in the flow of her deep red blood, which stained the white pad on the gurney. The little girl's legs appeared to have been spared. Her Tinkerbell pajama pants weren't even torn. My breath lodged in my throat when I saw the grease-stained tennis shoes.

Dread filtered into my bloodstream, filled every nook and cranny with its dark presence when the little girl's right eyelids fluttered open. Bright blue irises so much like her father's were glazed with the pain she must've been experiencing.

*No.*

Memories came back to me of another time, the clouded eyes of my baby girl just before she died. It was almost too much for me. Panic set in as the puzzle pieces came together in my mind. She was missing her headphones. They were her comfort. If Maddie was here, Blake had to be in the same car.

Where was he? I darted to the hall and scanned the other gurneys coming in through the doors, but there were too many. I couldn't exactly go outside and start triaging the ambulances as they arrived.

Focus on Maddie. I moved back to the side of her bed, lifted her shirt, and palpated her skin. Her skin was tense. Distended.

"I need the ultrasound."

A nurse wheeled the ultrasound cart next to me. I grabbed the hand-held probe and rubbed it against Maddie's abdomen. Space gapped between the kidney and the abdominal wall.

*Crap dammit!*

Blood pooled uncontrollably inside of her.

"Start O neg blood, now." Maddie had minutes at the least, a couple of hours at the most.

The nurses scrambled to get the rapid transfuser running. Lab techs ran into the room carrying bags of blood and handed them to the nurses.

In less than two minutes from when I gave the order, Maddie had blood transfusing into her body, and we rushed her to the OR.

Where was Blake?

As a physician, I understood Blake's absence either meant he was in good enough condition to wait for treatment, he'd been sent to another hospital, or it meant—

I shook my head. I had no time to think about Blake now. Maddie needed me, and I would do everything in my power to keep her here. I refused to lose another baby girl.

Maddie gained some awareness on the elevator. Her visible eye was unfocused, and she looked terrified. I placed my hand on the less damaged side of her face.

"Look at me, Maddie."

Her eyebrows creased together. "Lili?"

"Don't talk," I ordered as the gash on Maddie's cheek began to pour out fresh blood. She started to hyperventilate and pull at the braces.

"Do you remember the day we played pirates in your backyard?"

Maddie stilled and looked at me.

I moved my hand to hold her cold fingers. "I want you to think about how fun it was to play pirates with your daddy and me. Try playing pirates in your head, and don't worry about anything else. I'm going to take care of you." I stopped at the operating doors. "Maddie, I've got to go wash my hands. When you wake up, I'll be with you. Don't worry."

The moment I let go of her fingertips, a brief flash of panic returned to Maddie's eyes.

It was going to be all right.

It had to be all right.

I repeated these six words in my head over and over as I scrubbed my hands up to my elbows.

Pete walked beside me and started sterilizing his arms. If I told him I knew Maddie, would he let me in on the surgery? By the end of the operation, he would figure it out anyway.

"I've called in the pediatric surgeon to take the lead on this surgery." Pete finished washing and held his hands above his waist. "Dr. Patel will be here as soon as she can."

With an event of this magnitude, the operating rooms at both the children's hospital and ours were beyond full capacity. It was a miracle we had a peds surgeon free to come help with Maddie's operation.

"This one's special to me."

"You know her?" He looked up from his hands to my face, already shaking his head.

Tears fell, unchecked. "Her name is Madeline Richardson, and I can't let her die. Please."

I sensed Pete's immediate wariness. His bushy white hair burned my eyes. "Lil, maybe you shouldn't—"

"Don't," I interrupted. "Please don't tell me I shouldn't be part of the operation. If I thought I was a danger, believe me, I would walk out of this door and leave." I took a breath. "I have to do more than what was done for my daughter."

His white eyebrows lifted, wrinkling his forehead. "Fine. I'll assist you until Patel gets here. If you show signs of cracking, you're done. I'll finish on my own."

"I promise, I will be in control," I said, then backed into the operating room.

# Chapter 38

## Blake

I jerked awake. Sweeping the blinding light out of my vision with my left hand, I shoved the man standing above me with such force he stumbled backward. Contorted metal statues of once ordinary vehicles scattered around me. Where was I? What had happened?

Blades of a helicopter thudded in the distance. The man approached me again, this time with caution. My defenses were up. I was ready for battle, but I was missing something.

Two more men flanked me, and I catapulted to my feet. A sharp pain shot like a flaming arrow up my right leg into my spine, the metallic taste of blood filling my mouth. My brain scrambled, an emptiness that I'd never felt before filled me.

Maddie. Where was my daughter?

"*Maddie!*" I yelled, praying for a response.

"It's all right, man." The person I'd shoved stood next to me with his hand out.

It was then I recognized who, or rather, what he was. A paramedic.

"The little girl in your car was life-flighted out of here."

I looked behind me at the men who were on my flanks, but they were just onlookers with cell phones out, recording the destruction. No better than flies attracted to a dung heap. I rubbed my hand on the wet spot on my forehead and moved it in front of my face. Bright red blood smeared across my palm.

"Where? When?"

"St. Louis Children's Hospital. About ten minutes ago." The paramedic walked to me and smiled his teeth brilliant white against his black skin.

"My daughter. How is she?"

The smile faltered on his face, and all the air squeezed out of my lungs as if I'd stepped into a vacuum. *Not my little girl.* The pain in my leg was the only thing keeping me from falling to my knees.

"She was alive when we put her on the chopper. The docs will fix her up right." He was close enough now to put his hand on my shoulder. I read his name badge on his shirt pocket. *Dejon.* "But we need to worry about you now. Make sure you're all good and ready when that little girl wakes up."

She was unconscious. No. No. Please, God. *No.*

My eyes locked onto the remnants of the Hemi 'Cuda. Through the distorting rays of the late afternoon sun, the Barracuda's cavernous skeleton stretched open toward the heavens. The jaws of life had ripped it open. I'd spent countless hours restoring that vehicle to mint condition, and I'd lost it. It didn't matter. I could replace a car, but I'd never recover if I lost Maddie.

I staggered into a puddle, evidence of the torrential rainfall. Lightning flashed in the distance, dampening the low, radiant sun. Puffs of evaporating water wafted from the ground.

*Please, God, save my baby girl.*

"Let's get you over to the ambulance." Dejon's voice took on an edge of authority. "You aren't going to win any fights in your condition."

I tightened my lips into a flat line and walked with Dejon to the ambulance. The ache in my leg annoyed me. Dejon helped me into the back and placed a rough gray blanket around my shoulders. I shrugged it off.

With the humidity from the storm, I could barely breathe in this heat. I almost relaxed against the gurney, but then I heard the cry of a baby, a newborn.

Dejon paused right before he put the blood pressure cuff on my arm and turned toward the sound.

"Did you hear that?" I asked.

"Yeah." He held his hand up. "You wait here, and I'll go check it out."

I pulled out my wallet and searched for my EMT card. I showed it to him.

"I can help." I neglected to mention the volunteer part.

"Not before I check you out." Dejon shook his head. "My partner and I will go get the baby and take you to the hospital."

"Where's your partner?"

Dejon looked out of the ambulance in all directions. "I'm sure he'll be right back."

Without asking again, I stood, ignoring the pain in my leg. Hopefully, the adrenaline in my body would keep the pain at bay for a bit longer. I couldn't sit idle when someone else's baby might die. I scanned the area for other rescue workers, but they were all involved in digging through the rubble, absorbed in their efforts. Either Dejon ignored my following after him, or he realized that he needed the help.

We followed the sound to a Chevy Cobalt balanced on its side on the front bumper of a Cummins Ram 3500. The Ram reached toward the sky. Its under-carriage leaned into the back of a semitruck's multi-car trailer. The Cobalt had to be at least thirty feet from the ground, its front end completely gone.

"Whoa," Dejon breathed.

Together, we made our way up the wreckage, using the ramps on the car trailer to get as close as possible. Dejon reached the driver's side of the Cobalt before I did, my leg slowing my progress. A woman lay unconscious in the driver's seat. Her long hair and arms dangled toward us, both front and back driver side doors were gone.

Dejon hollered down to a few others to come assist. At this point, I would have called in a chopper so we could place her on a brace board and lower her to safety. With the scale of this pile-up and the precarious situation of the car, we couldn't afford to wait.

I placed two fingers on her jugular artery. "I found a pulse."

Dejon pulled a neck brace out of his bag, slipped it on the woman, and snipped her seat belt. All the while, her baby wailed in the backseat.

"Let's lower her down to Ryan." Dejon shoved his thumb toward another paramedic climbing the wreckage beneath us.

While he supported the woman's upper body, I carefully freed her legs from under the steering wheel and handed them down to another paramedic.

"We got her." Dejon scaled the large black beams of the semitruck's trailer with one hand while holding onto his patient with the other. "Work on getting the baby free, and I'll be back to help. Don't do anything to get yourself killed, or I'm in deep trouble."

The infant car seat was installed without a base and the seat belt was jammed. I felt the wreckage sway.

*Move faster, Blake.*

One slip and both the baby and I would have a clear path to the steaming asphalt below. The baby had quieted, making me more nervous.

The passengers of the Ram were nowhere to be seen. I hoped they'd been able to get to safety. I reached into the backseat and checked the baby for a pulse, my fingers giant against the minuscule neck. The baby couldn't have been much older than two months, and a small blue blanket with "Tyson" on the tag was wrapped around his legs. After a heart-pounding second, the tiny flutter of his heartbeat pulsed against my fingertips.

I pressed on the latch release, but the seat belt didn't dislodge. I pulled out my pocketknife and sawed at the straps.

"I'm coming up!" Dejon shouted from somewhere down below me, and I glanced down at him.

When Dejon put his weight on the tire of the Ram, the Cobalt jolted and shifted. Dejon fell back, and I teetered on unsteady footing, my arm slamming against the infant car seat. The thick strap snapped, and the car seat careened into the windshield of the Cummins. The baby boy started crying. Spiderweb cracks snaked their way out from the wailing infant, the splintered glass barely supporting its weight. I grabbed the frame of the Cobalt between where the driver's side windows would be.

"It's all right buddy. I'm going to get you." I spoke in soothing tones, hiding the rising tension.

Pain throbbed in my knee, but I shoved my right foot, my injured leg, into a more secure foot hold while I held fast to the metal. Suspended on a cliff of wrecked cars, I leaned down to the car seat. Broken glass sliced deep into my right palm. My left leg dangled in the air as I stretched my left arm as far as I could reach.

My middle finger brushed the handle of the car seat. Warm, sticky blood flowed down my other forearm. I caught the car seat as the windshield gave way. The shards of glass clinked down the pickup bed, exploding onto the pavement.

Fuel pooled on the tailgate of the Cummins, licking its way toward a flaming Escalade a few yards away. Fumes and smoke lodged in my throat as I hung there, a literal human lifeline to a screaming baby.

Flames danced at the edge of the diesel fuel, eager to be fed. At any moment, they could ignite the fumes, and both the baby and I would be engulfed.

"Dejon, we've got to do this fast," I panted, my strength all but gone. "Are you anywhere near me?"

"I'm here." Dejon steadied himself on the wreckage of the Cobalt.

"All right. I'm going to push him up to you on the count of three." I breathed hard. Briny sweat dripped into my mouth adding its flavor to the blood.

"Ready."

*Please God, help me.*

"One."

*Give me strength.*

"Two."

*Help me save this boy.*

"Three."

With all the remaining strength left in me, I curled my left bicep and pushed the car seat into the air. The weight lightened as Dejon removed the baby.

"I got him, Blake. Hold tight, I'll be right back to help you."

Strength waned from my arm. The car seat broke out of my grip and tumbled down into the wreckage beneath me.

*Thank you, God.*

With a deep sigh, I swung my left foot onto the back tire of the Cobalt, but it slipped. My right leg wrenched in the opposite direction of my body as gravity pulled me downward. Pain exploded and shot up my leg to spread throughout my body. Black dots danced through my vision, and I vomited.

Still hanging above the Ram, I swiped my free hand across my mouth. After a few deep breaths, I placed my left foot next to my lodged right and pushed against the twisted metal. My foot slid free, and my lower body swung away from the car with the force I'd used dislodge my right leg. I managed to maintain hold onto the frame before I somersaulted into the pavement.

Struggling to hold onto my slight grasp on consciousness, I clung to the Chevy with one injured hand, both feet now dangling free. I couldn't find a secure foothold with my right leg all but useless.

*"I'm crazy, I can't do this."*

Lili's voice came back to me from the day on the cliff. *Nothing is secure up here.*

I couldn't help but chuckle as my left foot skidded off slick metal again. Nothing was secure up here. I slipped again and sobered. The wrecked Ram beneath offered me no help.

My pinky finger slipped as the flame ignited the gas far beneath me. I did the only thing I could do—the only option I had left ... I prayed.

*Thank you for saving that boy.*

My ring finger followed.

*Please make sure Maddie remembers her daddy.*

All but the center of my vision submerged into blackness.

*Please, somehow, make sure that Lili knows I love her.*

My last two fingers, glazed in blood, slipped off the metal surface of the car. In the millisecond I was suspended in the air, my life flashed before me. My regrets, accomplishments, Maddie's birth, and my hopes for the future. Lili's face reached my mind and I latched onto it.

Beauty. Love. Hope. She had given all of it to me, and I would never be able to tell her.

# Chapter 39

## Liliana

The doors of the operating room closed behind me. I'd repaired the bleeds in Maddie's abdomen, set the bone in her arm, and stabilized her blood pressure. After the sedatives wore off, Maddie only regained awareness for a brief time before she drifted away again. The MRI had shown an epidural hematoma. Blood pooled between the sac surrounding the brain and the skull, adding pressure—causing potential brain damage.

The neurosurgeon had told me the surgery went well, but he wasn't exactly verbose. His team shaved a small portion of her head, drilled into her skull, and put in a drain-tube. Now all we could do was wait.

*If* she ever woke up. It was hard to be optimistic when I'd lived through the worst-case scenario.

After her surgery, the nurses had taken Maddie to the Pediatric Intensive Care Unit.

I pulled off my blood-covered surgical gown and gloves and threw them into the biohazard bin. The steady stream of cases flowing into the trauma OR had slowed to a trickle. I walked into the bathroom; my bladder filled to the point where sharp pains shot through my abdomen.

The Emergency Room quieted, still with no sign of Blake. The post-adrenaline rush settled in my stomach, making me feel sick. I moved to the sink to wash my shaking hands, and the warm water soothed my tremors. I glanced in the mirror; dark circles under my eyes stood out against my pale face.

In the operating room, I'd barely been able to keep my fear for Maddie and Blake under control, but in the poorly lit bathroom I met them head-on. Worst possible outcomes came to the surface. Blake torn up, lifeless, on the pavement—bleeding out in his car—trapped—his tanned face colorless in the rigor of death.

I covered my eyes with my still-wet hands, and water funneled down my face.

"Stop it!" I yelled. My breaths came in sharp, uneven gusts. I shut off the water and focused on breathing.

I pulled air in against the tightness in my chest.

Air hissed slowly through my teeth.

Some people had been DOA—Dead On Arrival. Could one of them have been Blake?

Breathe in and out.

I didn't have the courage to find out right now.

I shoved the door open, walked to the fifth-floor sky bridge connecting our hospital with St. Louis Children's, passing patient rooms with televisions echoing the news of the accident. I couldn't look at them. Would I see the bright orange paint of the Hemi Barracuda? Or maybe the deep blue of his truck?

Walls, chairs, and stools transitioned to brighter colors as I crossed to the elevators and pressed the button for the eighth floor. The PICU nurses paid little attention to me. They continued to rush about, trying to keep up with this shift from hell. After a brief stop at the nurse's desk, I found Maddie's room. The large glass doors framed her tiny body against her white hospital bed. The picture wasn't one unfamiliar to me.

My Bug.

Dark braids versus blonde.

Tanned skin versus porcelain white.

Both girls were precious to me. I couldn't survive the loss of another one. What determined which child lived and which one died? Earlier in my medical career, I'd thought it was half a person's will, half my skills, and sheer determination that kept them alive. Could I be missing a significant part of this border between life and death?

I rested my hand on the doorknob. My shift had ended, and I needed to pass off my patients to the oncoming physician. Instead, I silenced my phone and entered Maddie's room.

The beeping of the monitor rang in my ears as I sat in the seat next to the bed. A partial fiberglass cast splinted her forearm, ending at her mid-upper arm. The orthopedic surgeons must have repaired it while I'd been in other surgeries. White gauze wrapped around her head and secured the bandage the neurosurgeons had placed there. The chill in the room seeped through my scrubs. I held Maddie's uninjured hand, wanting nothing more than to drown out the constant beeping.

"Maddie," I spoke only after the last of the nurses had left the room. "Did you know that I used to be a mother? I had a baby girl. I only got to know her for two years, but we loved to play games together. Do you know what our favorite game was? We loved to play dress up and spin in circles together."

I brushed my fingertip along the saline drip line and followed it down to the IV taped to her hand. Careful not to disturb the IV, I laid Maddie's hand across my palm and rubbed my thumb along its side. "You want to know the craziest thing, Maddie? I used to call my little girl Madi too."

The ventilator pumped air into Maddie's lungs, the endotracheal tube fastened around her face with Velcro straps.

"Madison Paige Chase."

My throat clogged. It had been almost eleven years since I'd said my daughter's name out loud. It hurt much more than I thought it would. No matter how many times I called out her name, Madison Paige Chase would never come running into my arms. Madison Paige would never reach out to hold my hand. Madison would never walk by my side. Madi would never curl up on the couch next to me and fall asleep again. My Bug was lost to me.

"You have helped me so much. You've allowed me to love another little girl." Nothing but the sound of my sporadic breaths echoed in the room, out of sync with the beeping of the heart monitor. "I used to sing a song to Madi, one that I wrote for her, every night before she would fall asleep. I sang it to her when she got hurt," I added in the barest of whispers. Words I'd created for my baby ricocheted through time and flowed out of me. *"Hush little Maddie, don't cry, my dear. Mommy is with you; she'll always be near."*

Maddie's hand remained limp in mine as my alto voice carried through the room. I waited for a sign, the smallest twitch, or a smile—anything to show that Maddie still existed in this world and wasn't moving onto the next. *"If you are weary, she'll rock you bye until the stars are high in the sky. Oh, hush little Maddie there's nothing to fear. Mommy is here."*

I stopped singing. Silence hummed against my eardrums alongside the droning machines. Somehow even the constant beep of the monitors calmed me.

*Mommy is here.*

A stray hair had fallen across Maddie's stitches on her cheekbone. I carefully brushed it away. "I know you're going to get better, Maddie. I know it. In a few days, you are going to be romping around this hospital with your father chasing after you."

I wiped the tears from my eyes as more flooded to replace them and rested my forehead on the bed.

"Please, let him be alive."

# Chapter 40

## Blake

I was jarred into full awareness when my body connected with the passenger seat of the Ram. Just as I was about to topple even closer to the flames, I clutched onto the steering wheel. After I caught my breath, I pulled myself to relative safety. The heat was nearly unbearable. I searched around me for possible escape routes. I moved my good leg into position and kicked at the truck's wedged door.

With every kick, the wreckage groaned and shifted as if it were alive. The truck began to fall. Dejon reached in from the broken windshield and grabbed my arm.

"I told you I'd be right back!" he shouted over the popping fire as he worked me free of the truck.

With his help, I clambered out of the Ram. Putting as little weight on my right leg as possible, I slid down the multi-car trailer and landed on the asphalt.

The truck teetered to the side.

"Move!" Dejon yelled.

I dragged myself along the pavement as the truck slammed onto the ground, what was left of the Cobalt following its descent. Dejon helped me to my feet and pulled me away as fast as I could possibly run. The truck erupted into hungry, orange flames; the heat scalded my exposed skin. A black plume of smoke rose high in the air.

My breaths came out hard and fast. I collapsed on the ground, leaned my head onto the asphalt, and rolled onto my side. I lifted my head. The flames had overtaken the seat I'd vacated, burning hotter and brighter the more of the truck they consumed.

"You're one wild dude." Dejon kneeled next to me and put his hand on my shoulder. "And that baby owes you his life."

I looked to the heavens.

"Take me to my daughter now. Please," I said between breaths. "But I need something out of my car. A floor mat. In the back seat."

Dejon eyed the remnants of the 'Cuda. "That thing?" He shook his head. "You are seriously messed up in the head, you know? But Baby Boy over there is alive because of you, so I guess I'll have to forgive you."

Dejon assisted me to a standing position as bystanders and another paramedic ran toward us. My world swayed as my right leg buckled under me, unable to hold any more weight. I would have fallen back to the ground had it not been for Dejon's support. My head sagged forward.

The next thing I remembered, I was in an ambulance with Lili's stained car mat on my chest. Dejon was by my side checking the monitors. An IV dripped saline into my veins, an oxygen mask covered my mouth, and the siren blared.

# Chapter 41

## Liliana

Someone shook me awake. My head rested next to Maddie's hand on her bed. I looked up in confusion. My med student, Amy, stood there with wide eyes, her chest rapidly pumping air in and out of her lungs.

"There's a man ... in the ER. He's yelling. Won't let us ..." she gulped in air, "... touch him until he sees you."

I bent over Maddie's hand and kissed it.

*He's alive.*

I rubbed at the dried tracks of tears on my cheeks and bolted out of the room, vaguely aware that Amy followed. I ran from the PICU, back through the sky-bridge connecting the Children's Hospital to Barnes. The hallways blurred as I sprinted to the stairwell and down into the ER.

"I told you. Don't touch me. Where's my daughter?" I heard Blake's voice coming from bay three. "You can't take that. I have to give it to Dr. Chase."

Stressed voices clashed in the same room.

"We can't take you to your daughter until you're examined."

"I'm only checking your vitals."

"Sir. We're here to help—"

"I need to see Dr. Chase." His deep voice carried over all other sounds, my ears attuned to its familiar intonations.

"Blake!" I yelled and ran to the third bay.

Conversations through the whole ER died.

"*Lili.*" His response came seconds after mine.

My co-workers' stares burned into me, their eyes wide and jaws dropped, but I didn't care. I ran past them and pushed my way into his room, out of breath and panting.

All the workers stilled when I entered. I took in the sight of his scorched clothes, his strong jaw covered in stubble and dried blood, and his splinted leg. Then I ran to him. He cupped the side of my face, his thumb wiped my tears, and guided my lips to his.

Starved for the feel of him, I pressed closer to him, threading my hands through his hair, careful of his injuries. Tears tingled my tongue with their salty taste, and I savored his warmth, his arm tethering me to this world. I rested my hand under his chin along his neck and relished the thud of his heart against my fingertips.

Blake pulled his lips off mine. "Maddie, she was with me—"

Tears cut through the grime on his face leaving a clean track of skin behind. He was broken. Afraid. More concerned for his daughter's life than his own.

"I have her—we operated—I can take you to her."

The nurses whispered and pointed, Amy stared with her mouth open, but it was as if they didn't exist. The world consisted of two people: Blake and me.

"You shouldn't have come." I touched my forehead to his and placed my hand on his chest, at once noticing the rough texture of—carpet? "My floor mat? That's why you—"

He nodded. "You run, and I'll follow. I told you before that I was falling in love with you. I lied. I *have* fallen in love with you. And I don't fall easily, remember?"

My chin shook as I recalled what he'd said on our rock-climbing date.

*"You mean, I'm supposed to be able to hold your weight and keep you from falling?"*

*"Yes. If I fall. It won't happen."*

It looked like he could fall after all.

My hand moved along with every breath he took. *He's alive.*

And he wanted me, a broken-down excuse for a person who hadn't figured out how to live. My eyes connected with Blake's, but his glazed with pain, his concentration waning. He relaxed against the pillow with a grimace that he couldn't hide from me.

I took the car mat, shoved it into his bag of personal belongings hanging on his bed, and started barking orders. "I want non-con CT of the head as well as contrast CT of the chest, abdomen, and pelvis. Get x-rays of his right knee. Give him another liter of LR with one milligram Dilaudid IV and draw CBC, CMP, carboxyhemoglobin, PT/INR, and a blood type and screen."

Blake's eyelids took longer and longer to open each time he blinked. "Maddie ..." He shut his mouth tight against the pain and swallowed, his Adam's apple bobbing with the sharp movement.

"Let me make sure you're stable. Then I'll take you to her. I'll try to convince them not to admit you. That you'll be under my care."

"I'll leave. They can't stop me. I need ... to see ... my daughter."

"I know." I ran my finger along the side of his face, leaned close to his ear, and whispered, "Don't worry. I'm going to take care of you."

# Chapter 42

## Liliana

Florescent bulbs hummed against my eardrums and seared my eyes. I hadn't rested them in days. I hadn't rested them much in years. The call room was suffused in the harsh light. With the door securely locked, I fell back onto the foam mattress.

Traces of the scent of hospital laundry detergent perfumed the room. I couldn't stop the tremor in my hands. My mind wandered to the first time I'd spent the night here. Bright-eyed, bushy-tailed, and yet, perpetually terrified one mistake would cost me my fellowship and the future spot on their trauma surgery staff. Not a single day on the job had challenged me like today.

Much had happened since my first day in this residency and fellowship program, but the most drastic changes to myself had occurred in the past month. Blake, Maddie, Mom, Angie, and even Chuck and Pedro had wormed their way past my safety net. And it frightened me.

I'd experienced so much loss already in my life that I wanted to scream to the heavens, *again*? Why did I have to suffer so much?

I waited to hear an answer, but none came. I braced against the same abandonment I'd felt the day my family died. Yes, this time I had more control, but Maddie's care rested primarily in the hands of the Pediatric

Intensivist. My responsibilities were limited to checking on her surgical incisions. I couldn't know or do everything. At some point, I had to rely on someone else.

A knock sounded in the small room.

"Lili, are you in there?" Tiff's voice muffled through the door.

I straightened my scrubs and opened the door.

"Oh, my goodness." Tiff brushed passed me. "I stopped by the PICU to see your Idaho Blake. He's doing fine. I can see why you ..." She paused, and her gaze trained on my face. Her tone changed. "I'm sorry. How are you holding up?"

She pulled me into a hug, and despite my best efforts, my eyes kept leaking. "Why is it so hard?"

Tiffany didn't say anything. For a few minutes, she held me tight and let me cry. "I don't know." She dropped her hands to her side and leaned against the desk in the corner of the room. "I've prayed for you since you told me about your little family. I didn't know what else to do."

"You've done so much for me."

"Not nearly enough." She hesitantly touched my shoulder. "I know you miss Michael and Madi desperately. Although it feels like it, I don't believe they're gone forever. You haven't lost them. They're just waiting for you in heaven. Love is eternal after all. It stands to reasoning, we must be as well."

Much like in the myth with Orpheus and Eurydice, Michael and Madi resided in a realm I couldn't reach in this life. Sometimes I thought that I felt their presence close by my side. Other times they were as distant as the farthest star in our galaxy, and I lost hope of ever seeing them again.

Tiff continued without waiting for a response from me. "I think you have shed enough of these." She wiped a tear from my cheek and held it on the tip of her finger. "Michael would want you to be happy. Get out of this room and go be with Blake. He needs you as much as you need him. You've been given a second chance. Be brave and take it." Tiff crossed her arms. "Of course, that means you'll be seeing more of your mother."

I laughed out loud, and some of the tension from the last hours drained out of me. "Actually, Mom's not so bad. I think you'd like her. She's blunt like you."

"Wise woman. I'll have to visit again when I can stay longer than twenty minutes." Tiffany stood and placed her hand on my shoulder. "I've got to go check on one of my patients. Do you need me to stay? I could get someone else to cover for me."

I shook my head. "No, I'll be all right."

"Call if you need me." Tiff paused in the doorway.

After my nod, she shut the door, leaving me alone.

I sat for a while on the uncomfortable mattress covered in cheap hospital sheets. My past had been hell, but I still had the power to change my future. In the cramped call room, of all places, I finally had the strength to admit to myself I'd fallen in love.

I'd fallen in love with the life I'd found in my hometown. I'd fallen in love with Maddie and especially with Blake. I even gained the willingness to work on my relationship with my mother, something I thought was lost to me. I raised my eyes to the ceiling. *Help Maddie to live.* I prayed to whatever divine being existed.

As a doctor, I'd done all I could. Hopefully, Maddie had the strength to come back to us. It'd take a long time for her to recover full function of her arm, but it could be done with physical therapy.

But the unknown of her head injury cut into my momentary optimism. Was her brain damaged? What if she didn't recover, and I had to face the same torture I'd barely survived when Bug died?

I slid off the bed onto the floor. Cold from the tile leached through the thin fabric of my scrub bottoms. Another prayer formed in my mind, one coming from my core.

*Help me not to be afraid anymore.*

Tiff was right. Michael would want me to be happy, and my little Madi would have loved this man who'd worked so hard to keep her memory alive. With Blake's love, maybe I would finally find the real kind of happiness again, not like the kind in fairytales, fickle and trite. The kind of fulfillment that only came after years of slugging through todays only to survive tomorrows.

For ten years, ten months, and twenty-some days, I'd avoided falling in love. Tired of living in isolation, and as if it were a natural thing for me to do, I pulled out my phone and called Mom.

# Chapter 43

## Blake

Monitors beeped out of rhythm with the throbbing pain pulsing throughout my body. Textured gray walls and unforgiving white tile combined with the frigid temperature gave this place an arctic feel. Earlier, I'd convinced the nurses to help me get situated on the edge of Maddie's bed, which was barely big enough for me to fit. Lying on the covers next to Maddie, I looped my hand around her head and propped my leg on a pillow at the end of the bed. The smell of strong sterilant filled the air.

I couldn't wait until I could manage to take a simple shower to scrub the filth from the accident off my skin. The wipes they'd given me to clean up hadn't been sufficient. Rubbing at my cold arms, I tucked Maddie's blanket more securely around her chin. The aching in my body was nothing compared to the raw agony searing through me as I stared at my unconscious child.

A tube ran out the corner of her mouth to the machine preserving her life, the opposite side of her face covered in white bandages. The bruises, broken bones, and gashes on her delicate skin were out of place on my daughter who barely settled down enough to sit through a thirty-minute show.

I should have known she wouldn't have given up so easily on going with me. If I'd only been more diligent, I could have prevented her from getting into the car. Then she would have been pissed at me, but healthy, waiting for me to return home.

Tears formed in my eyes, my throat constricted, and I drew in shallow breaths, easing the sting of my broken ribs. The emotion I'd managed to hold in check until now broke free. A level of hopelessness I'd never experienced before invaded my life.

I gained new understanding of the torture Lili dealt with every day. How had she lived with pain like this for all these years? With each sob, fresh waves of pain washed over my body. I deserved every ounce of hurt. This was my purgatory for the wrongs I'd committed.

Leaning my head against the pillow, I closed my eyes and drifted between waking and dreaming, praying that sleep would take away my torment for a moment, but it followed me into my brief dreams until pain snapped me awake.

The latch of the door clicked. I kept my eyes closed, figuring if the medical people wanted me to move, they'd wake me up. Soft footsteps echoed toward me and paused at Maddie's bedside. The scratchy fabric of a hospital blanket slid over my arm.

Opening my eyes, I turned and looked up. Brown wavy hair brushed against her blue scrubs; her familiar green eyes met my own.

"Lili?"

"Yes?" She leaned against my empty futon, placing her hand gently on my arm. "Do you need anything?"

I shook my head and groaned as I shifted to a seated position. The speeches I'd rehearsed on the drive here filtered through my mind. Nothing had gone the way I'd expected, but I still needed to tell her the words

I'd driven all this way to say. "I've been waiting to tell you I'm sorry for what I did to your car."

She waved her hand in front of her face, dismissing my apology. "It doesn't matter now."

Placing my good leg on the ground, I tried to maneuver to her on my own, but she stood and slid under my arm to support my weight before I did more damage to my right leg. Grabbing the blanket that'd fallen onto the floor, she arranged it over us as she sat next to me on my makeshift bed.

"Yes." I looked at Maddie and then back to Lili. "It does matter, and I'm sorry."

"You're not responsible for Maddie's condition." Her soft voice sliced through the quiet room. "You can't blame yourself. Like what happened to my family—"

"If I could change one moment in my life it'd be fixing the Bronco's brake line." I cut her off, not willing to hear the end of her sentence. Not when I could have prevented their deaths. Tucking her hair behind her ears, I held her face in my hands. "I can't go back and make it right. I know, I should have told you sooner, but I didn't want to cause you unnecessary pain, and then I didn't want to lose you." Remembering how she'd run to me in the ER—how she'd kissed me—gave me courage to voice my next words. "Will you be able to forgive me?"

"Only if you can return the favor." She ducked away from me and ran a hand through her hair. Dipping her chin to her chest, she bit her bottom lip. "I shouldn't have left the way I did, and I shouldn't have written that note." Suppressed emotion choked off her words, but then she drew in a ragged breath. With an almost imperceptible nod, she straightened her back, and locked eyes with mine. "It was easier to be angry at you than to be in love with you."

"Wait." I gripped her upper arms, relying on her to keep me steady. "Say that again."

The light from her smile radiated into her eyes. "I am hopelessly, sincerely, and eternally in love with you, Blake Richardson. I love *you*."

I took in a sharp breath and held it. Chills overtook my entire body. Though gravity still secured me to this world, its effect lessened, as if everything inside of me became weightless for the briefest of moments.

Lili was in love with me.

How could it be possible? I'd taken so much from her and yet she'd still chosen me. The loneliness that had dogged my heels since childhood dissipated. The internal voices telling me I was unworthy, undesirable, insignificant—that I had to twist myself into a pretzel to deserve love—quieted.

I'd found my other half.

I tugged Lili toward me, but she pressed a hand against my chest, maintaining her distance.

"I have something I need to tell you." The seriousness in her tone compelled me to lock eyes with her. "Michael and Bug's accident wasn't your fault."

With my mind still stuck on the L-word, I'd nearly missed what she'd said. A persistent buzz hummed in my ears.

"What do you mean?" I studied her and rubbed my thumb along her cheek, trying to decipher her non-verbal cues.

"I found the police report." She pulled a crumpled piece of paper from her pocket and handed it to me. "The brake line broke due to off-roading damage. You didn't overlook anything."

My hand fell away from her face, and I glanced at the paper, my gaze fixating on the words ... *damage due to off-roading*.

I *wasn't* responsible.

This crinkled, aged, simple sheet of paper washed my soul clean of guilt's dirt. I'd been under water and finally my lungs were able to expand, filling with pure oxygen. Thoughts clashed in my head. I tried to formulate a response.

"It wasn't my fault," I repeated out loud.

"No." She placed her hands on the back of mine where they clutched the paper in my lap. "I shouldn't have acted the way I did. I'm terrified of losing you, like Michael. I can't go through that again." She leaned into me, and I wrapped one arm around her back. "I'm so sorry," she said against my chest.

Lili was nothing like Cindy, who'd chosen to leave Maddie and me because of her own selfishness. Broken and still healing, Lili had run simply because she'd been afraid to lose me.

Letting the report fall to the floor, I tilted her chin up and placed a soft kiss on her lips. "Don't ever leave me again. Promise?"

"I promise." She rested her head on my shoulder.

Her presence lessened the sting of my injuries more than the pain meds. The only light in the room came from a lamp on a table where I'd placed the car mat. Its halo illuminated the stain.

I gestured to it. "I didn't understand how much a stained floor mat could mean, but now I'm facing the possibility of losing my Maddie and—" I stopped and cleared my throat. "Everything she touched is precious."

Lili's love proved the existence of miracles, and if God granted me this one, then maybe he'd throw me another and heal Maddie.

WHAT HAPPENS IN IDAHO

A few deep breaths shuddered out of her. "Thank you for bringing it back to me."

I placed a kiss on her head, savoring the feel of her against me.

"I dug through the dumpster to find it." I spoke into her hair, then lifted my head and rested my chin where my lips had been. "Only to have Maddie tell me she'd hid it in her playhouse." I breathed out a laugh, but the motions of laughter shot sharp pains through my midsection.

"Really?" she asked. "You searched through piles of garbage, for me?"

The incredulousness in her voice proved she expected nothing from anyone she associated with. She'd been forced to forge her way through life alone, but not anymore.

"I will do anything to make you happy," I whispered against her ear. "All you have to do is ask."

I briefly closed my eyes and pulled her against me, carefully wrapping both of my arms around her. Nothing stood between us now. Nothing would keep me away from her ever again.

I squeezed Lili tight, ignoring the sharp twinges snaking through my chest. My whole body was bruised, but I couldn't lessen my hold on her. "Thank you." I rested my cheek against the top of her head. "Thank you for being here for Maddie—for being a part of my life."

She angled away from me. "I was so worried. I ... I thought—" Her whisper carried over the sound of the monitors.

I brushed my fingers along her arms. "I'm okay. I'm here, and I'm not going anywhere."

Exhausted, I rested back onto the pillows, taking Lili with me. Running my hands through her hair, I closed my eyes and fell asleep with her soft body pressed alongside mine.

# Chapter 44

## Liliana

Every morning for two weeks I stood beside the pediatric intensivist and the pulmonologist as they stopped Maddie's sedative. It was the most trying time of the day. Blake and I, and sometimes Mom, would wait as the seconds ticked by, waiting for any sign of life from Maddie. Every morning, she failed the Glasgow Coma Scale.

Some mornings, Maddie's eyes would open to pain, others to our voices. Yesterday, she'd even withdrawn from painful stimuli, but she still made no attempts at making a sound or remaining lucid.

Off and on, images of my Madi lying on a similar hospital bed would enter my mind. On the bad days, they never left.

The doctors were hopeful for Maddie, though, unlike how they'd been with my daughter, and in my limited experience with PICU patients, I saw signs leaning toward an optimistic outcome. Having lived through the trauma of losing a child once, doubt clung to my every move.

I reached out my hand to Blake. He held it securely. A week ago, he'd been released from the hospital. His bruises had faded, and his crutches leaned against the wall since he sat next to Maddie's bed. I stood next to him, holding his hand.

The staff had allowed him to continue to sleep in this room while Maddie recovered. Her vitals crumped any time he wasn't around. Sometimes I slept here too, curled up next to him or in the recliner by the door. I monitored every vital sign, every hour of every day. The hand of the clock ticked to nine o'clock. The peds team had everything set up.

"It's time." I squeezed Blake's hand.

Mom chewed on her cuticles against the far wall of the room. The pediatric intensivist shut off the valve on the IV administering the sedative. Thirty seconds passed, and Maddie showed no signs of waking.

Blake rubbed the side of his daughter's face. "Maddie, it's Daddy. Wake up, honey."

Blake ran his thumb in small circles on my palm keeping me connected to them. A minute passed. *Come on, Maddie.* My chest tightened, I breathed in deep and hummed Madi's lullaby.

A minute and a half.

*Hush little Maddie. Don't cry my dear.*

Two minutes.

Maddie's eyes fluttered and lifted. Her irises grew and shrank in and out of focus.

"Can you hear us, Maddie?" The intensivist asked as he poked her fingers with a pointed object.

Maddie rolled her head, first to Blake and then to me, but she didn't maintain focus on our faces. Air wheezed out of the tube as she tried to speak. She winced and yanked her hand away from the intensivist. Her eyes widened in panic as she scrambled to pull the tube from her mouth.

"She's awake." I dropped to my knees as Blake crushed me to his chest.

I sagged into his arms. My little girl had finally woken up.

The PICU team spoke with animation as they removed the endotracheal tube. I covered my face with my hands as Blake buried his head in my shoulder and sobbed.

Maddie's rough voice quieted the room. "D-daddy?"

I stood and backed away as Blake leaned closer to the top of Maddie's bed. "I'm right here, baby." He took one of her hands in his.

Maddie's panic faded, and she relaxed against the pillows. The heart monitor slowed as he rubbed her arm. Up and down. Calming. Loving. Doting. All things a parent should be.

"Thank you, God," Mom whispered from the other side of the bed. Her cheeks were wet.

"Can you tell us if you recognize anyone else in the room?" The intensivist spoke over-loud to Maddie. I never understood this type of bedside manner in my fellow physicians. The patient was waking up from surgery or a coma. They weren't deaf.

"That's my daddy." Her arm twitched as she tried to lift it to point to her father. "And Renee." Her eyebrows drew together. She looked back at her father. "Daddy, where's Lili?" Her words were faint.

"I'm right here." I crouched next to the bed.

"Why did you leave?"

"I'm so sorry." I held her hand and kissed the back of it.

"Daddy was really upset."

I sniffed and laughed and looked at Blake. He matched my gaze. "Was he now?"

"Yes. You can never leave. Ever again."

I held firm to Blake's hand. Life without them was not an option. "I promise, I'll never leave again. I'm going home with you."

I spoke to Maddie but looked at Blake. His eyes widened and a big smile lit up his face. He didn't speak and planted a firm kiss on my mouth. Then he kissed his daughter on her cheek.

"Can you sing to me again?" Maddie's eyelids hung heavy over her eyes.

Maddie *had* been able to hear me sing. "I've been singing a lullaby to you."

"I like it. Maybe you could sing it while you and daddy tango." Maddie's words slurred.

I laughed along with Blake's chuckle.

"You're still so focused on that." He smoothed Maddie's hair away from her forehead.

"Well, how else am I supposed to get a brother?" Maddie rested her cheek on the pillow.

As she closed her eyes and drifted off to sleep, I stared at the cord to the ventilator curled on the ground—unplugged from the wall and shifted my eyes to the rise and fall of Maddie's chest.

# Chapter 45

## Liliana

*O* *ver a year later...*

Flickering flames captivated my attention as the warmth of the fire seeped into my toes. The hem of my white dress brushed the rug on the wood floor. The rush of the day was over. Caterers and decorators, dresses and flowers, all had done their respective jobs creating the most optimal outcome.

I was married.

Blake sighed in the chair next to me; he propped up his feet and undid his bowtie. Closing his eyes, he leaned his head back and let out a long sigh. He reminded me of a cat with a belly full of milk, curled up in front of the stove. Firelight danced over his face, softening his features. His eyelashes cast small shadows on his upper cheek, his hands hung loose over the armrests, black ringed his cuticles, the contours of his muscles tested the fabric of his white shirt. I memorized every detail while he was wearing a tuxedo, and not just a blue shirt, jeans, and cowboy boots.

Yet, I'd have him either way. My husband. My mechanic. My Blake.

A coyote called in the distance. The white snow reflected the moon outside the window. It almost looked like a framed picture of the wilderness surrounded by the brown logs of the hunting cabin.

The crystalized flakes slowed and settled around the cabin, silencing all other creatures, and making it feel like Blake and I were the only two people in existence. We'd driven to the cabin at the base of the Tetons before the snow had become impassable. Our weeklong honeymoon might be extended if we got snowed in.

"We survived," he muttered without opening his eyes.

"Do you think Maddie will be all right this week without us? I mean she still has her physical therapy and—"

He opened his eyes. "The last thing on my mind right now is my daughter. She'll be fine with your mother and Irene."

As his eyes burned me with their hot stare, I changed my mind. I preferred him without a lick of clothing on—no jeans or cowboy boots and definitely no tuxedo.

"Oh," I whispered and placed my feet on the floor. I walked over to his chair and stood over him. "In that case, I have a problem."

"What problem is that, Mrs. Richardson?" He pulled me to him and rubbed his hands along the back of my legs and up to cup my butt.

Mrs. Richardson. That would take me some time to get used to. Of course, in my professional life I'd still be Dr. Chase, but I'd chosen to assume his name. To become one with him, in love and in life.

"I'm still in my dress."

"I believe you and I share the same problem." He leaned into my abdomen and whispered, "But I think I can help you."

"You think?" My words came out breathy. Tingles of warmth, having nothing to do with the fire, emanated from where he touched me through the fabric of my wedding dress. It made me impatient to feel his hands on my bare skin.

He kissed me along my body until he stood, his hands on my hips, still holding me against him. "Have you seen how many buttons are running down your back? I might get frustrated halfway through and rip your dress."

I laughed. "It doesn't matter if you rip it. It's done its job. I won't need it again."

I pulled his lips to mine, and he crushed me against him. His lips devoured mine, bringing me to the heights of desire until I couldn't take the sweet torture anymore. I broke contact and turned my back to him.

He started at the top button. With each button he undid, he kissed my bare skin. This continued.

Unbutton.

Kiss.

Unbutton.

Kiss.

Finally, the heat of the fire warmed my unclothed back. He ran his hands along my exposed skin, reached under the fabric of my dress, his hand warm against my abdomen, and caressed me in all the right places.

Waves of pleasure washed over me with each brush of his lips, each touch of his fingertips. "Rip the dress already." I groaned in impatience.

He laughed against the goosebumps on my back and kissed his way to my ear. "Don't rush me," he whispered. I closed my eyes and arched my arm around his head as he kissed the curve of my neck. "I don't think you understand how beautiful you are, or how much I love you."

I couldn't dream of being any happier. This was the fairytale kind of happiness. Maybe it did exist after all.

"I love you too."

He turned me to face him. Raw desire, need, and love all blended in his eyes. He focused on me as if nothing else in the world mattered to him.

"I think ..." I kissed his lips. "It's time ..." I kissed his jaw. "To take you to bed." I pressed my lips to his again, allowing more passion to flow into my kiss. "Husband."

He looped one arm under the back of my knees, his other hand still securely inside my dress, and lifted me off the ground. I squealed as he ran to the bedroom with me in his arms.

"I couldn't agree more." He laid me on the bed and covered the length of my body with his.

# Epilogue

## Blake

The bedroom was illuminated by the rising sun. Its pink rays brightened the floral arrangement and the framed snapshots that Lili had placed on the mantel of the fireplace. The picture of the three of us at the pumpkin patch became clear, followed by the one taken at the Japanese steakhouse for the anniversary of the day we met. Frozen images—of Renee teaching Maddie how to swim, of Shasta, our new cat, curled up by the fire, and of Lili's first roller coaster ride, with her mouth open in terror and me shamelessly laughing at her—zigzagged across the polished wood.

Two chairs sat on either side of the fireplace with a decorative, pale-green throw draped over the top of one. A sheepskin rug laid on the floor between the chairs. She'd added her touches around the house, and I liked seeing reminders that she lived here with me in every room. Lili rested her chin on my naked chest as I closed my eyes and pretended to be asleep. She twirled her fingers in my chest hair.

The rest of my life would be filled with mornings like this. What had I done to get this lucky? I opened my eyes and flipped her full body onto mine, the thin silk of her pajamas doing little to shield her from my view.

She laughed and squirmed against my chest.

I stretched my legs and yawned. "What time is it?"

"Seven."

"Then I have ten more minutes before my alarm goes off." I rolled over and took her with me.

"How can you sleep on a day like today?" She playfully slapped my shoulder.

My hand spread possessively over her abdomen, and I kissed her neck. "Easy. I close my eyes and snuggle you close like this." I stopped kissing her, rubbed my chin into the side of her neck and hummed.

As always, it made her laugh uncontrollably. She drew her shoulder to her chin and tried to push me away. "Stop tickling me," she said in between laughs.

She pushed against me. I held her tight as I rolled back and forth across the bed until she pressed her hand to her mouth and made a gagging noise. I instantly stilled.

"I'm okay." She sat up in the bed and curled her knees to her chest. "But maybe we should stop wrestling."

Mornings had been rough on her, but thankfully at night, she didn't have any problems. I brushed my hand through her hair along the side of her face and let the tips fall through my fingers. "Thank you for last night."

She bit her lip and glanced at our clothes still scattered on the floor around the sheepskin rug. Only faint embers remained from our fire. Her lips lifted into a smile. I'd never tire of her caresses or the way she made my body sing.

A few months had passed since our wedding day, yet it felt like she'd been in my life forever. She traced the line of my jaw with her fingertip and lifted my chin for a kiss. I forgot about her morning sickness and let my body take over. The kiss took on a life of its own, seasoned by practice.

"I thought you said ..." I nibbled her ear. "We should stop wrestling."

I didn't stop and left a trail of kisses down her neck. She looped her hand around the back of my neck and arched herself closer to me. My body ached for more than a kiss. She made a sound in the back of her throat before I pushed her onto her back and pulled myself on top of her.

"I changed my mind." She closed her eyes.

"I better lock the door."

Maddie burst into our room with her hair tied in messy pigtails, and her headphones looped around her neck.

I groaned and flopped back onto the bed. Lili heaved a sigh and laid her head against the pillow.

"It's snowing." Maddie ran to the window, plastering her face to the glass. The only evidence of the car accident was the fading scar on her cheek. "Do you think they'll cancel school?" she continued, unaware of my frustration.

"Since we're only supposed to get an inch of snow, I don't think so." I laughed and pulled the blankets over the top of Lili and me. "You better be ready to go in twenty minutes. Grandma Renee will be here to pick you up."

"All I have left to do is eat breakfast and brush my teeth." She turned away from the window but didn't leave the room.

I put a hand over my face and shook my head, causing Lili to laugh. She sat up and leaned against our headboard. "Why don't you go fix yourself a bowl of cereal?"

"Okay, Mom." Maddie paused by the bed to kiss Lili on the cheek before she left the room.

"Thank heavens it's cereal Tuesday," Lili muttered.

"You want to pick up where we left off?" I asked as soon as Maddie was out of hearing range.

"Nice try." She kissed the top of my head and hopped out of bed. "But we can't be late for our appointment. I don't know how I'll get someone to cover another shift this month."

"Crap dammit." I used her curse words, and she giggled. I stalked out of bed to the bathroom and started the shower.

She followed me into the bathroom and watched me undress. For a couple of moments, I could tell she thought about joining me in the shower, but then she disappeared into the closet.

Lili was waiting for me in the kitchen with two mugs of hot coffee by the time I'd dressed and shaved. Maddie's half-eaten cereal sat at the bar counter next to her lunchbox. While Lili's back was turned, I peeked inside. I did most of the cooking, but Lili insisted on packing lunch for Maddie.

A note sat on top of the bagged food.

*Don't forget how much your mom loves you while you're filling your brain with spelling words.*

Lili'd drawn three hearts on the paper. What she'd packed didn't matter any longer. My eyes grew watery, and I fell even deeper in love with my wife. I closed the lunchbox as she turned to hand me my cup of coffee.

The doorbell rang.

Maddie sprinted past us, grabbed her lunch, and ran to the door. "Bye, Mom. Bye, Dad. See you after school."

She swung the door open, and Renee waved briefly as fat, lazy snowflakes drifted to the ground behind her before the door closed. We planned on telling Maddie about the pregnancy after school. I barely had enough time to finish my coffee before Lili pulled me out the door and into the Audi.

We made it to the OB's office a solid fifteen minutes before her appointment time. Damn, we could have finished our tango this morning and still been on time.

The front desk clerk handed us an iPad loaded with forms to fill out. While we sat in the waiting room, I thought of all the ways those ten minutes had been squandered.

"Hey, Lili." Angie wore bright pink scrubs and stood in the doorway leading to the back to the ultrasound.

Lili had told me that Angie'd graduated nursing school, but I didn't know she worked on the mother-baby unit. We hung out some, but I wasn't involved in their girl talk, and didn't want to be.

"Blake! Did Lili tell you? I'm now *Nurse* Angie Johnson. I finished my final exams last week. I took a little longer than everyone else because of a family crisis, but my heavens, you two surely understand."

I didn't ever have to wonder about anything where Angie was concerned. She had a way of filling in the gaps. We followed her into the ultrasound room.

"Now, when you're done in here, get dressed and I'll be in to take your vitals. I sound so official, don't I? Vitals." Angie laughed and closed the door.

"I can't believe Angie's your nurse." I sat in the chair by the side of the bed while Lili got undressed from the waist down and pulled a sheet over her. "I think we need to go pick some beans. Right now."

Lili shot a sideways look at me. "Will you ever let that go?"

"Probably not." I mentioned it in one way or another about fifty percent of the time we were around Angie. They'd finally confessed what transpired in the bathroom of the bowling alley during our long-ago trout date. I'd be forever grateful for what Angie had done for me and Lili.

When the ultrasound tech entered the room, I moved closer to the bed to hold Lili's hand and get a better view of the screen.

"Relax against your pillow and we'll check on baby." The tech pulled out the stirrups for Lili as she scooted to the edge of the bed.

She sucked in her breath when the tech inserted the speculum, which did *not* look pleasant. I would never understand why a woman would want to get pregnant once, let alone multiple times.

"All right, here we go," the tech said.

A faint whooshing filled the room. The baby's heartbeat. I stared at the monitor as the image of a little jellybean came into focus. I touched the screen. The fast little heartbeat became the center of my world. "Look at our baby."

"Hello there." Lili waved her fingers at the tiny image. A smile brightened her face.

I rested my forehead against hers. "I love you so much," I whispered before I kissed her.

I never thought I'd experience creating a life again. This time it was so much better, because I was making a baby with the woman I loved, a baby sure to be spoiled beyond all belief. I hoped it would be a boy for Maddie's sake. My little boy would never doubt the love I showered on him, or the love I whole-heartedly gave to his mother.

"Well, actually ..." The tech's bubbly voice reverberated in the sterile room. "That's baby number one. And right over here ..." she adjusted the ultrasound probe, "... is baby number two."

How few of us really appreciate love~
~its immensity ~ its universal availability
and the wonderful circumstances it provides!
It is the great reality of life and without it
we have nothing.

There seems to be too many who do not
recognize the tremendous value of love, and
suffer for not knowing how to give and receive
it. For what other purpose could the 'Supreme
Architect of the Universe' have created what
we enjoy?

Love brings us great joy when we accept
it and give it. There is no other facet of
life so valuable.

—Hazen W. Hamlin

# Acknowledgments

First of all, I'd like to take a moment acknowledge how hard it is to compile a list of people who helped me write a book with a sixteen-year publishing journey. The village for on this one is large and absolutely miraculous. (Unless you're interested in seeing how many people it took to craft this novel, feel free to skip to the last paragraph. Lol.)

Even in the darkest moments, when I doubted pursuing my dream of being a published author, my husband, Richard, supported me and made it possible for me to go to conferences, workshops, and meetings where I learned the artful craft of writing. You are the reason I can write about finding true love. I love you always and forever. Throughout it all, my kids, Emma, William, Olivia, and Genevieve learned to be self-sufficient, taking the burden of cleaning the house off my shoulders and often, when I was on a deadline, you fed yourselves and brought me sustenance. Thank you for being the most amazing kids a mom could ask for.

I can't even express how incredible my publishing company is. To all the authors in my Rising Action family, you are the best! Alex, you believe in my book as much as I do, and for that I'll be forever grateful. Thank you, Tina, for being an amazing editor with a great taste in classic cars. Mar French, your edits were spot on, and I loved reading all your thoughts about my book. Kayla and Miruna, thank you for any time you spent on this project. Emmy thanks for being gifted at seeing the errors which have slipped past so many others. I'll always have a debt of gratitude for Katrina Escudero for giving me the most uplifting professional feedback I've ever received and championing my book in Hollywood. I cannot thank Miss Nat Mack enough for my absolutely perfect cover design! Your artistic talent combined with your knowledge of what sells in this industry astounds me.

I'll forever be indebted to my librarian mother. Mom, you always had a book in your hands and gifted me with the love of reading. Thank you for using your grammatic and story powers to edit my manuscript. Your tireless work helped this book become what it is now. I'm grateful for my dad who fostered my drive for scientific learning. You shared your passion for all things STEM, helping me create a like-minded character in Lili.

One of the greatest men in my life is my brother. A good portion of the inspiration for the heroes in my books comes from you. Thank you for being a remarkable example to me and for also being a voracious reader, even if I'm still developing a taste for the high fantasy novels you love.

I wouldn't be who I am without all my sisters who share the love of the written word with me. My oldest sister Tamera is there for me in my day-to-day life, reminding me not only to write about life, but to live it as well. Heidi, thank you for being one of the first to read over my roughest draft and for being my herbal tea buddy. I can't help but send a big hug across the country to my foreign exchange sister, Tamara! Love you, sis! Naomi, what can I say, you are the most unique, charismatic person I know. Newanda! Thank you for always being there to support me no matter what.

Marci, I love how much you believe in my books, yet hold me accountable for anything that could be better, and for always finding ways to insert humor into my life and into my novels. I'm especially indebted to Kelsey and Kayla. Kayla, our almost daily chats keep me focused on writing and give me the boost I need to keep going. I can always count on you to be there whenever I need last-minute edits. And Kelsey, I called you when my patience for myself and this book hung by a thread. You refused to let me give up on Blake and Lili and without your unwavering belief and dogged feedback, no one would have the privilege of reading their story.

I have the best in-laws! You have all been so supportive in my writing career. A special thank you to my mother-in-law, Polly, for opening my eyes to my 'that' problem in my first draft, and to Grandma Genevieve, now an angel in heaven, you're one of my earliest and biggest fans, and you showed me what having a grandma's love truly is like. Marcie Davies, my wicked awesome cousin-in-law, you make me so happy with how much love you shower on me any time I get good book news.

Being a part of a large family also gives me the support of the greatest aunts and uncles (in-laws included), cousins, brother and sisters-in-law, nieces, and nephews. Every text, reply on social media, call, hug, and smile means the world to me. Thank you so much.

This book traveled with me across the United States. Drafted in St. Louis, edited in Florida and Virginia, then published in Idaho. Countless friends I met along the way helped in the birth of this novel.

Natalie Lukens, you had the (not so lucky) joy of reading this book chapter by chapter as I wrote it. You're the first person to ever read the terrible sentences I strung together, yet you became my cheerleader, giving me the confidence and the courage to keep writing. Thank you.

I'm so grateful for my Florida mom, Felicia Pye. Thanks for being as excited for my every achievement as if I'm your actual daughter. My BFF, Kristin Pete, listened to me every morning for years during the dark days spent in the query trenches and welcomed my daily therapy sessions. I may have scared you away from ever writing a book, but your unwavering belief and support means the world to me.

Mary Behre, Tracey Livesay, and Avery Flynn came into my life in an important time when I was deciding whether or not to take writing more seriously. Through your guidance, I joined the Romance Writers of America and the Virginia Romance Writers and found my people. Thank you.

All my wonderful Virginia friends who loved and encouraged me during my final years in the military family, thank you. Especially Shelbey Waite, who had the courage to read my novel after going through the greatest loss of your life. What you told me about Lili's path to healing impacted me most in my journey to publication and became my driving force to never give up on this story.

My SP writing group helps me keep a pulse on the publishing industry and always adds humor to everything. Without your connections and help with my query letter, I wouldn't be getting published. A special thanks to Lindsay Maple, Amanda Nelson, Jackie Khalilieh, Crystal A. Hill, G.S. Brouwer, Angela Joy, and Maren Soderbeck for taking the time to read my manuscript and offering me priceless feedback.

I'm grateful for my romance critique group full of talented writers. L.M. Potter, thank you for reading and critiquing my work. Megan A. Clancy, thank you for coaching me and tightening up my submission package. Hannah Sharpe, you read the beginning of my book and believed in it enough to brag about it to the right person. Thank you!

A big thanks to my writing support group. Alli Anderson, Lindsay Hiller, my Sisters Prim, Natalie Kraus, Sally O'Keef (the proofreading goddess), Tarry Perry, and KayLynn Flanders. You're all so great!

I want to give a shout out to my Storymakers peeps. Serene and Jolie thank you for helping me with my social media skills, Megan Clements for being awesome and sharing my love for volleyball as well as writing, and Alan for always being ready with a smile. Chelsea Hale, I still have the sticky notes you stuck to my hotel door. I adore you so much! Shari Phippen, you give the best hugs! Traci Hunter Abramson, I'm so glad I met you in Virginia and get to continue to be your friend. Julie Wright, I'm humbled by how excited you were for me when I told you about my publishing contract. Melanie Jacobson, I love your bright smile and stellar dresses. Rebecca Gage thank you for teaching me about poison and being so welcoming. To Jennifer Nielsen, you are an inspiration to me and to everyone around you. A big thanks to Lisa Mangum for editing the first pages of my manuscript two times over. Gina! Thank you for spending a weekend doing nothing but combing through my manuscript after I'd given up and thought it was "good enough." For anyone else I didn't specifically mention, I love and appreciate you!

To my regency/historical author friends, Joanna Barker, Jentry Flint, Esther Hatch, Ashtyn Newbold, Kate Condie, Anneka Walker, Amanda Taylor, Martha Keyes, Deborah Hathaway, Megan Walker, Sally Britton, Emily Inouye Huey, Anneka Walker, Sian Ann Bessy, Sarah M. Eden, Jess Heileman, A.L. Sowards, and Arlem Hawkes, who offered support and answered any of my questions along the way, thank you. I'll never forget our romantic dance, Megan.

I'm so grateful for my Coeur Du Bois RWA chapter in Boise for your continued support, expertise, and enthusiasm only writers understand how to give! Donna, you developmental editing queen, thank you so much for finding the gaping holes in my storyline. You were right on every count. I'm privileged to be on the board for the Idaho Writers

Guild, and I'm thankful for the effort you all put into creating a community for writers in the area.

A huge thank you to my volleyball friends! You're all so supportive and keep me in shape!

For any writers out there looking for a great way to connect with professionals in the community, Manuscript Academy is where it's at. Jessica and Julie thank you for providing me with so many opportunities. Jessica, thanks for taking time out of your very busy schedule to meet up with me in New York. Mary Murchie, I always look forward to your positivity calls. You are a bright light in this industry.

Thank you to Erin Merrill, Jolene Lyon, Layne Beckner, Elizabeth Hull, and any other beta readers I haven't named. Your feedback helped shape my book into what it is today.

To all bookstagrammers, reviewers, and everyone else who helped publicize What Happens in Idaho, thank you for sharing my novel with the world!

For writers still struggling to find the drive to write, to feel appreciated, to feel valued for your effort, keep going! Don't give into the dark days. I believe in you! Your stories matter!

Most importantly, I'd like to acknowledge my immense appreciation for you, my dear reader, for picking up this story that lived only in my head and on my laptop for almost two decades and welcoming my characters into your life.

From the bottom of my heart, thank you,
Bonnie Jo Pierson

## *About the Author*

Gifted with a short attention span, American romance author, Bonnie Jo Pierson, wants to experience and do as much as she can. Using the great powers of YouTube, she's taught herself how to knit, crochet, paint with oils, acrylics, and watercolors, coach volleyball, play the piano and cello, ride a motorcycle, renovate a house, raise livestock, sing, sew, bake, and most importantly how to write. As a member of Romance Writers of America, the Storymakers Guild, Idaho Sister's in Crime, Idaho Writers Guild, and Manuscript Academy, she's won the Heart of Denver's Molly contest, placed third in the Orange Rose contest, was a finalist in the Shiela and Four Seasons contest, and placed multiple times in the contest at Storymakers. She also earned a spot in the RAMP mentorship program. With a degree in biology, she's a lover of all things science, especially in the microscopic world. She and her Navy veteran husband have four children and spent several years as military nomads. Now she's made her home in small-town Idaho, where she's attempting to resurrect her great-grandparent's one-hundred-year-old farm. *What Happens in Idaho* is her debut novel.